5TH&HOPE

NATHANIEL SEWELL

Copyright © 2017 by Nathaniel Sewell

All rights reserved.

Interior Design by StandoutBooks.com

No part of this book may be reproduced in any form or by any electronic or mechanical means, including information storage and retrieval systems, without written permission from the author, except for the use of brief quotations in a book review.

Dedicated to my grandparents, Hazel and Sewell.

CHAPTER 1

As I stood near the jagged cliff edge, I reflected on how the news I had been expecting for years had, on a rapturous Carmel Bay morning, managed to come unexpectedly. My sister had told me the facts during a brief smartphone call. She was one of the few who had my personal phone number and one of the few whose incoming calls I always accepted. She was, in fact, one of the few who I suspected I loved. I wasn't sure what love meant, but I had a vague notion because of her and our maternal grandparents. Her low whisper caused the back of my throat to burn. It was as if I had known the news before I heard it. Maybe it was her tone; perhaps, from within her hesitant breath, I heard finality. Of course, I did. My mother was dead. I shut my eyes as I flipped the ubiquitous device onto a repurposed, cast-iron table. If it shattered, it could be replaced.

Even though I hadn't spoken to the woman in decades, I wanted to cry. I thought it was what I was supposed to do, but I suspected my emotions were connected to a myth rather than reality, as if I had Stockholm syndrome. My grandfather, Stephen, would not have cried. At least, he would not have cried in public view. It wasn't his way. And he was never called 'Steve'; he was always 'Stephen'. A red-tailed hawk shrieked down at me, as if my grandfather spoke through the wild animal, telling me to buck up and get right with the Lord. It was perched high above me in a mature live oak, defending a nest that was intertwined with dry vegetation. Within, newborn chicks chirped for breakfast. As a routine, this was my favorite spot to watch the daily human and animal goings-on. It offered beautiful views of the frigid Pacific currents. I gripped the warm mug. The black coffee tasted bitter, as if it had been brewed from bourbon-barrel char, but I liked it. My mother was dead. I nodded acceptance at a God hidden within the wind, hidden by a perfect, pale-blue sky; a God I didn't believe existed. My preacher grandfather wouldn't have been pleased. It was a fact: she was gone. My sister wasn't the type to play horrible practical jokes. I leaned back against the table and sucked in the salty air, looking up into the predator bird's dark eyes. I wondered if it sensed something permanent had happened.

For several minutes, I watched the pastoral, white-frothed sea line as a blond-haired boy menaced a golden retriever with a driftwood stick. I wondered what it would have been like to have been a parent. My only attempt had been reduced to ashes, now contained within a cypress box. I had no idea what it all meant; to love a human being you helped create, to love them beyond reason. I sipped the warm coffee and shrugged as the ocean's thunderous sounds reassured me like a mother's hug. But then, my mother had never been the hugging type. In fact, I had always wondered if she even wanted me. I wasn't sure I felt anything as I strolled back across the stone walkway and into our kitchen. I told Rebecca, my wife, the news with a simple sentence, staring down at our butcher-block countertop. She hugged me, and the house staff disappeared from my view. With her encouragement, we journeyed back to Kentucky one last time, to pay our respects.

* * *

I twisted the SUV's steering wheel, gazing up through the panoramic windshield at a resplendent fall afternoon. The trees prepared for another harsh winter; the oak, sycamore, and maple leaves were dying from thirst, but the tree family had shared one last stunning color palette of reds, yellows, and oranges that blanketed the dense, Appalachian forest.

We drove along the twisting, two-lane road, past the tiny town of Jackson, and toward my grandfather's chapel, the natural canopy blazing above us. The moist roads were rutted with the concave imprints of coal-truck traffic; traffic that splattered coal dust across our rental. It sounded like the truck drivers were throwing wedding rice, but we drove toward the past, not toward an abundant future. I glanced over at Rebecca.

"Thanks for coming," I said. "Haven't seen my grandfather's chapel in eons."

"Of course," Rebecca said. She reached for me. "What was he like?"

"Authentic. My grandparents chose to mission here," I said. "Out here—"

"Missionaries? I thought you said he was a minister and she was a nurse?" Rebecca asked. She stared over at the modest homes and the weathered people.

"He was born here, but yeah, they were really missionaries," I said. "They met in downtown LA. I thought I mentioned that?"

"Never. It's beautiful here, a bit rustic," she said. "Love does make you do strange things."

"Cute," I said. I glanced over at Rebecca. "My grandfather had taken trains out to LA to study at Biola."

"That sounds familiar."

"'Bible Institute of Los Angeles'," I said. "1926. Remember the 'Jesus saves' signs?"

"Oh, yeah," Rebecca said. She nodded. "Neon sign?"

"That's them," I said. "They were all-in; he was out there before those signs went up."

"Would he have 'healed me'?" Rebecca asked. She grinned as she smacked my thigh.

"No, he wasn't like that," I said. I looked forward as another hulking coal truck approached at a sharp bend. "Met my grandmother out there, they married out there, in SoCal. Think about that."

"She loved the boy," Rebecca said. She pointed at the dirty truck. "That thing is scary."

"Yeah, it is," I agreed. The truck's diesel engine growled out gray fumes as it thundered past us.

"Just keep your eyes on the road," Rebecca said.

"Hazel and Stephen," I said, grunting. "They're buried up on a hillside, not far from the chapel. We can go up there, after the service."

"We'll see," Rebecca said, shifting in her seat. "Sorry, funerals are never easy for me, as you know. Let's not ever have one, for either of us."

As I nodded, I thought of our lost child. I wondered what my grandmother Hazel would have said; if she would have approved of us having the body cremated. I suspected she would have told us we'd prevented our child from participating in the great rapture when Jesus returned, but perhaps she would have deferred all matters of theology to my grandfather. She must have had a simple faith in Stephen. *His* faith had been in God; he had found his conviction in the Holy Spirit early in life, after his brother's tragic accident. My faith was in money and math. I thought math ruled the universe. If it were proven that the almighty God my grandparents had worshiped was a complex mathematical equation hidden within the universe, I'd have perked up, but I had my doubts.

A rusty pickup rolled past us, going in the opposite direction, and the wrinkled driver waved over at us with the back of his left forefinger. He wore bibbed overalls and he clutched a burning cigarette between the fingers that gripped the steering wheel. By instinct, I waved back.

"Do you know him?" Rebecca asked.

"No," I said, shrugging. "It's what they do here."

"Oh," Rebecca said. "That was odd. The smell... Did you?"

"We're not in California, my dear, and no, I did not." I smirked at her. "That smell is sulfur and coal smoke from potbelly stoves."

"Oh," Rebecca said. "Potbelly stoves?"

"It's how they heat the house," I said. I turned the SUV left onto a familiar road; the same road my family had driven to visit my grandparents for Christmases, Thanksgivings, and summertime weeks past, when I would watch their everyday lives unfold. It amazed me that, in 1930, when the large, white sign on the south side of Mount Lee read 'HOLLYWOODLAND', my grandparents had chosen to drive over 2,200 miles in a Ford Model A. They had travelled together, without air-conditioning, over dirt, brick, and aggregate roads that my grandfather had described as 'like driving over corduroy pants'.

They started their life's journey together from the then-termination-point of the newly opened Route 66. It was before World War II; the beginning of the Great Depression, before commercial air travel, television, and the pervasive Internet. They left behind their West Coast friends, her entire family, and a new cartoon character named 'Mickey Mouse', but it was their choice to go back east and leave behind the hot Santa Ana winds of modern progress. They could have easily just stayed in California and saved souls as they soaked in the sun, but they didn't, and I got to exist.

After we succeeded in not having the windshield shattered by jagged coal chunks from the parade of dump trucks, or being crushed by a random limestone boulder from the steep hillsides, I turned left onto Route 15. We drove a few miles, and then I steered left onto County Road 476, which was barely wide enough for two-car lanes. It snaked deeper and deeper into the mountains.

"As a child, I hated this road," I said, leaning forward to glance up into the leafy hills, which were covered in dense, green kudzu. Then, I focused on the road, which was carved between a sheer, dark-gray rock wall and a trickling creek bed with a steep, grassy embankment.

"They called that creek 'the Troublesome'."

"Why?" Rebecca asked. She tapped her hand on the window, indicating a rickety bridge strung together with wood and thick rope. "What's that about?"

"Oh, swinging bridge. A redneck, sorry, *hillbilly* method of getting across," I said. I smiled over at her as sunlight flashed at me between gaps within the dense tree limbs.

"Big surprise," Rebecca said while she studied her mobile, "I have zero coverage. What's the difference between a redneck and hillbilly?"

"It's complicated," I said. "It's like asking why the Hatfields hated the McCoys."

"Kind of dangerous, here?" Rebecca asked. "Any Boss Hoggs?"

"The road is, but the people are nice, for the most part," I said, shrugging. "I used to get car sick, on this road. My grandmother was always oblivious, until I'd vomit."

"I can see why," Rebecca said. In an unfamiliar, twangy voice, she added, "This is like driving across a python's back, *right?*"

"'Python's back'?" I asked. "Who are you?"

"My inner 'hillbilly'. I've watched *The Dukes of Hazzard*," Rebecca said. "Isn't that how they talk here, all twangy?"

I tried to remember how my grandfather had sounded, the

cadence of his words, his mannerisms. Then it occurred to me; he had never sounded 'twangy'.

"Some do, my grandparents didn't," I sighed.

"Sorry," Rebecca said, touching my arm. "Just trying to lighten things up."

"It's all right," I said. "She got to be old. Maybe I'll get well into my nineties, too."

As we drove along, I saw the old post office and the general store where I'd been exposed to Moon Pies and RC Cola. Several double-wide trailers were set beneath the road surface, tucked into open spots near the creek bed. Around the bend and a quarter-mile further, there was my grandfather's once-vibrant, wooden-planked chapel in a large, flat clearing. We parked outside, on the gravel lot, and I said a brief prayer, because I thought it was what I should do. We held hands as we stepped inside the modest, double-door sanctuary. The oak floorboards creaked from age and loosened nails. My mother's closed, cherry-veneered coffin had been placed beneath the same simple pulpit from which my grandfather had spent over four decades conducting worship services, weddings, and funerals. The tiny seating line of pine pews smelled of fresh funeral flowers and a certain dampness that only comes from dense humidity and age. My sister acknowledged me as she sat nearby with her family, her expression telling me that we were late.

"I guess there's an advantage to growing old," I said. I glanced down the empty row. "No one's left to come to your funeral."

"This place is rather quaint," Rebecca said. She placed her hands on top of the casket, whispered a quiet prayer, and made the sign of the cross.

The funeral was low-key. It was what I'd expected, down to the music: *How Great Thou Art*. I'd heard that song played by my grandmother numerous times, seated behind the same upright piano that was set over to the left of the pulpit. The one thing I knew about that piano was that my grandfather had carved a heart around my grandmother's name, on the inside. He had told me that, with a mischievous grin, when I was a child.

"If that piano could talk," I said, fiddling with Rebecca's wedding ring.

"What would it say?" she asked, grasping my hand.

"Nothing," I said. I nodded over at my sister, Ruth, and her family. She looked down at the wooden floorboards. "Never mind..."

After the service, four sturdy, young pallbearers hired by the funeral home led us outside, and then we drove up the hillside, behind the hearse, to the family cemetery. It was a quiet ceremony. After, we strolled between the tombstones, protected by a rickety wire fence. The barnacled, contorted tree branches had twisted and intertwined in an uncomfortable embrace.

"I have a question," Rebecca said. She pointed down at two headstones. "These, and several others, say 'CSA', but only in this area, not near your mother."

I reached from behind to hug her close.

"Confederate States of America, 'CSA'," I said, pointing to her left. "That one was my great-great-great-something-or-other. He was a colonel for the gray side."

"For real?" Rebecca asked. "You never told me."

"Ah, not worth talking about," I said. I leaned down and pulled out the grass clumps that had begun to grow on the tombstone. "They say he was buried in his uniform."

I stood up and stuffed my hands into my jacket pockets. We walked over to my grandparents' shared headstone.

"I wish you'd met them," I said. I tapped the marble monument. "I still miss them."

"Me too," Rebecca said. She took in a deep breath. "It's beautiful up here, nice view of the valley, but I wouldn't want our baby boy here, all alone, in a cemetery."

"Yeah, I know," I said. I stared down the hillside at the simple chapel. "Weird, that's been there for almost a hundred years, now."

"Hello, Brother," Ruth said. "Glad you're still alive."

"Hey there," I said, hugging her. Her once thick, blonde hair was turning gray, but her blue eyes were still as vibrant as a cloudless summer day.

"You never call, I'm surprised you came," Ruth said. She hugged Rebecca. "We never see you."

"I'm just really busy," I said. "You know, I don't know why I came, Rebecca thought it was a good idea."

"Well," Ruth said, "it's all behind us, now."

"I promise I'll call," I said. "Promise."

"That's what you always say," Ruth said. "You're welcome at the house, don't be a stranger."

"I won't. I think we better get back," I said. "I'll try to call more often."

Her eyes told me she didn't believe me, and she turned and walked away. The fall breeze had turned a bit cooler, the warning that wintertime approached. Soon, the ancient trees and the land would be stripped bare, awaiting the colorful springtime renewal. I hated winter. Rebecca stepped between the markers and headed toward the back of the cemetery. The shadows had begun to creep forward like the leafy kudzu that covered parts of the mountain. We paid our respects to my mother's permanent spot, hugged my sister, and then drove back toward Lexington.

"I think you should go back," Rebecca said. "Home—"

"Why?" I interrupted, grimacing. "My home's in California."

"Closure," Rebecca said, grasping my hand. "For me?"

"I think bulldozer that place, it was a house of horrors. Just scrape it away, down to the dirt, and start over." But I dutifully nodded. "You're right, don't want to dump all the mess on my sister."

By instinct, I navigated the SUV back toward the old house. After I parked on the shifting driveway, I glanced at the big yard hidden within the darkness, where I used to mow the bluegrass lawn with a ten-horsepower tractor that belched fumes. I took in the spot where I'd practiced punting a football over a large oak tree, now reduced to a stump, and the spot where I'd learned to chip a golf ball, because I thought that was a game for rich folks, and I wanted to fit in when I became rich. I grinned, remembering this was where I'd stolen my first kiss from a giggly ten-year-old girl named 'Laina', just behind a line of old dogwoods.

The brick house was silent; it was as if we'd walked into a museum exhibit on the 1970s. The darkness outside caused the incandescent lights to cast a milky glow down the narrow hallways. They were the sort of hallways a character in a horror movie shouldn't investigate.

"I guess we should make sure the place is secured," I said as we walked further inside. I was careful not to touch any of the living room furniture, unwilling to be pelted with dust. "I think I'll get a security service to monitor the place, you never know. I'll call my sister."

"The utilities are in our name, right?" Rebecca asked. She stared down the dark basement stairwell and then glanced back at me. "Spooky! It could be fun to explore."

"Sure is, but be careful, Mom was a hoarder," I said.

I flicked on the kitchen lights, and everything appeared in perfect disorder. I turned down the back hallway and opened the first door. It was my bedroom, a room where I used to stare out of the locked windows at the lamppost on the street corner, thinking I had a different destiny. The room was cold and full of boxes; some contained relics, others were half-filled with newspapers. The boxes blocked the bottom half of the windows, and I quickly shut the door to block out any memories. I continued to peek into the other bedrooms, checking that the windows were locked. I walked past my high school senior photo. I examined it and decided to take it with me, thinking Rebecca might get a laugh at my Dutch-cut. After I inspected the rest of the windows and doors, I stood on the top step of the basement stairs. After a few minutes, Rebecca appeared. She smiled up at me, clutching a corrugated box. She dropped it at my feet.

"Guess what I found," she said. She flicked the box's top off. "Check this out."

"Leather-bound books?" I asked, kneeling down. "Let me guess, southern recipes?"

"No, they're diaries," Rebecca said. She snapped one open and shoved it at me. "Read it."

"Here," I said. I handed her my high school photo.

"Oh, look at you," she said.

I held the book and glossed my fingers across the old leather. It smelled musty. The pages were covered in writing, all in black ink. The handwriting was consistent, intentional, and legible. It took me seconds to realize who had written the words: my grandfather, Stephen. It was as if he was standing in front of me, talking to me in his plain, direct way. I could almost smell his Aqua Velva aftershave; I could see his black-and-gray hair smoothed neatly down with Vitalis.

"My grandfather," I said. I bent down and put it back with the other journals. "Let him rest. I don't—"

"Are you kidding? This is a goldmine," Rebecca said as she pulled out another diary. She set my photo aside and leafed through it. "See? Here's his picture. Guess what?"

"I have nothing to say. These creep me out."

"He was quite detailed," she said. "I know his address."

"Ah, so do I, I was there when they buried him, and her too," I said. "Let's get out of here."

"No, I have his address when he was in Los Angeles, in 1926," Rebecca said. She waved the diary in front of my face. "Guess who he met in 1926? They were down there, just waiting for me to find them. Look at him."

"I know how this story ends," I said, reaching for the front door. "Don't forget my picture."

"This is your family," Rebecca said. "I bet it's a love story, in these pages."

"Gross," I said. "You're talking about my grandparents."

"I know," she said. "Haven't you ever wondered what they were like, when they were young?"

"No," I said. I leaned down to retrieve my picture. "Let's go. I have all I want. Give them to my sister."

But I should have known better, and Rebecca packed the box full of my grandfather's diaries onto our private plane. As we flew back toward California, she hardly said a word to me or the flight crew, immersed in reading each and every page.

"You should read these," she said. She licked her forefinger, carefully turning each page. "They're like reading a living history, the words he used."

"No," I said. I stretched out my legs. "I closed that chapter of my life a long time ago. I don't look back."

"Why?" she asked.

"Let the dead," I said, "remain dead."

CHAPTER 2

After we returned home, I stood in my backyard contemplating the universe. The gray evening fog billowed across my vantage point, and I moved closer to the cliff edge as the red-tailed hawk squealed its high-pitched warning. I leaned against the waist-high, stone wall that separated me from certain death and peeked over the side into the cold, soapy gloom. I couldn't see my feathered friend within the mists, along the meandering sea line, or above me in the swaying trees, but I knew the predator bird was out there. The half-full, crystal wine glass that I grasped in my right hand bobbed and weaved for its life. I steadied it like a cargo ship captain fighting a white squall, certain from years of experience that a navigation point would emerge from the darkness. It did; Rebecca sat next to a blazing fire. She nodded over at me, sitting behind our sprawling Mediterranean-style house with its red-clay-tiled roof.

"Are you coming back?" she asked, from across the lawn. "I think I need more wood."

"Yeah," I huffed. "We have plenty of wood."

Thanks to Nikola Tesla, the nearby estates cast enough electrical light that I could swirl my crystal glass. I examined the wine's thick, tributary legs, which streamed down to settle into a dark-red, half-full bottom. I smelled hints of juniper, currant, and velvety blackberry. My grandmother had loved springtime junipers. She would never have imbibed; the vessel's contents would have been abhorrent to her, even though wine was a part of Jesus' biblical journey. Last I read, he'd even had wine before he was executed for telling the masses they were allowed to think and were free to worship the one God.

"Maybe another log?" Rebecca asked. She studied the fire.

"We're good," I said.

I started to walk back toward her. My well-worn, Italian-leather shoes were covered with oval globs of residue. They had seen better days, but they were my favorite pair, because they were like me; a bit old and wrinkled, but confident. During the summers, my grandfather used to hoe his Kentucky corn before he preached at his one-story, white-planked chapel. I remembered his black wingtips were always covered with brown mud. He would try to knock off some of the dirt on the church's painted, concrete steps. He wasn't concerned if the mud didn't come off. He told me he wasn't in control, God was. If he had mud on his shoes, he was supposed to have mud on his shoes.

"We should drive down to LA," Rebecca said. "Go see where your grandfather lived, you know."

"No," I said. I sipped the wine.

"Why not?" Rebecca asked, stoking the fire. "It'd be fun."

"Careful," I said. The flickering shards from the fire reminded me of when my grandmother would teach me to hunt for summertime fireflies and trap them in a mason jar. "Those aren't fireflies."

"I think you should reconsider," Rebecca said.

"No, that's enough," I said. My mother's funeral was almost forgotten. I had left my childhood behind. It was the best way I'd learned to deal with pain; hide it inside my brain and forget the spot where I left it. I grimaced over at Rebecca, and then walked back inside and shut my office door behind me. Within moments, she had followed.

"Sit up, your posture's terrible," she said. She waved me back onto my home office's soft, leather couch. "I have exciting news."

"Please don't burn the house down," I said. I wondered if her plan would involve me selling shares of stock to fund her newest adventure. "Remember, I may be sort of retired, but I do have work in the morning."

"Not much of a retiree; we never have fun anymore. Close your eyes," Rebecca said.

I squinted to watch her pull out one of the diaries she'd lugged back from Kentucky. She opened to a page that had a blue-ribbon book marker, then she stepped forward and handed the open diary to me.

"Look, there."

"What?" I asked. I stared down at the thin, rice-paper pages. On the left page, behind the front cover, was an old, black-and-white photograph of my grandfather. It was taped to the bottom center beneath a handwritten note that advised that this was his diary. He was quite young, in his early twenties, and smiling. He wore a newsboy hat and had the gaze of an infinite future within his eyes.

"Handsome fellow," Rebecca said, nudging me.

"I remember his eyes were brown," I said. "He told me he was part Cherokee." I glossed my fingers across the picture. I thought it must have been a big deal, early in the twentieth century, to have your photo taken. He must have been proud, to have taped it to his diary for safekeeping. "I always thought he resembled Gregory Peck, after I watched *To Kill a Mockingbird*."

"Really?" Rebecca asked. After examining it closer, she added, "He does have some similar features."

"Yeah, that mix of hard and soft," I said. I handed the diary back to her, then crossed my arms and inspected my damp shoes. "And he had a dark side. Really dark."

"Interesting," Rebecca said.

"Can we stop this?" I asked. "I'm not amused."

"Look at this page," Rebecca said. She tapped her forefinger at the top of the right-side page with force. "See? See?"

"Yes, dear, I see an address," I said. "I guess this was *his* address."

"That's our starting point!" Rebecca said. "1926!"

"What?" I said. "No."

"I've read through most of his diaries. Not every word, mind you," Rebecca said. She started to stroll back and forth across the ornate Persian carpet that centered the office. "We start at 536 South Hope Street, in LA. It's perfect."

"For what?" I asked.

"Here goes," Rebecca said. She stood square with me. "We drive down to Los Angeles and retrace your grandfather's steps. Go visit where he lived, worked. It's all here, in these diaries. It'll be fun."

"You've lost it, right?" I asked. I started to walk toward my office bar. "I don't have time for this nonsense."

Rebecca moved in front of me, blocking my path to the land of sour mash, bourbon, and distilled aging with associated blurred vision.

"Nonsense?" Rebecca asked. "Oh, no; this is your life, and you now have the time to learn who your grandfather really was. We have the resources to do what millions would kill to do, and you're not saying 'no'."

"Better! How about 'no way'," I said. "Drink?"

Rebecca shrugged and faked a cough.

"I've already called your staff," she said. "I even called some board members."

"You're out of your mind," I said, staring at her intently. "This isn't funny!"

"Listen to me, don't get mad, please, try to remain calm," she said, grabbing my hand. "We have all the stuff we want, but I don't have you. You don't even want to hug me. It's like I'm here, but not here."

"Really?" I said. "I'm… it's not on purpose, I'm just distracted. Sorry—"

"I miss that boyish man," Rebecca said. She began to cry. "I miss that happy guy, I miss your stupid voices."

I stared away, out of the office and down a dimly lit hallway decorated with finely crafted wainscoting.

"Lost, huh?" I asked. I gripped Rebecca's fingers.

"I need more," Rebecca said.

"I know," I said.

"You've been given a gift, in those pages," she said. She released my grip and stepped back. "The gift of understanding your life, his life… I just want to come along for the ride."

I walked to the back of the bar and chose a tumbler from the first shelf, filling it with a handful of shaved ice. I let the bourbon marry with the ice and release a taste that always reminded me of horse racing, tobacco barns, and pretty girls.

"Let the dead remain dead," I said. I sipped the master-crafted beverage, but Rebecca just stared at me. Suddenly, she pointed at me, turned, and brought back another leather diary. It was segmented with numerous colorful ribbon bookmarks.

"Dead? Like you? Our boy?" she asked. Her finger glided toward a yellow ribbon, and she opened the diary. "Dead, right?"

"What's your point?" I asked. I took a significant gulp, and my throat burned from a raging, liquid fire.

"You don't understand," Rebecca said. "What kind of preacher was he? He was brutally honest?"

I closed my eyes and thought about sitting in his chapel.

"He sounded a bit gravelly; his voice was like a whisper, if that makes sense. He was never loud," I said. I thought about his distinct jawline. "He had a fire, though; this smoldering conviction to him."

"I thought so," she said. She moistened the tip of her forefinger and moved a page back. "After I read this, you tell me if he's dead."

"To Grandpa," I said. I raised the tumbler, took a sip, and expressed acceptance.

"Okay, this is what he wrote about your grandmother, the day he met her, the very first day," Rebecca said. She coughed, and then she began to read my grandfather's diary. "My first full day in Los Angeles. I am alone. I am not sure how to feel, for I met another believer, today. She told me she believed. Her name is 'Hazel'. She is pretty. She wore eyeglasses, like me."

"Stop," I said. I was no longer interested in the bourbon. It was an odd sensation to have their faces appear in my mind. I hated the fact that I could remember them in their coffins. "Fine, we'll do this, someday soon."

"No, now," Rebecca said. She dropped the diary on the bar. "You're not listening: now."

"Fine," I said. I nodded as I closed my eyes. "If it means that much to you—"

"Thank you," she said. "We have the Pierce-Arrow ready; we ride in 1929 style. And I've got a secret."

"Ah, no," I groaned.

"Sorry, but yes. I don't demand much, but I am now," she said, walking behind the bar. "Don't worry, you're already packed. We drive in the morning."

"Come on, now, it's not highway worthy," I said. My pulse started to thump as I imagined the terror of driving that car on the

101. "It's scary enough on the slow, seventeen-mile drive on parade day."

Rebecca waved me away and walked toward the main office's six-panel doors. She faked a yawn.

"Morning will be here before you know it," she said, and she shut the door behind her.

"Come on!" I said.

I walked back and slouched onto my leather couch. After I'd watched my alma mater lose another college football game, I was consoled by the thought that basketball season approached. I weaved my way to our bedroom. Rebecca had drifted off to sleep, or she pretended to be asleep. If I had any questions as to the conspiracy she had instigated, all I needed to observe were the clothes missing from my closets and that my bathroom had been rearranged. It seemed I no longer had any control. I got into bed and tried to snuggle near my wife. I was terrified she would leave me.

"But the Arrow?" I whispered. "It's my baby."

"You'll see," Rebecca said. She sighed. "Goodnight, my love. I want my man back." — *When has she lost him?*

"Night," I said, pulling the warm bed cover up to my neck. It had been decades since my grandfather had died, but over the years, I'd thought of him often. It wasn't a restful sleep, because snapshots from my childhood flashed in my brain. I remembered my conversations with my grandfather about Kentucky basketball and the Cincinnati Reds. He loved baseball, and we'd had endless conversations about our favorite players. My grandmother would grin over at us as she sat on a cushioned recliner and read under a tall lamp. I would memorize all the batting averages from *The Sporting News,* and we'd wonder if they were going to get to the series and beat the Yankees. It was a time when radio brought baseball to our ears, and the only baseball game on the black-and-white television was on Saturday afternoon, the *Game of the Week* hosted by Curt Gowdy with expert analysis from Tony Kubek. I closed my eyes. In truth, I wasn't worried about the antique car. I could replace it. What I was worried about was what I might find out.

CHAPTER 3

The next morning, just before six, my eyelids snapped open. I gazed up at our coffered ceiling, which had been painted with a rendering of the moon, earth, and stars. Rebecca had thought it would help us fall asleep with wonderment and perhaps trigger the creative sides of our brains. I was showered and quickly clothed in my comfortable khakis and patent-leather sneakers. I scampered downstairs through our custom kitchen and then toward our vast garage, a full mug of coffee in hand. I hadn't noted Rebecca's whereabouts as I navigated through our high-ceilinged house. She was already out of the bed, which did concern me, because she wasn't an early riser, but I was too late. I swung open the door and frowned. It was obvious; my ruby-red 1929 Pierce-Arrow Dual Cowl Phaeton had been loaded with our suitcases.

I walked into the garage from the portico side, and a few friends' backsides could be seen. I heard them laugh as they escaped through the fourth garage door. I strolled over to the car, and its eight different-sized headlamps seemed to question me with their gleaming. I sensed the car wanted to focus its lights on me so the archer hood ornament could have the best view in order to fire its arrow at me. Even the wide grill seemed to express an objection as I heard chuckles and sensed movement outside the garage doors.

"I saw you confederates," I said. I looked at the ornate car with its white-walled tires, long running boards, and a narrow, horizontal windshield. I moved to the side, where the term 'dual cowl' originated due to the solid wall between the uniformed chauffeur and the 'haves', the latter protected from society under a canopy roof. I thought there were a lot of suitcases on the back floorboards and within the rear baggage box, and I wondered why so many for a simple six-plus-hour drive down to Los Angeles, but I guessed my wife wanted to make it a long weekend at some swanky resort. It was her way of helping me to get over my mother's death. The death was already behind me, and I had total control over my thoughts. I pursed my lips and took a sip of my warm coffee.

"I hate resorts," I said to the well-maintained, classic automobile. This was not a *car*, but a rolling piece of art that had wanted its curvy exterior to be ogled by envious eyes since the time of Charlie Chaplin and my grandparents. I stood there, enjoying the coffee's aroma and inspecting my immaculate, antique, four-door touring car. I was quite aware that I'd accumulated several four-wheel, manmade toys, most of which were currently within my eyesight. The money I'd earned from my bloodless business career was simply the liquid to feed a passion. I loved cars. The area we lived in provided numerous low-key dining and drinking spots, and I liked the idea that success allowed us to choose to disappear. I guess, in a way, this wasn't unlike my grandparents' choice to drive back east through a hidden section of the United States. We, in contrast, wouldn't disappear driving this Roaring Twenties status symbol. And staying at a fancy resort? Rebecca had known I wouldn't enjoy listening to random people invading our personal space while trying to impress us. In those situations, I tried not to divulge anything significant about us, and I worked to listen to what they said so I could pepper them with questions about themselves. I had learned the technique from my grandfather. He had always told me to 'be ye kind', but he'd also taught me how to deal with strangers. It was easy for him; he was a preacher, a man of God, so he was expected to care about all of God's children and listen to them complain about how unfair life had been to them, or how wonderful their life was and how important they were. He treated them all the same.

As I paced around the garage, I remembered a comment he had made to me. 'Bobby, let people talk, it makes them feel better.' He had winked down at me. At the time, I didn't understand, but later in life, I had appreciated his wisdom. As I leant back against a tall, red auto-mechanic chest, I saw a note on the thin windshield. I walked over and opened the note, only to realize Rebecca had thought through each step of our trip to Los Angeles. In part, this was because my master mechanic, Wylie, had written a note to assure me he had inspected my classic girl, that he had made adjustments, pumped pressure into the gas system, and replaced the fluids necessary for our journey. In essence, Rebecca had anticipated my objections. At that point, I realized I had to accept this trip was going to happen. Her conspiracy had been fully fleshed out. And then Rebecca magically appeared.

"Watching me?" I asked.

"Well, ready to go?" she asked. She had strolled into the garage with a travel mug; black-framed, movie-star sunglasses; and her hair covered with a shimmering silk scarf. "I have a plan."

"You know, this car isn't safe on the 101," I said. I pointed over at her.

"But it's legal, right?" she asked. She giggled, because she already knew my answer.

"Yes, but that has nothing to do with danger," I said. I checked that the back luggage box was secured. "I'm concerned about the other cars and trucks. Not to mention, this isn't exactly a low-key car."

"I know, but we aren't taking the 101," Rebecca said.

"Good, okay, you got me," I said. My pulse slowed, and I nodded in agreement, understanding her clever joke: we were headed to the nearby executive airport. I felt stupid, having thought we'd actually drive this machine the six hours down to LA.

"We're taking 1, down the Pacific," Rebecca said. She smooched at me with an air kiss and pushed the garage door opener. She fished her right hand forward like a shark's fin schooling along the coast. "I love how it hugs the coast, don't you?"

"California 1?" I asked. "That'll take forever!" I stared at her through the driver-side window. "This is an open car; it won't really protect us from the weather."

"Do we have a clock on us?" Rebecca asked. She opened the passenger-side door and took off her sunglasses. "Get in, drive. I have a plan. It'll be beautiful; it'll prepare us to go back in time."

"Back in time?" I asked. I motioned back at the house with my thumb.

"Don't worry, our friends and security will take care of the rest, you know that, stop stalling," Rebecca said. She pointed at the driver's seat. "Like I said: get in, drive. Besides, I have the car cover packed, and I've already had the dual-ignition system cranked by Mr. Wylie. He's just a phone call away, so get in, we'll be just fine."

After a moment's hesitation, I glanced back. Then, I opened the driver-side door.

"You're crazy," I said. I turned the key and pumped a little more pressure into the gas system.

"You chose to marry me, remember? I gave up my career for you," she said, patting my shoulder. From her black purse, she drew one of my grandfather's diaries. "I'll read as you drive; I have several parts I think you'll enjoy, it'll set the mood."

"That's creepy," I said. As I'd already figured out, the keys were waiting for me. "But you'd have been a great lawyer. And mother, if things had been different."

"Not now, let's not go there," Rebecca said. She sat back on the soft, tan, leather bench seat.

"Ready," I said. I sipped the coffee.

"Yeah, well, anywho," Rebecca said. She looked through the open garage door and onto a street lined by our friends. They waved at us as if we'd just gotten married.

"You and your adventures," I said. I shifted the car into first gear, and we began to roll forward. As we passed across the garage threshold, I waved at our friends and honked the bugle horn at them. Rebecca waved back, and then she took off her sunglasses and gazed over at me.

"I promise," she said, beginning to tear up but fighting past her emotions, "I have a plan. I want my Bobby back. Right?"

I thought that, when you're aware of it, love has a weird way of emerging. But then, I was typically unaware. It might have been the look in her eyes, the cadence of her voice, or it might have been that instinctual sensation that the hawk would figure out a way to feed its family without me nearby.

"Alright," I said. I shifted into second gear. "Alright..."

CHAPTER 4

Typically, it was a bit chilly as the morning fog that blanketed Carmel Bay was burned off by the rising sun. I maneuvered our automobile away from the Pescadero Canyon and the lounging sea otters, avoiding a busy seventeen-mile drive as I turned the old car right and drove through the quaint seaside town of Carmel-by-the-Sea. We journeyed along Ocean Avenue, past the village boutiques and then onto Cabrillo Highway, better known at State Route 1.

"I cannot remember the last time I drove down the 1," I said. I kept the car in the right lane at a calm cruising speed. As I pressed down on the metal throttle, my right hand sensed that the car engine had opened up its straight-eight, three-speed, manual transmission. It was as if it enjoyed showing off, being freed from our garage, and driving along the California cliff edge in the salty air, past the blue Pacific Ocean.

"Just look around," Rebecca said. She adjusted her sunglasses. "It's amazing, think how lucky we are."

"Well, get comfortable," I said. I gripped the black-lacquered steering wheel. "It'll take some time to get to LA, depending on traffic, and State Route 1 is notorious for chunks of rocks sliding into the ocean."

"Don't be a fraidy-cat," Rebecca said. "We have all the time in the world."

"I think we both know I'm not a fraidy-cat," I said. "I'm the one with a warrant out for my arrest."

"Funny," Rebeca said. She slapped my right thigh. "I'll worry when a black SUV appears."

I ignored her comment, because I knew a security detail was always following me; the board of directors had demanded it after an unfortunate, but quite profitable, set of trades. Thankfully, they maintained their distance and allowed me to live, for the most part, a nondescript lifestyle. I loved being nondescript and rich.

"You know one of the cool things about this car?" I asked.

"Please inform me about your old mistress," Rebecca said. After she sipped her travel coffee mug, she started to leaf through one of my grandfather's leather diaries.

"The headlights are molded into the fenders," I said. I glanced over at her. She examined the diary, and then she looked through the side-folding windshield. Finally, she pointed at the hood ornament.

"I just like that little naked man, you used to look like that," she said. She tapped on the safety glass. "You need to find me a charm like that, for my bracelet, but in gold, not silver."

"The hood ornament?" I asked. "Figures; that archer was the symbol for Pierce-Arrow. I think I'll remove it. It's a rather desirable object."

"Why do you worry so much?" she asked. She slipped a page marker into the diary. "We've been married for eons, and you always worry about 'what if', but you don't have to worry anymore. If we lose it, so what?"

"I hate waste," I said. "Makes my palms sweat."

As we drove along the scenic highway, I thought about growing up hearing and seeing constant conflict. Back then, my first order of business each day was to survive. Going out into the world, all the while trying not to be noticed. The technique had helped me succeed in business. I had a few close friends, but I'd gotten used to being alone. After my grandparents had died, I'd had little to look forward to. There had been no prom for me, because I wouldn't risk allowing the girls I liked into my world. I'd thought they wouldn't understand, and I couldn't have borne the embarrassment. It had been a constant barrage, enduring my delusional father and my mother's passive aggressive. What I'd had was the hope to escape and create my own future; to control my world, to be left alone. By most measures, even my own expectations, I had succeeded, but, in truth, I didn't feel any different. It was like having a hidden tick suck your life away.

"Stop at Rainbow Bridge," Rebecca said. She dug down into her purse to retrieve her smartphone. "I want pictures from our quest."

"Quest?" I asked. I steered off the highway and into a parking area with metal picnic tables. Behind them, a fence line was set near the cliffs. "If we do this often, it'll take us until the next century to get there."

"Get out, I want a photo of you, your mistress, and the bridge. Read about the bridge, it's interesting," Rebecca said. She focused the camera lens on me and pressed against the touchscreen. "Perfect."

I obeyed her request, but I'd taken off my V-neck sweater as the morning temperature had begun to warm. Several cars sped past us as I stood against one of my favorite possessions. Behind me were the concrete, spandrel-arched bridge and the white-foam waves of the Pacific Ocean crashing against the rocky, Central California coastline. The seagulls above us appeared almost weightless, as if the breeze held them in place, before dive-bombing into the Pacific. The bridge had been built back in 1932 to connect Big Sur to the rest of California, because the road was almost impassable during winter storms. Looking down at the concrete arch, it occurred to me that my Pierce-Arrow was older than the popular bridge, and it might have made the journey across the bridge before I was born. A story was trapped within the car metal. If only the archer could put his bow and arrow down, what would he tell me about their journeys during the Great Depression and before World War II? My grandparents would have already made their journey from Los Angeles back to Kentucky.

"What are you noodling about?" Rebecca asked. She had stuffed the smartphone back into her bag and now walked over to hug me.

"I don't know," I said, hugging back. "Never mind."

"Stop lying," Rebecca said. She nudged me. "Tell me."

"Sorry," I said. I stared out across the Pacific to where the dark-blue ocean merged with the pale-blue sky, like a contemplative Rothko painting. "I was thinking about the fact that this car is older than the bridge, and that my grandparents had already driven back across the country along Route 66, in a Ford Model A, when it was built. Weird."

"That's not weird, it's sweet," she said.

"Get back in," I said, kissing her forehead. "We need to make some time, down the road."

"Love, love," Rebecca said. She waved me away, then walked to the passenger side as the constant ocean breeze caused those curvy lengths of her blonde hair not tucked under her colorful scarf to encircle her face. She grinned at me as she opened the passenger-side door. I turned the key to engage the battery, checked the gas pressure, made sure we had both the left and right sides of the engine on, and pushed down on the foot pedal starter with my right shoe.

"Just drive toward downtown Los Angeles," Rebecca said. She snuggled down into the seat. "But take your time; enjoy the surf, the seagulls."

"Seagulls?" I asked.

"Yeah," Rebecca said. "Look at them fly in place against the wind. Hear them? They're talking to each other. I bet they're looking down at us."

"Just searching for food," I said. "We're too big."

We traveled back along State Route 1 at a sensible speed, to protect my baby's engine from injury. We drove past Big Sur, acknowledged Hearst Castle, William Randolph Hearst's San Simeon vanity monument, and avoided any time-killing tourist traps, while Rebecca continued to read my grandfather's diaries. She would occasionally reach over to brush her soft fingers along my face and behind my ear. She said nothing. We spoke little as we traveled. There was no radio to invade our space. It was an odd sensation to feel content just being with her. It was hard to trust the feeling, but it was fun to share moments along the twisting road as we drove past coastal communities and collections of beach dwellers. Driving along the California coastline took me back to a time when the state was calm and pristine, and the future seemed limitless as we listened to the same, constant motion of the Pacific tides. As we approached the bustling metropolis of Los Angeles, we noticed progress had happened; the Cabrillo Highway now merged onto the Ventura Freeway. We rolled past Thousand Oaks, Encino, and Sherman Oaks.

"Ventura Highway in the sunshine!" Rebecca sang. She clapped her hands and waved at passersby like she was running for mayor. "This is so much fun."

"I love that song," I said. I gripped the steering wheel and then cautiously drove onto the bustling Interstate 5. "So, we aren't going to stay on this for long?"

"We're not far," Rebecca said. She pointed forward.

The Pierce-Arrow wasn't made with the knowledge that it would someday have to share the five-lane-wide road with eighteen-wheelers, junkers, and four-door sedans being driven by texting mothers and teenagers through concrete spaghetti junctions. But there we were, thankful that the overcrowded interstate traffic was moving at a manageable speed. Now, I just hoped not to die from the noxious fumes.

"What's your plan?" I asked. It was loud enough that I had to ask Rebecca in the style of a carnival barker. She pulled out her notebook and thumbed through her secret itinerary.

"Biltmore," Rebecca said. "I think it's a perfect spot for us, it was built in the 1920s; they would have seen it."

"Weird," I said. "Never stayed there…"

"I know," Rebecca said, "but it's perfect."

By dusk, we had driven past Griffith Park and Dodger Stadium, unharmed by the dense city traffic. Our antique, ruby-red girl was getting an occasional honk of approval as Rebecca's smartphone navigated us toward our hotel. I suspected the car liked to be gawked at, that's what she was made for; that and to show them her owners had made it. She was a classic status symbol. I wondered if this wasn't her first trip to the Biltmore. As I turned into the valet station near the ornate, Greek-columned archway, had she rolled up to these golden double doors before, perhaps for the Academy Awards? Had she seen Shirley Temple, Clark Gable, or Walt Disney in the prime of their lives?

"You know, my love," Rebecca said. She waited for the valet to open her passenger-side door. "Your grandfather would have walked past this joint, almost daily."

"Stop, that hurts my head," I said. I handed the well-groomed, uniformed, Hispanic valet a hundred-dollar bill with specific instructions on how to treat my girl. I glanced back across the city street and wondered what it had looked like in 1926.

Rebecca and our talkative bellboy walked inside to the front reception area, and I glanced back at my car being driven off. I prayed for her safety.

"She'll be fine," Rebecca said, waving me forward. I stood next to our bags, which were stuffed onto a valet cart, watching the staff care for an array of guests. The colorful foyer had enough highly polished marble and finely crafted carvings to make a Roman emperor blush. I doubted my grandfather had ever stepped foot inside, even though his address was well within walking distance, but I was comfortable. I had an all-access ticket that they don't offer at Disneyland, anymore: simply put, money. I stared down at my leather shoes and then out through the front doors at the street traffic. For some odd reason, I felt like my grandfather was nearby, frowning at me. It all came back to my vanity. My grandparents wouldn't have approved. It was a sensation I couldn't explain to Rebecca, who was negotiating for an exact suite with the reception staff, but it was a sensation I felt following me, and now observing me. It was a presence that I had rarely sensed, but it was there, nearby.

We were escorted from the busy front foyer, built to express power, wealth, and prestige, and up into a quiet, one-bedroom club suite. It had more space than my grandparents had ever lived in, and it was fair to describe it as opulent. It was a collection of rooms on the tenth floor that provided comfort and safety from the humble masses below, who I watched scurry about the city streets through the smoked-glass windows. Rebecca dismissed the hotel staff and walked over to stand next to me.

"This view is perfect," she said. She tapped at the glass window. "Just down there—"

"Where?" I asked, an acidic feeling in my throat.

"Somewhere near that library, see the pyramid?" Rebecca asked. "That's where your grandfather lived, and down the block, he met your grandmother. Below that tall building."

"I think things have changed, since then," I said, looking down at the crowded collection of short, fat, and skinny buildings paired with cluttered alleyways and concrete side streets.

"Yes, they have," Rebecca said.

"I also think we own part of that tall building. Actually, I know we do."

"Let me read this. I love this entry. He repeats himself, like he's not sure," Rebecca said. She opened a diary written in a forgotten time and read, "September 15th, '26. My first full day in Los Angeles. I am alone. I am not sure how to feel, for I met another believer, today. She told me she believed. Her name is 'Hazel'. She is pretty. She wore eyeglasses, like me. I walked down the street, I think she was standing near 5th Street. I need to learn how to get around.

"She told me they had moved here from Kansas. They had lost the farm. She said nothing of anyone else, not of her father or others. I do not know what to think. She was pretty. She wants to be a nurse or missionary? I think that is honorable. She had blue eyes, dark-brown hair. Her eyes told me she never lied. I do not understand why? I had stood at the corner of 5th Street and my street, Hope. She was standing just down the street from my room, maybe a few blocks. It was my first walk, after the train ride. I thought 'Hope' was an odd name for a street, but the school found the room for me. I think there are so many streets here. I am tired. I am scared. I am alone. Outside my window, tonight, the street is quiet. I pray God shows me what to do. I wonder what Ruby would do. But he is dead. I hope he has found Heaven. I will pray for his soul. I think I should pray for Hazel, I don't know why. Is that wrong? I wonder if I will ever meet her again. Why should I pray for her? I should look for a job in the morning."

"That sounds just like him," I said. "He wrote like he talked, I'll give him that."

"And tomorrow, after a good night's sleep," Rebecca said, snapping the diary shut, "we go for a walk over there."

"Do you think I would have been a good father?" I asked.

Rebecca stared through the windows for several moments.

"Yes. Let it go, I don't want to think about it," she said. She turned and walked toward the bedroom.

For some reason, as I stared into the distance and the city lights began to flicker and twinkle like celestial stars, I wondered about my grandfather. He was all alone in LA. He was a scared young man living thousands of miles from his home. I could feel a thick lump in my throat, and I fought back the urge to cry. But I didn't understand why.

CHAPTER 5

The next morning, we dressed in our casual attire and comfortable shoes and had a quick pre-ordered breakfast delivered to our suite. We took steaming coffees with us and held hands as we exited the quiet Biltmore and entered the boisterous South Grand Avenue. It was warm, the sky was a perfect California clear-blue; a blue hidden most days by the marine layer, better known as smog. But the day lacked the one thing I had endured growing up in Kentucky: humidity. You hardly sweat in Southern California.

    We dodged the constant street traffic; it was just a four-minute walk around the city block, along the tree-lined sidewalks, off 6th Street, and onto Hope Street, then on toward my grandfather's old address, but all we found there were a stale, twenty-story office building, a half-full, gated parking lot, and a line of trapped valley oak trees shading the concrete sidewalk. A feral cat crossed the street that dead-ended into a side entry for the Los Angeles Public Library. An uneven mass of skyscrapers poked into the sky, casting long shadows across the library and daily city life. The only reason we knew this was the spot was because our smartphone told us so, and the address numbers sandblasted across shiny, black-marble signage near the building's bank of glass-front doors.

"Well, that's that," I said. I wasn't surprised that his one-room apartment in a modest house had been bulldozed long ago. "That's life."

"I knew about this," Rebecca said. She took off her sunglasses. "I told you, I have a plan! I don't know what to expect, but come along. It's an adventure."

"Where?" I asked. "There's nothing here."

"The library. I spent a day researching this place," Rebecca said. She started to stroll off the street, between vintage, twin-lantern street lamps and toward the cast-iron-gated entry. "Walk with me, I'll be your docent."

"I love fancy words for 'tour guide'," I laughed. "All right, please inform me."

"That's the spirit," she said. She waved her hands in the air at the hulking concrete-and-limestone building, which was topped by a decorative, tiled pyramid. "Guess what year this library was built?"

"I have not a clue," I said.

"1926. Your grandfather would have walked under street lamps like those and past this library," she said. She led us up the concrete stairs and toward the thick, iron double doors. "Hope Street was redirected, hence the reason we can't walk to 5th Street. The spot where they met is now occupied by the library and a tall building. Well, at least the concierge *told* me that it was one of the tallest buildings."

"So, they met on a fluke?" I asked.

As we stood near the double doors, Rebecca pointed upward at the building's façade.

"See up there?" Rebecca asked. "The inscription is from the Bible, a lamp to our feet, and whatnot."

"Grandpa would have loved that," I said. "Goin' all biblical.

The dude up there looks sad." I held the door open and followed her inside, into the air-conditioning and the smell of cleaning solvents. "Why do government buildings, schools, and public libraries all smell the same?"

"Don't we all meet on a fluke?" Rebecca asked, ignoring my comment as she stopped to pull out one of my grandfather's diaries. She put on her reading glasses and leafed to a faded page covered in my grandfather's black-inked handwriting. She began to read as other curious library patrons walked past us.

"It is never dark here. Outside my window, the streetlights are always on. I am amazed. They have electricity here. I cannot see the stars, like I can back home. I pray not to feel alone. I know God has a plan. I walk around the new library to be around people. I wonder if God is in that place. One of my teachers said the symbols on the pyramid are pagan, I don't understand what that means."

Rebecca closed the diary. We continued up a set of polished marble stairs and into a massive, high-domed rotunda.

"An architect named 'Goodhue' designed this library. It's considered an early example of art deco," Rebecca said. She stopped at the center of the rotunda. "He also designed the penis of the prairie, better known at the Nebraska State Capitol building."

"Yes, the phallic symbol for big government," I said.

Rebecca pointed for us to look up at an ornate chandelier.

"That is the Zodiac Chandelier, it represents the building's theme, 'light of learning'," Rebecca said. She poked my chest with her manicured forefinger. "Nebraska: 'N' is for 'knowledge'."

"Zodiac? Grandpa wouldn't have dug that," I said. I stared up at the chandelier and the tilework crafted across the arched ceiling. "Looks like a globe surrounded by tiny suns."

"'Light of learning', that's what it means. It comes from a Nebraska philosophy professor," Rebecca said. She grabbed my right hand and moved me toward the south staircase. "I told you, there's no place like Nebraska. The happy, peaceful people of the prairie are everywhere. By the way, the murals along the walls depict Californian history. Let's go; we have an appointment to make."

"Blind dates do work," I said. I glanced up at a mural of a menacing-looking group of Spaniards, helpless padres, and an unlucky Native American. "If only they'd warned me before I met you in Winter Park, you sneaky Nebraskans."

I walked with Rebecca and we found the hallway leading over to the Tom Bradley wing. We left the circulation desks and old Los Angeles behind for modern Los Angeles, walking across the green, terracotta-tiled floor and into a tall, sun-splashed atrium. Rebecca inspected the building's legend, and we stepped on the cascading down escalators. We glided down past the Art, Music & Recreation Department, the Children's Literature Department, and down to lower level 4. At the bottom, we stood in front of a sign: 'History & Genealogy Department'. Rebecca opened up her itinerary and tapped the center of the handwritten page.

"We're meeting with the department head, a Ms. Wilkinson," she said in a whispered tone. She walked forward with purpose onto the tan, zig-zag-patterned carpet that navigated us past rows of tall, metal shelves stuffed with books and artifacts, as we made our way toward the reference desk. Behind the circular desk stood a slender woman wearing a flower-print jumpsuit, her hair was dyed pale pink with aquamarine streaks.

"What up, my Biola peeps?" she asked. She had an expression that suggested her skin felt comfortable and content hanging around its host. Her smartphone rang, but she switched it off. "Sorry. Thirsty boy, you know. How can I help?"

"Yeah," I said. "We've come to save your soul."

"You're funny," she said, pointing at me.

Rebecca moved in front of me and tapped her fingers on the desktop, examining the nearby library workers and patrons.

"We're looking for a Ms. Wilkinson," Rebecca said. "We have an appointment, I called ahead."

"That's me, I'm Amy, I'm the director," she said. She nodded her head and put her hands on her slender hips. "You're the people, right? The Church of the Open Door peeps? Jesus saves!"

"Sorry?" I said.

"Hope Street? If not, awkward," Amy said. She inspected us. "You called asking about Hope Street and the 'Jesus saves' people, it's all good. Chill, bro."

"Yes, but... *what?*" Rebecca asked. She examined her notes. "'Biola', not 'Church of the Open Door'."

"Chill?" I asked. I looked over at Rebecca. "Promise her we aren't looking for L. Ron Hubbard."

"Bro, don't talk about those people," Amy said. She inspected the quiet library suspiciously. "I'll take the Jesus freaks, keep the *satantologists* away."

"Who are you talking about?" Rebecca asked. She took off her readers. "Biola was over there on Hope Street."

"Never mind," I said. I nodded at Amy. "I got y—"

"That's it! 'Bible Institute of Los Angeles', 'Biola', they had their meetings there, back in the day," Amy said. She kept nodding her head, smiling at us as she bounced, as if to have us agree with her. She waved her hands above her head. "Jesus saves! I found a whole bunch of photos for you. It's sad, the big building was down the street, thirteen stories or something like that, if I remember my research correctly. It's gone. But anywho..."

"Let me guess," I said. "Torn down, evil developers, I love the protests, right?"

"No, earthquake took it out, so all we have now are photos to share and some history books," Amy said. She frowned. "Sad that we lost so much; if it isn't natural disasters, we just bulldoze over it. Killing history—"

"We'll take what we can get," I said.

"It'd be perf if we could get one of those 'Jesus saves' signs," Amy said. "You know, for our collection."

"Ah, I had no idea," Rebecca said. She glanced up at me. "What's next? You have photos?"

Amy walked from behind the counter and waved for us to follow her down a narrow hallway. She acknowledged her co-workers, opened a gray-metal, interior door, and flicked on the ceiling lights. Attached to the far wall was a black television screen. Beneath the screen was a keyboard sitting on a yellow oak work surface.

"I have it all saved," Amy said. She wiggled the mouse, and the screen clicked on to reveal a file folder named 'Hope People'. She clicked on the icon and opened a black-and-white pictorial. "Very cool; we have a California index, and I found photos from the time period. I got so stoked, this is old-school LA, very cool, so this was totally fun for me."

"That's cool," I said. She started to scroll through the photos of street scenes of houses, buildings, and everyday life from the 1920s. "You're a native?"

"Yeah, for sure. Born in Pomona, way east," Amy said without shifting her gaze from the screen. "Then La Mirada, that's how I know about these people. Biola's out there now, saving souls. My masters at USC was Californian history, so I'm way all over this stuff."

"Pomona? My grandparents were married at a house in Pomona," I said. I didn't need to read my grandfather's diaries to know that; they'd told me, and I'd even seen their wedding photo. I could remember it as clearly as if I was holding it in my hands. It was a picture of them in front of a wooden mantel and fireplace, my grandmother holding flowers. What I remembered the most was that they looked happy, the opposite of my parents' wedding photo.

"Ah, cool, man," Amy said. She nodded her head. "P-Town's changed a lot since then, just saying."

"Show us what you got," Rebecca said.

We sat down near Amy on some wooden chairs and watched her display black-and-white photo after black-and-white photo across the large screen. They were from a time when Southern California beaches were covered with oil-derrick farms, some guy named 'Disney' had created an animated cartoon character named 'Mickey Mouse', and Charlie Chaplin was making silent movies with a bamboo cane.

"I found photos near the address on Hope Street," Amy said. She scrolled down into a sub-folder. "These are from the 1920s; they're rather random. Remember, taking a photo back then was a new thing."

"I didn't even think about that," Rebecca said. "Sorry, not much to go on, I guess."

Amy kept scrolling through the photo collection. There were street scenes with women and men wearing the latest fashions from the flapper era. Bell-shaped hats for women with short, curly hairstyles, who wore long, silk dresses adorned with strings of fake pearls. The men wore stiff, high-collared shirts and three-piece suits. It was a time when Prohibition – the noble experiment – had failed despite faith's presence in every aspect of daily life. My grandfather's neighborhood had a church or temple on street corner after street corner after street corner, and it was expected that you worshipped at your chosen religious flavor. But the once proud sanctuaries were all gone from outside the library; the photos were the only windows left to see into a time when being right with God meant something connected to your soul's eternal life.

"I guess it was worth a shot in the dark," I said, shrugging. "Thanks, I appreciate all your efforts."

"Can I see the diary?" Amy asked. She held out her left hand for encouragement, and Rebecca searched her purse.

"What are you thinking?" I asked. I watched Rebecca hand over a diary.

Amy smoothed her finger tips across the pimpled, leather surface.

"This is priceless," she said. She seemed moved by the mere experience of touching the diary. "This is a time capsule. This is our history, it's alive."

We sat near each other, contemplating her comment for several minutes, as Amy read the diary.

"He had good handwriting," Rebecca said.

"Can I keep this, for a few days?" Amy asked. Her voice squeaked at the end. She set the diary on the work surface and opened a side drawer, pulling out a pair of white gloves that she began to put on. "I promise to be careful; I should have put these on to begin with."

"Well?" Rebecca asked. She looked over at me.

"Sure," I said. My instinct told me to follow her lead, and I had learned to always listen to it. "What's your plan? You seem absorbed."

"This is amazing," Amy said. Her eyes appeared lost in each diary entry. "He's writing about his everyday life, right here, near where we're sitting. Do you understand? This is a living history, it's really alive."

"Got some ideas?" Rebecca asked. "I'm at, well, a loss."

"Do you have more of these?" Amy asked. She adjusted her eyeglass frames as she stared over at us.

"Several. They're from most of his life," Rebecca said.

"Interesting," Amy said. She sat back in her wooden chair. "I want to take pictures of them, so I can chronicle them and add the information to our database. It would be invaluable. What happened to them? They buried here? You all looking for that sort of thing?"

"No, they drove back to Kentucky," I said. "Brethren, missionaries, or something like that, he was a preacher, she was a nurse. They're buried up on a hillside, not far from the chapel they built."

Amy took off her eyeglasses and crossed her arms.

"Wait, they drove all the way back to Kentucky in the 1930s?" she asked. Her voice went up an octave. "Are you serious?"

"Yeah," I said. I leaned forward. "They drove a Ford, Model A Ford, the original Route 66, I think."

"I am totally stoked, they took Route 66 to get their kicks," Amy said. She laughed as she put her eyeglasses back on and tucked her hair behind her ears. "Let me analyze this, it's like finding an undiscovered country. This is so cool."

"Yeah," I said. I leaned closer. "No kidding?"

"Let me read these," Amy said. "I am way in, you don't know what's in these."

"Fine, but how long?" Rebecca asked.

"Oh, I just need this one, first. Give me, let's say, two days?" Amy asked. She tapped the top of the diary. "Maybe we can trade them as I work through them, and maybe I can give you something in return that might help you. You know, give you a list, find your family history."

"Now what could that be?" I asked. I was amused by her passion. "I don't need a list, I know how this ends."

"A road map," Amy said. She smiled. "That's what you really want, a road map to follow, to places that he was at, *they* were at. You all are just trying to understand them, right?"

"That's awesome," Rebecca said. She wiggled off her chair. "How much money do you need?"

"Oh, nothing," Amy said. She waved away the thought. "This

is my career, I'm not into money. I follow the footprints of the past to the present. I'd do this for free if I could, but the big peeps don't play."

"We have a deal. We'll make the big peeps happy; we can donate to the library," I said. I got up and shook Amy's gloved hand. She grasped my hand with both of hers, and for some odd reason, she made me feel calm.

"You'll call us when you're done with this one?" Rebecca asked. She shook Amy's hand.

"I have your contact information," Amy said. Her knees bounced, and she nodded at us. "I'll call you in a few days, cool?"

"Cool," Rebecca said. "We'll go play in the meantime." We started to walk toward the door.

"Want a recommendation?" Amy asked. She touched Rebecca's arm and moved a step closer to us.

"Sure," I said. I grasped the cold, silver doorknob.

"Go check out Biola," Amy said. She grinned. "I have a contact out there, I bet he could help."

"Are you kidding me?" I asked. I wasn't comfortable with the idea of being around *those* people. "They might try to heal my soul. Better; to extract money."

"Don't worry, my contact is chill," Amy said.

"Don't say 'trust me'," I said. I opened the door.

"You're funny, in a cynical way," Amy said. She waved me out the door. "They have records; I bet they can show you his grades."

CHAPTER 6

A day later, Amy called Rebecca to share her contact at Biola, a man named 'Deano Rand'. I had hoped she might have forgotten her promise, but I knew she was way too smart to forget. After they tag-teamed me with logic, I agreed to accept my fate: to enter Biola University's grounds. Once again, Amy promised me her contact was 'chill'.

"I'm not giving them an offering," I said. I stared down at Rebecca's smartphone as if Amy were standing in our hotel room. "No kidding around, no money."

"Jesus saves!" Amy said from Rebecca's smartphone speaker. "I'm kidding, just slow your roll."

I still wasn't sure what 'chill' meant, and now I was trying to figure out 'slow your roll'.

"You all don't get it," I said. I paced back and forth in the suite. "This is 'save a soul' university, they're smiling assassins, but they're not Mormons, or, you know..."

"So, you'll go?" Rebecca asked.

"Yeah," I said. I blew all the air out of my lungs. "I just need some time."

I took a mental health break and walked into the Biltmore

parking structure. I checked on my vintage, straight-eight, white-wall-tired, ruby-red girl. As I circled her, inspecting each metal curve for dents, the hood-ornament archer seemed to wink at me. She was safe and secure within the hotel parking garage. I had provided some extra economic encouragement, so the valets had taken special care of her. They'd even roped off a special section, to prevent her from being dinged or touched by an unsavory gawker. I wasn't prepared to risk her on Interstate 5 again. I was barely prepared to be near those kooky people at the Bible Institute who would attempt to save my mortal soul from eternal damnation. I had grown up with their Southern Baptist projected guilt, but my grandfather had been different; he was never about guilt. If I took her out there, they'd notice her shiny, chrome headlamps and label me a backslider. It wasn't my fault my gas-powered babe had style.

"We cannot be guilted," I said to my car. "That's just how we roll."

After, I returned to Rebecca, who was bemused by my troubled expression.

"I called ahead," she said. She took off her reading glasses. "We have an appointment with Deano, he sounded like a nice fellow."

"I'll bet," I said. "Just wait, he'll start asking questions, then you'll see."

"Stop it," Rebecca said. "I thought you were Evil Bob? Evil Bob fears no man, right?"

After a few hesitant moments inspecting the suite's crown moldings for any gaps along the ceiling, I sucked in a deep breath.

"Don't call me 'Evil Bob'. I'll call down and get us a car," I said. I picked up the room's telephone. "Not taking her out there..."

"Wait," Rebecca said. She waved her smartphone at me. "Let's use that Uber thing, it's on my phone."

"I've heard of this, we've been monitoring this," I said. I put the telephone receiver back in its cradle. "I've been curious; they have an interesting business model. Maybe I'll get something out of this, what's next?"

"I was at lunch with the girls, they downloaded it for me, they thought it would be good, for if I got stranded," Rebecca giggled. "As if! It's local people, they go through a process, it's safe, we pay them with my credit card, no cash."

"Oh, I hate dirty taxis, always willing to spend more for a professional driver," I said. "What's the next step?"

"Not sure," Rebecca said. She started to press the application icon and read the instructions. "There are cars nearby, I think."

"Oh, yeah, see, they're moving," I said as I stared down at her touchscreen. "Like little car-looking bugs, see them? My grandparents wouldn't believe this."

"But it's another adventure," Rebecca said. She kissed my cheek. "Right?"

"Well, I guess so," I said. I opened the suite's front door. "Let's go investigate."

After a few hesitant minutes, we discovered how to summon a driver. A person's face and a description of the car popped up on Rebecca's screen. We got onto the elegant elevator and went down. On the ground floor, we walked past the front doors and ignored the valets, then we trekked down to the street, as if we'd committed a heinous crime and were searching for our getaway car. The driver flashed the car lights, and we got inside a tan SUV.

"Hi, I'm Trey. You're Rebecca?" he asked. He was a happy, middle-aged man with thin, blond hair and a California surfer's complexion. He inspected our expressions. "Your first time?"

"That obvious?" I asked.

"Kinda, yeah," Trey said. "It's all good. This is my part-time job; helps me pay for my kids' tuition."

Rebecca looked at me and then back at Trey.

"How does this work?" Rebecca asked.

"Want a quick tutorial?" Trey asked, pushing his fingers through his hair.

"Yes," Rebecca said. She grabbed my left hand. "It's legal?"

"Totally. Okay, so the people at Uber checked me out to make sure I'm not an axe murderer or known felon." Trey laughed nervously. "I keep the SUV clean, and we do follow a procedure: no cash, no tips, got it?"

"Well, yes," I said. I squeezed Rebecca's fingers. "That's a good start, but how do you make any money?"

"When I drop you all off," Trey said, pointing at Rebecca's smartphone, "you grade me, that helps me get more rides, and they pay us directly from the credit card charge. It's real simple."

"Cool," Rebecca said. "That is so fun, so creative."

"I call that entrepreneurship," I said. I nodded over at Trey. "Business is good?"

"Not bad, heading to Biola University, right?" Trey asked. He winked at us with a large, white-toothed smile.

"Biola," I said. I stared back over at the Biltmore.

"Really?" Trey asked. "That's kind of a hike from here, hope we don't get any Sigalerts."

"Really?" I asked. I gripped the door handle. "Let's not take the scenic route."

"No, dude," Trey said. "Sig-alert: freeways blocked—"

"His grandfather was a student," Rebecca said. She clicked in her seat belt. "The school started near here, but they moved their campus, from what we've been told."

"The 'Jesus saves' people," I said.

"Whoa, I remember those signs," Trey said. He nodded back at us. "That's old-school, old LA."

"My grandparents met here, down the street," I said. I was certain Trey thought we were religious zealots about to put the pinch on him. "They were missionaries. Don't worry, we're backsliders. We like to drink and misbehave."

"Gotcha," Trey said. He turned forward, shifted the SUV into drive, and nudged the automobile into the constant city traffic. "You know, you're headed not far from the happiest place on earth."

"I wouldn't think of Biola as the happiest place on earth," I said. I watched Trey maneuver the SUV onto Interstate 5.

"He means Disneyland," Rebecca said. She smacked me on the thigh.

"I threw up there," I said.

"Teacups?" Trey asked.

"Teacups got me," I said. The teacups had been a blur, like the blur of common city life as we sped down the interstate. "We were spinning, my grandparents had taken us. I guess I was about eleven. It was a time when I thought I looked cool in a powder-blue, polyester leisure suit."

"You sound pretty stylish to me," Trey said. He checked the side mirror as he drove inside the interstate's center lanes. "Knott's Berry Farm is another option. I recommend the log ride, my kids like it."

"Oh, we did that too," I said. "I was lucky. I got to go to Dodger Stadium one night and then watched the Angels the next night. I had no idea about the number of Hall of Famers I saw during those two games."

He flicked on the blinker for the Valley View Avenue exit and a sign for Biola University.

"Nothing like a Dodger dog," Trey said. "My kids love Dodger dogs."

"Ah, good point," I said. "I like Dodger dogs, but to be honest, I grew up a Reds fan."

Trey drove the SUV along Valley View Avenue, past light industrial buildings, one-story strip centers, and modest office buildings. The random grouping of skinny palm trees that peeked above us seemed out of place within the concrete jungle.

"I never knew you were a Reds fan," Rebecca said.

"Not so much, these days," I said. "You know something? Everywhere I go, these days, it all seems to look the same. Same stores, same restaurants, except for the palm trees. The trees tell you where you are, think about that."

"Yeah, back in the day, this was all orange groves," Trey said. He drove down Biola Avenue, which was rowed with ranch-style houses, bishop pines, and laurel oaks. He stopped the SUV near the driveway that led into the main campus.

"This works, we'll walk in from here," Rebecca said. She patted Trey on the shoulder. "So that's it?"

"Yeah, you can find a ride back by doing the same thing with the app on your phone," Trey said. He turned around to watch us get out. "Remember to grade me. Five stars, if you please."

"You got it," I said. I shut the passenger door.

"That was a fun adventure," Rebecca said. We walked away from the SUV and I watched it disappear back into the traffic. The blacktop was hot in the arid desert climate. Rebecca had placed me next to the Biola signage for a picture that would only be seen after I was long gone and my ashes had been scattered. We went to the front entrance guard kiosk and asked for directions, then along a meandering sidewalk shaded by oak trees, under which students were either napping, studying, or gossiping, until we stood holding hands in front of a three-story, red-brick-and-glass administrative office building.

"This is the place," Rebecca said. Her smartphone vibrated. "Look at that, he wasn't kidding."

"Give the boy five stars," I said, crossing my arms. "No going back, I guess."

CHAPTER 7

As we transitioned through the double doors, the environment changed from the loud, suburban noise of busy campus life to almost total quiet within a tall, sunny, split-level foyer, save for the hum of air-conditioning blowing through a metal duct just above us. We walked forward, listening to our steps resonate off the terrazzo floor, and then up the front stairs to a door with a black sign that read 'Administration Office'.

"I can hear myself breathe," I said. I gripped the cold, metal doorknob. "But it doesn't smell like cleaning solvents."

"Stop," Rebecca said. She pulled out her notes. "You are so weird."

Within the office, the reception area was furnished with wooden seats and side tables covered with Christian magazines. Biola memorabilia adorned the cream walls, but there were no people; it was as if everyone had left.

"Do you think the rapture just happened?" I asked. I grinned at Rebecca.

"Behave, these folks are professionals," she said, staring down the dark office hallway.

"We should wait," I said. It was funeral-parlor quiet standing on the dark-brown carpeting. Over the walnut veneer, I spied a chest-high receptionist's desk. It appeared someone had been working at the dark, marble work-surface; the telephone had green lights next to names, manila folder files were in a wire rack, and a well-used coffee mug decorated with 'Happy Mother's Day!' was sat steaming next to a child's picture.

"I promise I called," Rebecca said. She tapped her watch. "We are maybe a bit early."

"What are we missing?" I asked. I stuffed my hands in my gray slacks and glanced over at a picture from the top of the original downtown building. "We wait, I guess. Remember the signs, over there: 'Jesus saves', 'you are *healed*'."

"You do have the hair. You should have been a televangelist," Rebecca said. Then she pointed at me. "But these people are serious, we don't want to get escorted off the campus."

"No worries, I'm a legacy," I said, chuckling. "My DNA gets us invited into the club."

After a few more uncomfortable moments, as if we'd been left at the altar, we heard someone talking and walking toward us from the hallway. He emerged from the doorway.

"Sorry, it's Morning Prayer," he said, smiling. He was a solidly built young man with thick, black hair. The school logo was sewn into his white dress shirt's breast pocket. He reached forward to shake my hand. "I'm Deano Rand, and you are—"

Rebecca cut in.

"I'm Rebecca, I called." She stepped forward in front of me to shake his hand. "This is Robert, the grandson, we spoke about him."

"Of course. Welcome, my brother and sister," Deano said. He looked at us without moving his head and put his hands up, as if to bless us. "I'm kidding. Amy told me to act like a stuffed shirt that might want to save your soul and guilt you into a donation."

"Thank God," I said. I exhaled. "You had me."

"I don't bite, but I do accept donations," Deano said. He grinned as he waved for us to follow him down the hallway. "We don't make you confess your sins, here. That's for the other guys."

"Did you find anything?" Rebecca asked.

"Absolutely," Deano said. He escorted us to his comfortable office. "Make yourself at home on that couch, and I'll bring my laptop."

Rebecca and I sat on a blood-red leather couch. We watched Deano walk behind his yellow oak desk as he retrieved his laptop computer. He sat down next to Rebecca, turned on the screen, and after a few moments, he opened a computer file.

"Amy sent me a few selections from your grandfather's diary," Deano said. He wiggled his forefinger on the computer pad. "Yes, there we go, let's read that one.

"December 25th, '26. Santa forgot to come, I was disappointed. I was in the lobby at half past nine but missed the stage to go to Pomona. Went to Hirsch's, worked all night for only fifty-three cents an hour. We had CE at First Baptist, learning about fundamentals."

It was an odd sensation to hear and see Deano read from my grandfather's diary. The words told us a simple story, but I felt emotional. I wasn't sure why; they were simple words written in black ink.

"You wouldn't realize how valuable this is, for us," Deano said. He pointed at his computer screen.

"Not sure I follow," Rebecca said. She inspected the computer screen. "Fifty-three cents an hour, wow."

"The fundamentals and he came and went before the 'Jesus saves' signs went up in 1935, we don't even have class photos from that time," Deano said. He sat back on the office chair and glanced at me. "I heard you out there; I think you've got skills. If you ever want a class for public speaking and preaching, I've got your back."

"Fundamentals for saving souls," I said. "Be healed."

Deano looked over at me curiously.

"I take it you're not a believer?" he asked. He rolled his long-sleeved shirt up to his elbows.

"Sorry, I'm a skeptic," I said. I felt the shame, as if my grandfather sat nearby, poking me.

"I don't judge," Deano said. He pointed over at the wooden barrister bookshelf. "Those books are originals, *The Fundamentals: A Testimony to the Truth*. They're the basics for our Protestant beliefs and the education he got while here. He earned his diploma to be a preacher; the records indicate he wanted to be a missionary."

"Fifty-three cents an hour wouldn't have been a bad wage in 1926," I said. I wanted to change the conversation before I ran for the door. "Any idea about Hirsch's?"

"I think it was a bakery on Main Street," Deano said. He clicked on a picture and it expanded. "Your grandfather lived next to the main building. We'd find students nearby work to help them with living expenses. We required the business to pay them a living wage."

"He worked all night?" Rebecca asked.

"That's what he wrote," Deano said.

"At a Jewish bakery?" I asked.

"We've always been welcoming and respectful to all faiths," Deano said. He looked over at me. "Even to those without faith."

"What's 'CE'? Is that Confederate, too?" Rebecca asked. She glanced over at me.

"'Christian Education'," Dean said, "but why would—"

"'CSA', 'Confederate States of America', on some headstones," I said. I laughed. "We have some Confederate ancestry buried near my mother. Not the same thing, my love."

"Oh, okay. He does mention taking the stage," Deano said. He opened a photo of a horse-drawn stagecoach from the period. "Remember, the automobile was just starting to take hold across the country. At the time, one of the more inexpensive ways to get around was these stages that intermingled with the automobiles. Traffic must have been very loud. Total chaos. And that was just outside; he was here during a very controversial time."

"It's like something out of a movie," I said. "What was so controversial here, at the time?"

Deano clicked on another folder.

"The dean at the time had written a book, *Peter the Fisherman Philosopher*. He started a national firestorm, because it was a rather liberal interpretation of Peter's role in the Bible," Deano said. He put his hands up. "I don't know exactly what happened, but they forced him out. We haven't found a copy of the book, because they were destroyed, but let me read you something else from the diary.

"Went to church at BIO with Hazel at COD, had CE on seventh floor, went to work, forgot to get transfer, had to walk home from Main Street, made it home by eleven."

"Is he writing in code?" Rebecca asked.

"No. 'BIO' was, of course, 'Biola'. He really liked that Hazel girl. Amy said she's in almost every diary entry. He worked like a dog, at that bakery."

"Grandma," I said. I thought about them in their youth, at a time when they were just getting to know each other. "Her father died, he helped pay her bills. The family was broke after her mother lost the farm in Kansas."

"Sorry, I've read many a history like that," Deano said. He contemplated for a moment. "What was it? 'Go West, young man'."

"Manifest Destiny," Rebecca said.

"Huh?" I said.

"Don't you remember high school history class?" Rebecca

asked. "Horace Greeley said, 'Go West, young man, go West and grow up with the country.'"

"But my grandparents went back East," I said. "Maybe that's why I'm a contrarian."

Deano ignored our conversation and continued talking about the diary entry.

"What's interesting is he mentions 'COD', or 'Church of the Open Door,'" Deano said. He tapped the computer screen. "He's writing about the original building, he was hanging out on the seventh floor. It was thirteen stories tall; at the time, it was the tallest in Los Angeles."

"Earthquake took it out?" Rebecca asked.

"Correct, but Biola had moved out long before," Deano said. He coughed to clear his throat. He opened some more folders with pictures from the time. "I bet he's hidden in one of these. Sorry, I wish I had some class photos, but they simply don't exist."

Deano flicked through old, black-and-white photos of the time. Each class image consisted of bare rooms full of students wearing dark clothes, sitting on hard, wooden chairs while gazing up at their instructor, who was standing next to a chalkboard. There were images of packed congregations in a four-thousand-seat auditorium. Then, he opened a photo that caused my breath to stop.

"Stop!" I said. I stared at a photo.

"What?" Rebecca asked. "What?"

"That's them," I said. I stared at their black-and-white images, tapping the computer screen.

"Really?" Deano asked. He inspected the photo. "Which ones?"

"Center left, the two holding hands, both wearing black-framed glasses," I said. I moved closer to Rebecca, then reached forward and pointed my forefinger at the old image. "That's them, I'm positive."

"Oh my God," Rebecca said. She hugged me. "You're not kidding, he's dead-on Gregory Peck."

"I told ya," I said. "I told ya!"

"Dude, it's like fate or something," Deano said. He leaned forward. "They're looking right at us, as if they expected us to find them."

"They're just looking at the camera," I said.

"No," Deano said. He sat back in the office chair, contemplating their images, and whispered a brief prayer. "My faith requires me to listen; to listen to those moments when God is talking to me. I swear, I just got the chills."

"I didn't hear or feel anything," I said, shrugging.

"I know," Deano said. There was the gleam of tears in his eyes. "But I did. I believe you can sense when God is speaking."

"Are you saying," Rebecca asked, "that they wanted us to find them?"

"Like a parallel universe," I said. "Quantum physics—"

Deano shrugged and nodded.

"God is both the alpha and the omega," he said. He got up and went over to his desk, where he opened his leather-bound Bible. He dabbed his finger as he leafed toward the back of the book. "Yes, here it is..."

"Here's what?" Rebecca asked.

I knew from where he was reading. It was the Book of Revelation. I hadn't been in Sunday school in forty years, but I knew the section of the Bible that every believer went to when the Holy Spirit moved them. It was written by John, a Jew exiled on the Greek island of Patmos. My grandfather had preached about the end of days many, many times. He never scared me; like the Southern Baptists, he wasn't a 'fire and brimstone' preacher. He simply assured his flock that, if they believed in God with all their hearts, they had nothing to fear.

"Revelations, 1:8," Deano said. He shook the Bible as he

walked back and sat down. "'I am the alpha and the omega, the beginning and the end,' says the Lord God. 'I am the one who is, who always was, and who is still to come – the almighty one.'"

"You lost me," Rebecca said.

"I believe God created everything," Deano said. He stared across his office toward the back window, which cast rays of pale sunshine across the desk and carpet. "God is the only entity that can talk to us across time, because God created time. In other words, I don't put God in a box."

"It's the other way around," I said. I looked down at my grandparents. They appeared young, happy, and in love. They had the same expressions that I'd seen from my youth – the end of their journey. They seemed content to be sitting next to each other. It was odd to contemplate that, before they were my grandparents, they had been friends, and then lovers, and then created our family.

"Indeed," Deano said.

"I'm glad you found this," I said, "but this is just random luck; they're just looking at the camera."

"Deano," Rebecca said. "I wish I had your faith, but they look so happy, that's what I love."

Deano set his Bible on the coffee table. He sat back with his arms open, as if to accept the Holy Spirit into his life.

"I will pray for you two," he said.

"Thank you," I said. "I appreciate your kindness."

"I know you doubt me," Deano said. He closed his eyes. "But God spoke to me, just now. I never question God when I sense Him near me."

"I guess we missed it," Rebecca said. She looked back at me. "I don't know what to say."

"I'll bite," I said. "What's God saying?"

Deano nodded his head. He held his right hand up, with the palm open, as if to bless us.

"Listen," Deano said. He put his hand down. "I don't have answers, but they're talking to you, from that photo. I think they're talking to you; you simply need to listen and follow."

"Thank you," I said. I felt my face blush.

"Can we have a copy?" Rebecca asked.

"Certainly, I'll email you one and anything else I find," Deano said. He smiled at us. "I'm glad you came. All I want you to remember: have a little faith in them. If you can, trust God. God always provides the way, the path."

"I will," I said. I got up and shook his hand.

We left Biola and strolled past the front guard kiosk. We passed a few students studying in a grass courtyard. One ran past us, clearly late for class. Rebecca found us another Uber driver, and we quietly returned to our hotel suite.

That night, I was unusually tired, but I couldn't sleep. My mind was clouded with confusion. Over the years, I had learned not to just lie in bed trying to make myself go to sleep. Instead, I controlled my insomnia as I paced the suite and gazed across at the red-and-white lights that lit up downtown Los Angeles. I questioned every cell of my being. I wondered if I really had understood my grandparents, their faith, and my concept of what God was. At that moment, all I wanted was to talk to my grandfather, to ask him for guidance. And in a strange way, I sensed he was nearby, but I couldn't see him.

CHAPTER 8

Mid-morning, two days later, we sat with Amy at a white-linen-covered table. I had downed enough high-octane black coffee to wonder if my bloodstream had turned a darker shade. I needed all the caffeine I could manage, as I had barely closed my eyes the night before. Deano's prophetic words had gotten the best of me, and I'd been left with a nagging sense that this journey wasn't random. The entire thought process made no sense to me, but I had to admit I sensed something. It wasn't as if I thought some interplanetary being was pushing us along a predetermined path. I thought it had more to do with thinking about people that had long since left my life's orbit. I knew they wouldn't have approved of my life choices, but, even so, I missed them.

Amy was telling us about all her discoveries from reading my grandfather's diary. I was content to listen and watch her as she put on and took off her horn-rimmed reading glasses between reading sections from the first diary, but her smartphone kept ringing. The guests at nearby tables would glance over at our rather odd-looking friend, who had decided to color her shoulder-length hair a deep purple. I suspected she had several colorful tattoos hidden beneath her long-sleeved, vintage blouse, but discovering that would be work for a much younger, much hipper man or woman. I wasn't sure what her preference was. I shrugged; it was none of my business. I also thought there was a sadness, a loneliness, to her. It was a look in her eyes, a look that I recognized from my own journey.

"Thank you so much for sharing this with me," she said. She handed the green-leather diary, a memory stick, and a folder with paper copies and historical explanations over to Rebecca. In return, Rebecca smiled over at me and handed her the rest of the diaries. Amy clutched them. "Really?"

"Yeah. I was thinking, last night," I said, pointing at the diaries. "We can read them, but you understand the context, we'd miss that part."

"I promise, I'll take great care of these," Amy said. She gazed down at the collection of diaries, and her smartphone rang again. "Sorry, my sort-of-boyfriend's a bit crazed, these days."

Some of the diaries were the same green leather as the first, but others were a soft, brown leather.

"If you need some getaway money, no worries, I had a few goobers, back in the day," Rebecca said. She sipped some orange juice from a tall, crystal glass. "By the way, we're happy to help the library."

"Maybe. I don't know. Thank you," Amy said. She examined each diary before she placed them into her duffel bag. "Lucky I brought this; I was worried they might not allow a big bag inside this place. Might, you know, think I'm an anarchist. I've never been in here, it's like a museum. Think I can take some selfies and get away with it?"

"Yeah, just not of me, but I'll tell you the trick," I said. I fiddled the tip of my fingers along the soft linen edge. "Money. Even terrorists need that, to get past the front gate."

"Librarians don't get rich," Amy said.

"Even so. Are you happy being a librarian, maybe be a historian?" I asked. "Nothing wrong with being a librarian, maybe a professor?"

"Yeah, for sure, I think so, just really expensive," Amy said.

"Do you believe in God?" I asked. "Sorry, I don't know why I asked you that, maybe it's on my mind. Just tired, sorry."

"Robert, why would you ask that?" Rebecca asked. She just stared at me. "Who are you?"

"Sorry," I said. "I just got curious, I guess."

"Shots fired, shots fired, I get it, I'm not an atheist," Amy said. She stared over at a group of waiters attending a large business group. "I think there's something beyond us, but I don't practice organized religion, like your grandparents. I got tired of feeling guilty. It was a drag."

"Good, we understand each other," I said. I tapped on the table. "My story is just older, with more wrinkles."

"You are so cynical," Rebecca said. She shook her head. "How old are you, Amy?"

"I thought you weren't supposed to ask?" I said.

"Twenty-six," Amy said, glancing around the fancy room. "I just finished my master's in Californian history. I was lucky to get scholarships, but I got it done before thirty, so that's cool."

"Now time to make babies, I guess?" Rebecca asked. Her voice trailed off. "Funny how time passes."

"You all right?" I asked Rebecca. She nodded.

"Yeah, my mother can't wait, the struggle is real," Amy said.

She glanced at me but then looked at Rebecca. "Can I tell you something?"

"Sure," Rebecca said.

"My boyfriend wants to get married," Amy said. She slouched back on the chair and gazed up at the ceiling. "That's why my phone is on fire."

"But you don't?" Rebecca asked.

"Yeah, like, no way," Amy said. She shook her head. "I think he wants to protect me from what he calls my 'bohemian lifestyle'. I'm just like everybody else."

"What does that mean?" I asked.

"Robert," Rebecca said. "Quiet."

"No big thing," Amy said. "I like to explore, you know, swipe right, swipe left, maybe hook up."

"Great, I think travel is a good thing. I wish I had that artistic nature, just backpack Europe," I said. I picked up the coffee cup as Amy studied my face.

"I like to explore my sexuality," she said. She looked back at Rebecca. "I feel empowered, I feel alive, a woman, when I'm, you know, exploring. He's not into it."

"Oh," I said, blushing.

"I didn't expect that," Rebecca said. She winked at me. For some odd reason, I thought she was enjoying the moment. "He wants to settle down, have kids?"

"Yeah. I hooked up with him, so what? I get hit on daily, had to turn off the app at work," Amy said. "But I don't hate kids, I take my piercings out for work, so I don't scare anybody at the library."

"Wait, 'app'? Like Uber?" Rebecca asked. "They call Uber an app, right?"

"Ah, man, I'm in way over my head," I said. "But if you need protection, if he's being abusive? We can help."

"Thank you," Amy said, "but I've got it. Yeah, I turn the app on, they see me. If I'm in the mood, maybe a bit turnt, I go explore."

"Be happy, I guess, in whatever form it takes," I said. "I'm not sure what to say. How 'bout those Cats?"

"Listen to you," Rebecca said.

Amy gripped the strap of her duffle bag.

"Hey, I was thinking. This place was built before he arrived in Los Angeles. He would have walked past this front door many times." She cinched her duffel bag closed. "If you like, I could drive you all around town, show you where they went, lived. I know exactly where. I have a list."

I sat back in the upright chair and grinned over at Amy.

"Seriously?" I asked. Then I reached forward to shake her hand. "You have a deal, but I have a better idea; I'll drive."

"Whatever, that's cool," she said. "I'm curious, too. I learn a lot, each time I go to historic spots. If I just chill, be present, you'd be amazed what soaks in."

"Deal," I said. "You can talk to Rebecca about boys."

After I took care of the breakfast bill, we stood together in front of the hotel while the red-vested valets walked and ran to help arriving patrons out of their cars, drive them away, and return with another guest's car.

"Where's your car?" I asked Amy.

"Down the street," she said, pointing at a modest, four-door sedan.

"That won't do," Rebecca said.

"Give me the keys," I said. I walked over to the valet station and directed them to retrieve my ruby-red girl and drive Amy's car into the valet parking area. I walked back. "Amy, today you drive in style."

"Cool, but," Amy said, bouncing on her toes and watching the valet drive her car away, "does parking cost a lot, here?"

"No worries," I said. "I'll cover it, my treat."

I watched Amy's expression as she wondered what I meant by driving in style and, as if on cue, my Pierce-Arrow made her mark as she arrived on the scene. The valet hopped out and stood next to her.

"No way," Amy said. "This is for real?"

"My dear, for real, this is how you drive in style, old-school," I said. The valets moved to open the side doors. "You and Rebecca get in the back, and I'll be your chauffeur."

"Whoa," Amy said. She glanced up at me and then inspected the car's flowing, silver curves and the white-walled tires around her wooden artillery spokes. "I've never—"

"He loves this thing," Rebecca said. "It was his first. Some people have children; we have cars." She held the valet's hand as she got into the back bench seat. Amy got in next to her. "He spent a morning showing the valets how to properly maintain and start her. He's mental."

"This is a 1929 Pierce-Arrow Dual Cowl Phaeton convertible," I said. I tapped the thick wall. "This body-style kept the rich from having to interact with the servant. I will be your servant, for today."

Rebecca smirked at me as we watched Amy looking around the interior like a little girl, aware she was the center of everyone's attention. A passerby honked his horn at us, and we heard several whispered comments from those passing us on the city sidewalk.

"Get used to that," Rebecca said. She opened the folder Amy had given her.

"Amy, where to?" I asked.

"This is like sitting on an antique couch," Amy said. Her fingers glided along the soft, button-cushioned seat.

"Where to, madam?" I repeated. I inspected the dashboard and shifted the car into first gear.

"Oh, let's start at his old apartment address, I made a bunch of copies," Amy said. She pointed at the paper Rebecca was holding. "He spent most of his time there."

As I drove away from the hotel valet station, hidden by a Greek arch and tall, concrete columns, I glanced over at a slender young man who wore work clothes with his name stenciled over the right breast pocket. He was holding a petite, brunette woman's hand, and they examined my classic car. He looked me in the eyes, and my neck shivered as I drove past him, aware that, in 1930, my grandparents could have been standing at that very street corner at South Grand Avenue and West 5th Street, watching movie stars entering the Biltmore Hotel for the Academy Awards. They could have seen Charlie Chaplin waving at the adoring crowd in a similar make and model. I shifted into second gear as they disappeared behind us, still standing at the street corner, watching us drive down the busy street.

CHAPTER 9

After I parked the car along Hope Street, near my grandfather's original address, we sat silently. The windshield and silver headlamps faced the LA Public Library side entrance. We were shaded by a slender laurel oak's leafy branches. We listened to the antique automobile's engine idle; it sounded like an out-of-breath metronome. I used the black dashboard plunger to keep the gas pressure high enough to prevent the engine from stalling.

"Stop fiddling," Rebecca said. She tapped me on the shoulder. "It's fine; worst case, we have an American Express card, and maybe one of those Uber drivers rescues us."

"No more taxis," I said.

"Dude, like..." Amy said. She leaned forward over the thick barrier between the passenger compartment and the chauffeur section to examine the spartan, dark-gray dashboard. "This thing's like flying a plane or a space ship."

"Yeah. Cool?" I asked. I pointed down at my right shoe. "That silver peddle is the starter, this is the three-speed shift, and it has a dual-ignition system, side A and B. Over here, you can alter the gas mixture."

"Whatever, hero man, it looks complicated," Amy said. She

pushed back into the passenger bench seat. "You all want me to read some sections, you know, from when he lived here? He was, like, right here."

"I think that's a terrific idea," Rebecca said.

"Cool that," Amy said. She slipped on her reading glasses and chose a piece of eight-by-ten copy paper. "This was after that first entry, with the address, okay?"

"Got it," I said. I turned around and looked back at Amy as she began to read.

"September 15th, '26. My first full day in Los Angeles. I am alone. I am not sure how to feel, for I met another believer, today. She told me she believed. Her name is 'Hazel'. She is pretty. She wore eyeglasses, like me. I walked down the street, I think she was standing near 5th Street. I need to learn how to get around."

"I read that one earlier," Rebecca said. She pointed out toward the street. "They were just over there."

"Yeah," Amy said. She tapped Rebecca and pointed up at the tallest building in California. "Right where that building sits, but back then, it would have been churches and wooden houses, and next to us was the Biola building."

"Keep reading," I said. I leaned my elbow on the barrier. "That was before 'Jesus saves', right?"

"Yeah," Amy said. She studied the page. "October 17th, '26. Went to school, studied fundamentals, COD, went to work until ten, walked home, missed the stage."

"We know what that was," Rebecca said.

"Yeah, your chili-dude, Deano, explained," I said. I smiled at Rebecca. "'COD' was not 'Cash on Delivery'."

"November 30th, '26. Same thing. School, work, didn't see her. She wrote me a letter about our fuss."

"I wonder what she wrote?" Rebecca said. "What did she say about the 'fuss'?"

"He doesn't say," Amy said. She pointed her forefinger down

the page. "He mentions going with her to someone's house in P-Town a lot. They must have had a close friend named 'Ruth'."

"'P-Town'?" I asked. "'Ruth' is my sister's name."

"Sorry, 'Pomona'," Amy said. She shrugged.

"Oh, yeah," Rebecca said. She waved her hands at me. "Got married there, right?"

"Yep," I said. "Do they have an address for the house?"

"Not from this diary," Amy said. She pushed her reading glasses along her nose. "He wrote a lot about COD, work, CE, and your grandmother, for the next year. Or, like this... He wrote about meeting friends at the library, being on the seventh floor, and having lunch with your grandmother in the dining hall.

"March 20th, '27. Blue. Why?"

"Blue?" I asked.

"Yeah, I think he means depressed," Amy said. She picked out anther page. "He would write 'Blue', or 'Nothing', or 'Rain', or just a question mark, but then all sorts of information, real random."

"I guess he was homesick?" I asked. "Just everyday life."

"No clue," Amy said. She folded over a page. "But then he wrote this.

"May 5th, '27. Went with Hazel to Long Beach, ate dinner at Mr. Hirsch's house on East 3rd Street, we looked at the ocean, came back, worked from ten o'clock to half past five, tired."

"Really?" Rebecca asked. She clapped her hands. "Well, that's a start. Driver, take us to Long Beach."

"Cool," Amy said. She opened another diary. "I can read and maybe find some other places as we drive down, cool?"

"Yes, madam," I said. I shifted the car back into first gear and drove out of downtown Los Angeles onto the concrete 710 Freeway. Amy sat next to Rebecca, studying another green-leather diary. The hulking downtown skyline faded behind us as if it sat on quicksand, as the freeway snaked through the dry, urban neighborhoods. I was aware that the sun-splashed modern freeway I was driving along hadn't existed in 1927. There wouldn't have been the flat, overpopulated habitat we drove past, but streets lined with modest homes and sturdy palm trees, churches, town squares with shops and businesses, and wooden oil derricks. They would never have seen the many container trucks speeding past us toward the commercial docks that had opened up commerce to the world beyond.

But it must have been a magical experience to see the horizon become a constant Pacific blue that merged with the sky. It only took us about an hour, even in our antique convertible, what had taken them several hours in a time when horses pulled stages, and Model T and Model A Fords moved along the same dirt path in a dusty dance. The Los Angeles River was free-flowing and hadn't been encased in concrete, but over time, the horses and the oil derricks had disappeared; the streets became highways and progress trampled the past.

"Well, it looks like we made it," Rebecca said.

I drove the car off the freeway toward the Queen Mary and down Ocean Boulevard with the Pacific on our right. I turned left onto Cherry Avenue and turned onto East 3rd Street. The narrow city street was packed with parked cars. Older, single-story homes, interspersed with two-story beach homes with parking underneath that dominated the area.

"Whoa, dude," Amy said. She pushed her smartphone forward. "This is Carroll Park; this entire area is a historic landmark, protected."

"Are you kidding me?" I asked. "This is prime real estate."

"Many of the houses predate 1940, the craftsman bungalows are protected," Amy said. She glanced around the dense neighborhood, smothered with old trees that seemed more like well-maintained, leafy, upside-down bushes hugging the thick-columned homes. "They would have seen many of these houses, but without all the power lines. They likely walked along these streets."

"It does take you back in time," Rebecca said. She searched her bag. "Could we take a photo, Bobby?"

"Yes," I said. "Don't share it, right?"

"I know," Rebecca said.

I stood beside our vintage car and felt the warm ocean breeze. I could hear the ocean breathe waves across the beach. Amy showed us pictures on her touchscreen from the time period, and I wondered what it had been like, standing here in 1927. The dark, woolen men's suits, women with curly hair stuffed under domed hats with flapper-style wavy outfits. I suspected there had been a clear view of the Pacific. Not far from our location, Signal Hill would have been covered with dirty, black oil derricks. The clean air that I breathed would have been heavier then, with the distinct scent of tar. It might have reminded my grandfather of home and the sulfurous smell of burning coal from potbelly stoves. The palms, the sound from the ocean, and the smell of salt air would have been alien to them.

"Where to?" I asked. I looked over at Amy. She leafed through a diary and waved for us to walk down the street toward the beach. As we walked toward the busy traffic, the constant waves crashed forward, only to recede back from the sands. It would have been a surreal moment for my grandparents, both born to inland lands of flat corn fields and tobacco farms, and marked by thunderous springtime tornadoes, for them to have stood, holding hands, where the yellow sun routinely extinguished the day in the blue water.

CHAPTER 10

As we drove back toward downtown, we luckily missed the commuter traffic that had been backed up from earlier in the day. We asked Amy if there was something that she'd always wanted to do, but which her modest means had made impossible. We encouraged her to pick something extravagant, as a thank you for her help, but it had to be historical in nature. Something that my grandparents could have done, if they roamed Los Angeles at the time.

"Have you all ever been swingers?" Amy asked.

"No," Rebecca said. "Are you kidding?"

"That's your idea of extravagant?" I asked. I grinned back over at Amy. I had taken my classic girl back to hide out with the Biltmore valets. We strolled along with Amy, across the downtown streets. "What's a swinger? Baseball reference?"

"Dude, sharing partners," Amy said. She pointed toward the Biltmore. "You're already staying in the most extravagant place from your grandparents' time, this place is old-school."

"I guess the thing to order is the French dip?" Rebecca asked, looking up at the iconic restaurant sign. "And a cocktail? I need it. It's after five, somewhere."

"I doubt my grandparents ever stepped foot in here," I said, stepping inside. I watched the bartender mix a fancy cocktail behind a long, mahogany bar. "The drinking would have been off-putting."

"Dude, I'm just curious, I'm open to learn," Amy said. She laughed. "Ever heard of Prohibition?"

"I get it," I said. I sat back in the blood-red restaurant booth that we'd found set deep in the heart of the dimly lit, vintage restaurant.

"Babies wouldn't work, for you," Rebecca said. "They didn't work for me. Tried it once, never again, it's like having your heart ripped out."

"Hollywood wasn't that big of a deal yet?" I asked. I waved for the busy waiter to come back to our table, and we all ordered the French dip. The globe lighting along the red-painted, metal ceiling cast enough light for me to inspect photos hung along the red-velvet walls.

"They would have been in here?" Rebecca asked. She sipped her drink from a tall glass.

"For sure, this was when movies were silent," Amy said. She pointed her thumb behind her. "We're in the Pacific Electric building. This was the terminal he'd have had to come to, to get the train. He has to have been here."

"Then, this was one of the first places he would have seen?" I asked. My grandfather had journeyed across the country using the railway system. His father had worked for the railroad. I imagined what it had been like, post-World War I; what it was like to be a young man, alone, riding past the emerging country for the first time. The young man realizing what was beyond the Kentucky forests and coal mines.

"Yeah, they had to come here," Amy said. She put on her reading glasses. "In later years, he mentioned getting on a Red Car; that was part of the Pacific Electric Railway. It was the cheapest and easiest way to get around. This was the main terminal. It was owned by Henry Huntington, the namesake of the nearby Huntington Beach and the library in San Marino."

"That makes sense," I said. I thought about the nearby museum that held *Pinkie* and *The Blue Boy*. "I like that place, good place to hang out for an afternoon, remember?"

"Yeah," Rebecca said. "It's a beautiful museum."

The waiter returned with three white plates, each dominated by a French dip. They had cut the roast beef sandwich in half; a cup of brown au jus set between each half to help support an upright, green dill pickle.

"The streetcars replaced the horses, and then the car took over. It's all in the historical records," Amy said.

We devoured our sandwiches, but I doubted my grandfather had ever come inside this place. He lacked money. Only the well-off are in a position to go out for dinner. If you work for your wages hour-by-hour-by-hour, you don't go out to eat. Even so, I felt his presence from walking the neighborhood. He might have just looked inside and wondered. He never mentioned the address for the bakery he worked at, and it had long since shut its doors, but it made sense to me now why he had written about missing his transfer and having to walk home. He was frustrated. He had worked all night, he would have been dog-tired, and he knew schoolwork waited at home. And then he would end up back at the bakery, before sunset. It was a grind, surviving day-to-day, and the Red Car would have meant precious moments to sit and rest.

"Bobby, you okay?" Rebecca asked. She reached over to caress my hand.

"You can feel him. Them," Amy said. "You really loved him."

"Yeah," I said. I blinked hard. "Where to next?"

"Bobby," Rebecca said. "It's sweet."

I wasn't about to cry in the middle of a busy diner. I sucked in enough oxygen to maintain sanity.

"They were the one stable force, growing up," I said. I stared down at the penny-tiled floor. "Whatever. Next, please."

"How about Griffith Park, the former location of the 'HOL-LYWOODLAND' sign?" Amy asked. "It's early afternoon. If we have enough daylight, P-Town, maybe?"

"That's where they were married," I said.

"I know," Amy said. Her smartphone rang. "I know, I know exactly where!"

"Then we'll go find it," I said.

CHAPTER 11

It was mid-afternoon, and the wind had gone silent as the sun warmly watched our tourist adventures, cruising along the active city streets of Los Angeles. We had risked our lives driving among cars that wanted a racing date with our girl, swiping past her in the right lane; the Model A hotrods and the lowriders, but she couldn't be bothered into moving out of the left lane. We'd stopped at spots my grandfather had mentioned in his diaries. The ones that were left were either decaying buildings or had been crushed under the concrete for modern progress. I had maneuvered our shiny car off Los Feliz Boulevard and entered Griffith Park along the busy, circuitous, tree-and-car-lined Fern Dale Drive. I was careful not to run over any hikers crossing the street.

We parked near Griffith Observatory and sat together in my beautiful 1929 automobile, who had enjoyed her rebirth into stardom. We had been waving like beauty queens on a parade route to her well-wishers, both rich and poor, on her behalf. Trundling along the hillside of Mount Lee, we contemplated the white 'HOLLYWOOD' sign affixed atop the brown and thirsty land that was blotched with green bushes. There are places and things in the world that transcend being iconic, because they define our temporary existence. They trigger emotions hidden deep within our mind's eye, connected to our happy and turbulent histories. I gripped the large, black steering wheel. When my gas-powered girl had been created, the sign read 'HOLLYWOODLAND'. I wondered what my grandparents had thought about it.

The sign's original purpose was as a temporary housing development advertisement. But through forces beyond our understanding, it had transformed, like a phoenix, into a new existence. It occurred to me, as I watched tourist groups scamper across the modest parking lot to enter the concrete, art deco observatory, that I had hoped for faith. For most of my life, it had eluded me. I hadn't been moved by what my grandfather defined as the Holy Spirit; I doubted it even existed. Beyond us was a terrific view of the flat, urban LA basin, centered by the dark, downtown shadows. I thought of all the sets of eyes – brown, blue, and green – that had stood near us, lived their lives, and passed on. All those people who had looked across the canyon and up at the sign. I could see the tallest building in California that marked the exact spot my grandparents had met, but pretty much everything manmade hadn't been here when they had met. From that day until the day they died, they had no money. They had believed, as my grandfather would have said, 'render unto Caesar what is Caesar's'. They had survived the best they could by trusting in God, as they spent their lives saving souls one at a time on his behalf. They believed their golden age would be after death; that they would be together in eternal paradise. I swiped a tear from my eyes. I hoped, as I stared up at the sign, that they had found it.

"You okay? Amy asked.

"Yeah, I've glanced at that sign a thousand times," I said. I hadn't turned to look back at Rebecca and Amy. "Our transportation was still young, when that sign was built."

"They never came up here," Amy said. She was immersed in reading one of my grandfather's diaries. Her smartphone rang, but she turned off the volume. "The observatory was built in 1935, and by then, they were already gone. He mentioned the Griffith Park Zoo, but mostly they would picnic at the park."

"They survived on a college budget, 'free' meant 'affordable'," I said. I turned to look back at Amy. "So, I understand we have an address to find?"

Amy gathered her notes together, but she averted her gaze.

"Yeah," Amy said, "but it's getting late, so it's not safe to go there. Maybe tomorrow?"

"What?" Rebecca asked. "It's not even four."

"We could check out Pershing Square or the old flower market?" Amy suggested. She fiddled with her reading glasses. "He used to take her there; he got her flowers, when he could afford them. It was within walking distance of the original Biola."

"Yeah," I said. "But they got married in Pomona."

"I know P-Town," Amy said. She shifted forward. "It's not a nice neighborhood, now."

I rubbed the back of my neck and thought about my grandmother. She had taken me on numerous adventures in the lush, green hills of Eastern Kentucky. We had traveled into places that seemed more like third-world shanty towns than stereotypical, Norman Rockwell, white-picket-fence homes with innocent boys and girls pledging their allegiance to the flag. She would leave me and my sister in her four-door sedan as she marched up to a front door. We would watch her from just above the dashboard. Her mission was to care for the sick. If a shotgun appeared through the front door opening after she had knocked, she would simply move forward into the house. And then she would return and grin down at us. She wasn't a big talker, and we would gaze at her in amazement.

She would laugh at us, in her gravelly way, and just say, "That was interesting, they wouldn't harm an old lady."

Then, she would start the car, and off we'd go to her next appointment along the narrow roads, dodging coal trucks and ignorance. I grinned as I watched a little, brown-haired boy stare up at the figures of the Astronomers Monument, topped by what I thought looked like the eye of divine providence staring over at us. His father stood close behind.

"Cute kid," I said. I wondered what it felt like to be a parent, to protect a child from harm and yet not smother them.

"What's that?" Rebecca asked.

"Never mind. I have a small window of time, here," I said. I started the car. "Let's go. I've seen worse, I promise."

"Seriously," Rebecca said. She nudged Amy. "He's not kidding; parts of Eastern Kentucky have breathtaking beauty, but some parts *are* dangerous."

Amy glanced up at the observatory's re-tracked, copper-sheathed dome, which had a tubular telescope poking out from within the arched gap. She nodded her head and, with the benefit of opposable thumbs, punched in the address. She handed me her smartphone.

"There, drive to that address," Amy said. She sat back on the bench seat. "But let's not stop, maybe just a drive-by. It's not like we won't be noticed."

"That bad?" Rebecca asked.

"You'll see," Amy said. She crossed her arms. "In this thing, we can't exactly hide."

I put on my reading glasses and examined the digital map.

"Well," I said, "let's channel our inner Hazel. Amy, don't get too worked up. If need be, I can call in the cavalry, I have resources at my fingertips."

"Okay, dude," Amy said, frowning.

What Amy couldn't understand was that I wasn't just another

upper-class dude with a fancy car. For the most part, we were faceless to the world, but my every movement was monitored. My smartphone was more than a modern convenience, because I was a target. Our wealth could open any door, in any country, but it also meant there were those who would threaten us because my name was written on a 'top one hundred' list buried inside a business magazine.

We left Griffith Park behind. I drove along Ventura Freeway, past lonely palm trees and brown-brick retaining walls that kept out the freeway noise from the busy concrete-river traffic that we navigated beneath the San Gabriel Mountains. We drove past the green exits for Glendale and Pasadena, and took the Santa Ana exit heading south and on into downtown Pomona.

"People here make their living with their hands," I said. I acknowledged a group of young, Hispanic men standing at a street corner; they all wore black baseball hats pushed down behind their ears.

They yelled at me, "Hey homie, nice ride."

I waved back at them.

"You know, they have a classic car show, here. Never been. I should put it on my calendar."

"Sure, ignore them, just turn left down there," Amy said. She had leaned forward to backseat drive. "I know a safer shortcut, from now on, we need to avoid street thugs."

"Ah, car people understand each other," I said.

I drove down a tree-lined, two-lane city street, past a mix of old and new one-story homes with the occasional tumorous addition of a second floor. I turned the black steering wheel left at the stop sign Amy had pointed at and drove toward the address that she was certain was where my grandparents had married. Rebecca glanced over at a 1920s bungalow with thick front columns. The tiny front yard was gated and manicured.

"Is that a Mexican flag?" she asked.

"For sure," Amy said. She tapped me on the shoulder. "That's the one, by the way. The name 'Pomona' comes from the Roman goddess of fruits and nuts. And we *are* nuts, being here."

"Ah, I thought that's what 'San Fran' meant," I said. I slowed the car down to a walking speed. "Kidding…"

"Citrus was king, when your grandparents were here," Amy said. She opened one of my grandfather's diaries. "Yeah, this is it. Most of the area was covered with citrus crops."

"I'm surprised it's still here," Rebecca said. She moved close behind me. "It's a time capsule."

I parked near a pink-painted cinderblock wall with an iron gate that extended across the front property line. Behind it was a line of bursting rose bushes. It was a preserved, A-framed craftsman bungalow. A short, concrete path segmented the green grass; it led up to two steps in front of a wide, wooden-fronted porch. From behind a rectangular window, an old Hispanic woman with pure-white hair pulled back a sheer curtain. She was watching us.

"Let's drive," Amy said.

"Got it," I said. I shifted into first gear, but just as I was about to drive away, a young man with jet-black hair, wearing a white t-shirt advertising an auto body shop, walked out from within the house.

"Sorry," I said, waving over at him. "We'll move along."

"Wait, are you the Christian people?" he asked. He was expressionless as he examined us and the antique car. "My grandmother wants to know. Nice ride."

"Thanks," I said. I shifted into neutral. "I'm not sure; I think you have the wrong people."

"No, you come inside, my grandmother's waiting," he said. He waved us forward and opened the locked gate. "Your car's safe here."

We slowly got out of the car and moved together past the front gate. As we stepped up onto the front porch, the wooden flooring creaked with age, but it felt solid under my feet, and the boards were thick. We walked into the front parlor and heard Spanish. A diminutive, brown-skinned woman with dark, sparkling eyes grinned at me. She pointed her aged forefinger in my direction as she spoke to the young man.

"My grandmother says," he said, nodding down at his grandmother, "si, you're the one. Your grandparents were the happy Christians, no?"

"They were," I said. It only took me a second to recognize the mantel behind them. It was mahogany, topped with a mirror. "They were married where you're standing. I remember the mantel, from the black-and-white photo, but how'd she know? I'm confused."

The young man translated, and she smiled at me. With the aid of a metal cane, she wobbled toward us, and we walked closer to them. She reached forward with her free hand to grasp mine. Her hand felt like the hand that took great care of the fragrant rose bushes that adorned the front yard. She spoke to me.

"My grandmother says your grandparents came here, many years ago," her grandson said. He nodded down at his grandmother. "They just wanted to see the house where they were married."

"Ah, that makes sense," I said. I stared over at the mantel that a master carpenter had built almost a hundred years before.

"But, how does she know him?" Rebecca asked, pointing at me. The young man asked his grandmother in quick-cadenced Spanish. She spoke back to him. He nodded at her.

"She says you were with them, the last time she saw them," he said. "You have eyes like your grandmother."

"I don't remember," I said. I felt myself blush.

"Yeah," he said. He patted me on the shoulder. "She said you were stylin' in a powder-blue, polyester leisure suit, homie. She didn't say, 'stylin'. I added that."

"Ha," Rebecca said. She covered her mouth with her hand. "Sorry, you were so cute, I've seen the pictures."

"Si," he said. "She says your grandfather was a handsome man."

The old woman began to speak rapidly, then wobbled toward her kitchen.

"She wants you all to sit with her," he said. He waved at us to follow. "She wants to make you her chicken with mole poblano. It will change your life, seriously."

"Dude, you're like an honored guest," Amy said. She nudged us forward. "It would be an insult not to eat with her, it's the way she was taught."

"Si," he said. He grinned at me. "I know you, your face. You have been on television, no?"

"Oh, business shows, maybe," I said. It felt strange to be recognized by someone with colorful tattoos along his forearms.

"Guess you're famous," Rebecca said. She pushed me further into the home. "Let's eat."

"I thought so," he said. He shook my hand. "I watched you talk about business; your advice helped me."

"Mr. Dude?" Amy asked. She put her hands on her hips and stared over at me. "Who are you?"

It was a strange sensation to have my snow globe penetrated. I inspected the heavy furniture, thinking that it hadn't been moved in a generation. But the old lady had kept the family photos neatly together, and the house smelled of fresh flowers and homemade cooking. The inside of the home was as spotless as the outside.

"I've done really well," I said. I patted her on the shoulder. "I would prefer you just called me 'dude'."

"Dude?" the grandson laughed. "*He* no dude."

"By the way, my friends call me 'Bobby'," I said. I shook his hand. "And you?"

"Si, si," he said. He gripped my hand. "Ricardo. They like to call me 'Rico', but I don't like it."

"Nice to meet you," I said. "Ricardo."

He cocked his head a bit, then looked over at Amy.

"They call him 'the Humble Billionaire'," Ricardo said, but then Ricardo's grandmother barked out instructions in machine-gun Spanish, and he sprinted into the kitchen.

CHAPTER 12

The old woman's name was 'Isabela'. She had lived in the three-bedroom, one-and-a-half-bath bungalow since 1965. She and her husband, Diego, had made their way into the United States from their native Puebla. They had come for work; he had a strong back and a good mind, and, in time, they had saved enough money to buy this modest home. They had built a life together in the same home in which my grandparents had been married. In those days, though, the nearby population was mostly Anglo-Saxons who had come west. I thought they all sought the same thing: the American Dream. A dream that wasn't about the wealth that I'd accumulated, but about the freedom to be left alone.

As I sat near the sturdy kitchen table, which was covered with a well-used, plastic, flower-patterned tablecloth with long fold creases, I found myself immersed in three separate conversations. Isabela was recounting her time with my grandparents in happy Spanish, which Ricardo would then translate. I would respond with a nod and a grin. Whenever he wasn't passing messages back and forth, Ricardo peppered me with questions about capital formation, the corporate tax on foreign income repatriation, and what 'fully diluted earnings per share' meant. I hadn't imagined these questions might be coming. As I tried not to appear amused, I was embarrassed that I had judged him. He had money to invest, just like any other human being. Finally, Amy was curious how we had just roamed into her life; she was certain there must be an intergalactic conspiracy for her to have crossed paths with an almost-anonymous multi-billionaire. Her smartphone rang.

"The boy is at least diligent," I said.

"He's just a lovesick puppy," Amy said.

"Puppies can be trained," Rebecca said.

The longer Amy roamed in our life, the more I was interested in her. I thought she was hiding behind her colorful hair and overt sexuality; she worked in a world that always looked backwards, but she used her body to explore for something unseen. Like me, Rebecca watched Amy; she had not said to Amy what was on her mind, but I saw it in her eyes. It was about Amy's age and a scar that would never heal. In truth, I had the same scar. Eventually, after a wonderful homemade meal, she cleared the dishes. She had been quite amused, watching me squirm.

I thought there was nothing like a meal prepared with loving hands. It was something a well-known chef had taught me; if you put the right ingredients together, any simple cook can be transformed into a culinary artist. He was right. Isabela was a wondrous cook. It wasn't any different to investing; be quiet and allow the basic truths behind a business to emerge. It was all right there in the numbers – the ingredients, in this case. But the key element I searched for wasn't in the financial statements; it was passion. It was what made me feel alive, that night. She had taken me into her home.

"Do you have magic mindreading powers?" Amy asked. She wiped her face with her hands. "How'd you get so rich?"

"Luck," I said, leaning towards her. "I just got lucky."

"Si, you got lucky," Ricardo said. He shook his head. "You took crazy chances, but smart ones, Mister Humble."

"It was your grandfather, helping you out," Amy said. Her eyes were wide open, and she pointed up toward the ceiling. "Whoa!"

"Yes, Amy," I said, grinning. "I guess you're right."

But then Isabela, who only remembered me as the boy with thick, brown hair and straight bangs, started to talk to me in a whisper, her cadence slow and deliberate. She stared down at the tabletop, and her fingertips stroked the tablecloth's frayed edges.

"What's wrong?" I asked. I reached toward her.

"She says your grandfather prayed with her and Diego," Ricardo said. He sucked in a deep breath. "She says he saved my grandfather's soul, right where you are sitting, not long before my grandpapa died."

Isabela wiped tears from her face with a kitchen towel. She blinked her eyes, but then she smiled over at Rebecca.

"She says your grandmother did the same thing," Ricardo said. Isabela watched Rebecca remove more dishes. "She says he had fire in his brown eyes, when he talked about God. It wasn't loud; just plain, ah, direct, honest."

"Yeah, that's him," I said. It was odd; I could hear my grandfather's voice calling me 'Bobby', saying, 'be ye kind' as if he was standing nearby, watching me.

"I wish I had known my *abuelo*," Ricardo said.

For a moment, I watched Isabela stare behind me at the wooden hutch filled with her best china, but I had no words to say. My grandfather had done all the talking. For some strange reason, I felt he was nearby, and I couldn't shake the sensation.

"How did you learn so much, business-wise?" I asked Ricardo. "Those are unusual questions. I hope you don't think I'm insulting you. I thought you'd ask me about my car, you know."

"Oh, no, I know about it; big eight, car for the rich man." Ricardo nodded. "I like working old Chevies. I have a shop. But I hope for more, maybe a family. I study the markets on the

Internet. It's free. I have saved and invested carefully, like you say."

Amy started to cry. She sniffled and wiped her eyes.

"What's wrong?" Rebecca asked.

"You aren't real, is what's going on," Amy said. She had her long fingers shielding her eyes.

"I thought I was," I said. I tapped on the table. "Dude? You're the one who should 'chill'."

"Are you all right?" Rebecca asked Amy.

"Hormonal, I guess," Amy said. She glanced over at me. "I'm just emotional, you know? I get emotional about history."

"Yeah, I get that," Rebecca said. She shrugged.

Isabela began to talk again, and Ricardo nodded with her. He gripped his hands together in front of his face, staring down at the wooden floor.

"She says the dead are talking to you, they are calling you," Ricardo said. He wiped a tear away and scowled. "My mother, last time they came, they talked to her, your grandmother told her drugs were bad, to stop. She was very honest, the time you were here, in your blue leisure suit, she took her out back, out there. You know, she tried."

"Whoa, intense," Amy said. She stood up and paced toward the fireplace mantel, waving her hands as if trying to catch ghosts. "This is so bizarre."

From behind them, Rebecca gazed over at me. She winked, then she turned back to wash dishes in a white, porcelain sink, drying them with a threadbare tea towel.

"She's gone?" I asked. "Drugs?"

"Si," Ricardo said.

Isabela talked to us in her normal cadence. She gripped her hands together and prayed the Lord's Prayer in English. After the prayer, all we heard was the air conditioning unit cycle on and then off. Suddenly, I felt as though my grandparents were sitting next to me, at an address I had flown over time and time again. They seemed to talk to me, from some other place, from some other time, but I couldn't understand what they were saying.

"Thank you for sharing," I said. I breathed in and then blew the air from my cheeks. "Thank you for your hospitality, but I think it's time for us go."

"Si, si," Ricardo said. He talked in Spanish to his grandmother. She nodded. "But you will need to follow us; it can be unsafe to drive in a car like yours, here. Especially at night."

We expressed our goodbyes to Isabel. She took off her white apron, and then she hugged me.

I got back behind the black steering wheel. As my ladies got into the back, I went through the process of starting the old car. I pumped the dashboard lever to increase the gas pressure. I smashed on the starter with my shoe, and the engine began to cycle. As I let the engine warm, Ricardo called his friends. They appeared in a pack of loud, exhaust-firing lowriders to escort our Pierce-Arrow to the freeway ramp. There was a purple '57 Chevy that looked like the back bumper was dragging on the concrete, a turquoise '58 convertible Bel Air Impala, and twin early '50s pickup trucks with enough chrome to blind a sailor on a sunny day. We drove along with our new crew until we reached the freeway entrance, and then they stopped city traffic and put on a thunderous show. I waved over at Ricardo and thought I would track him down, someday. It was always a good idea to have an independent voice to ask about an investment. I wondered if our corporate office had ever had an employee with a neck tattoo.

I drove back to the Biltmore. The valets saw us coming and opened the doors, escorting our vintage car back to the concrete parking barn. We strolled into the front lobby, and I glanced over at the quiet concierge station. My heart thumped, the hair on my arms stood up, and my skin tingled.

"Drinks?" Rebecca asked. She looked around the lobby for an open bar. "Maybe over there..."

"I'm exhausted," Amy said. She started to back up, toward the front doors. "Thanks for the ride, it was an awesome day. Can you help me get my car?"

"Amy, you want to see Kentucky?" I asked. I stared over at her.

Rebecca clapped her hands. She hugged me.

"I knew it! I knew this would wake you up."

"Have you ever been across Route 66?" I asked Amy.

"Don't worry, we can fly there," Rebecca said. "Be back in no time, we'd love your company."

"Ah, that's cool," Amy said. She bounced on her knees but kept backing up. "But I have like, a job, rent, food."

"And a boyfriend?" Rebecca asked. "He can come."

"I'll take care of that," I said. I waved Amy to come back. "I'll make a donation to the library, they'll be happy to give you some time off, I promise. Maybe write a book?"

"Money talks, yeah. Tell them you'll write a book about the trip?" Rebecca said. She pointed at me. "But what about your girl? Leave her here? Call Wylie?"

I walked forward and grabbed Rebecca's soft left hand. It was the first time in my life I'd ever trusted whatever was beyond me. I wasn't sure what it was, but it had my attention, and it wouldn't be denied.

"No, she's coming, too," I said. I stared up at the fancy ceiling and laughed at the idea. "We're going the way they went. If my grandparents made the trip in a Model A Ford in 1930, damn it, we can make it in a Pierce-Arrow."

Rebecca pulled away and stood over by Amy, hugging her.

"Are you crazy?" Rebecca asked.

"Amy, you in?" I asked. I could tell she was afraid. "You want to really explore history?"

"I'm chill with it," Amy said. "But I don't know..."

"My love," I said. I pointed east. "We ride to Kentucky, old-school."

"But..." Rebecca said.

"I need to do this," I said. I almost began crying, but I didn't understand why. It was as if my grandfather was calling me; as if he demanded I pay attention. "I need this, I don't know why. I don't have a plan. You just have to trust me."

"Seriously?" Rebecca asked. "I did open the diaries..."

"I never knew them, but now..." I said, shrugging. I stared out of the front doors and across the street, as if my grandparents might appear under the street lights. "I want to. I have to."

"You okay?" Amy asked.

"I'm all right," I said. I turned and walked toward them. "But I'm restless. Maybe I'm just hormonal, too, but I'm doing this. I have no reason why."

CHAPTER 13

It was an early November morning, just past dawn. The downtown LA life that emerged from the dark shadows had begun the daily recycle along the city streets, and the sounds of progress belonged firmly to the modern day. I had essentially kidnapped Amy; I'd had the valets take her car back to her home. I had contacted the library; actually, I'd looked up the board of commissioners. I knew several, and it was a surprisingly simple call. It amazed me how easily people were motivated with money as a carrot.

As I sat behind the wheel, I wondered what my grandparents had thought, when they started their own journey back across the country. But then, they had known exactly what they were doing, and I had no clue what I was about to try or even why I was so energized to drive into the unknown.

"Are you sure?" Rebecca asked. She had her hair bundled in a fashionable, multicolored scarf. "It'll be cold. What's your plan? You always have a plan."

"Yes," I said. "I'm certain. I can't wait another day."

"Well, we're going to get to know each other," Rebecca told Amy. "I rarely go shopping anymore; could you take me to one of those vintage markets? Maybe I can help you by taking notes or photos?"

"For sure. The library must be stoked," Amy said. "I got an email from my boss; I'm not allowed to come into the office, until you say I can. You must really be a gnarly dude."

"Yes, I am," I said. I gripped the steering wheel. "You're coming along, unless you don't want to?"

"I'm in," Amy said. "Of course I'm in, but I'll need to get some stuff, like clothes, toothbrush."

"Told your friend?" Rebecca asked.

"Yeah," Amy said. "He's not chill with it."

"He'll be here, when you get back," I said. I pressed down on the throttle as we drove forward.

"I have a really cool section from his diary," Amy said. She fumbled her fingers along the pages. "Just after they were married, just before they left."

"Oh, great," I said. I shifted into second gear.

"I did start this, but I wasn't planning to drive cross-country," Rebecca said. She pointed forward. "Are you sure about putting mileage on her? It'll be cold, right?"

"It's way before Thanksgiving, we should be all right. We can get coats, whatever we need. Let's let our old girl experience freedom," I said. We drove away from the Biltmore; our first stop was my grandfather's old address. "Go ahead Amy, let's start from here."

Amy cleared her throat and slipped on her retro-framed reading glasses. The car engine rattled rhythmically. She held the diary close to her face.

"I thought he might write about the stock market crash in 1929, but reading these, I realized he was just talking about his daily life. He just kept his head down and worked and studied," Amy said. She dabbed her tongue with her forefinger. "Later, I realized why he worked so hard: he helped your grandmother pay for her nursing education, as well. He really loved her."

"Yeah," I said. I stared up into the cloudless, powder-blue sky. "That's him, just being him."

"Here it is," Amy said. "I am a married man. I am responsible for taking care of Hazel. I came here, and I will miss it, but it is time I go back home, to mission. It is our calling. I trust the family will accept her. It is not about our wants, it's about God. We are one now. It was a moment of pure love, for both of us. The Lord has provided us a new road, and a car; a Ford. Somehow, we are blessed."

"Wow," I said, chuckling nervously. "It's weird to hear about your grandpa getting laid for the first time…"

"Stop," Rebecca said.

"He doesn't write every day," Amy said, flipping forward. "I guess he was busy, but he'd write when he felt like it. You know we missed a spot?"

"Where?" Rebecca asked.

"We should drive across the street," Amy said. She pointed up at a tall building. "We should go over there, before we leave. I found a spot we should have investigated."

We drove from Hope Street onto 5th Street, maneuvering over to behind the tall building I was certain we owned part of through a real estate investment trust. We parked along the street and walked down concrete stairs into a square, green space set just above where the original 5th Street and Hope Street would have crossed. I looked over the side at busy 5th Street, and then over at the LA County Museum.

"Like, they sort of met here," Amy said. She stood near some ironwork art. "But down at the street level."

"Weird, I've been here before," I said. "I didn't even pay any notice, but this was almost the spot."

"Still want to do this?" Rebecca asked.

"Yeah, even more so, now," I said.

We left and drove down South Broadway, past City Hall, and then it occurred to me that I had no clue where to drive. I had a vague idea where our journey would end, an idea where the route crossed the country, but no idea where we should start. I parked in front of City Hall. I realized there weren't many obvious signs to guide us along Route 66. At least, they weren't obvious to me.

"This is City Hall; it dates to their time here," Amy said. She pointed up at the tall, concrete tower. "There's a cool observation deck, up there."

I turned to look back at a startled Rebecca and Amy.

"I'm lost, I don't know where to start." I shrugged. "Got any ideas?"

"You're serious?" Rebecca asked. She took off her glasses.

We drove to a nearby coffee shop that Amy was familiar with and sat near a square table. At that moment, the Internet had become as important as the air we breathed.

"Dude, how did you get so rich?" Amy asked. She was messing with her smartphone, searching for a good starting point.

"I was rather driven, as an angry young man," I said. I sipped the hot, black coffee. It tasted like charred wood. "Amy, ninety-nine percent of my life, I always calculated what to do; I took risks, that's how I got rich. But I'm flying blind. My instinct is to do this. I don't know why, I'm just asking for your help. Will you help me?"

"Who are you?" Rebecca asked. She crossed her arms. "You probably do need help."

Amy stared at me curiously. The difference between her and me was that I wasn't afraid. It's the one key component that separates the masses; when the big, bad wolf knocks on their door, those who are afraid try to hide, but I was never afraid of the wolf. In time, I had become the wolf. But Amy didn't know that.

"Sure, I guess," she said. She sucked in a deep breath. "This is super cool, but I kind of have to, right?"

"No," I said. I put my hand up, as if I were taking a pledge. "It's your choice; the money I promised will be donated, regardless of whether or not you come. If I make a promise, I keep that promise."

Amy kept fumbling with her smartphone. Rebecca grabbed it from her.

"This will not do," Rebecca said. She pointed it at me. "This phone will not work; we need to get you one of those fancy mobile computers."

"Genius," I said. I smacked the tabletop. "Sorry, I'm slow today. We have them all over the office. They're everywhere, you're right." I nudged her. "We have a huge stake in them."

"Dude, you could make a call and get someone – a real expert," Amy said. She studied my face. "You don't need me. I'm not a Route 66 expert."

"But you will be. I like you, it's that simple. You think my grandparents had their trip all mapped out?" I asked. I stared out of the coffee shop's front windows at the busy, sun-splashed city street. "They went one way, with what they could take, in a Model A Ford. They left the rest behind. They stepped off the cliff, not knowing where they would land. Think about that."

"To be clear, again, I don't specialize in this," Amy said. She sat back in the chair.

"I guess we're doing this backwards, not *Grapes of Wrath* style," I said. "We're heading east toward St. Louis, and then toward Kentucky, right?"

"For sure, I had some classes that, in part, studied the historical route, but I'm far from an expert. Yeah, though, *The Grapes of Wrath* was about heading here; California," Amy said. She looked behind me at a service counter and nodded, then she stared over at Rebecca. "But, instead of worrying about the roads, which are likely gone, we target places, maybe places he mentions in his diaries?"

"But only places they would have seen," I said. "So it would be 1930 backwards, right?"

"Yeah, I like that," Rebecca said. She sat up straight. "I can take photos of each location, to document the trip. This might be fun."

"Oh God," I said. "I didn't even consider that, just don't have me in any, okay?"

"It *would* help with my book," Amy said. Her smartphone rang.

"Exactly, yes dear, none with you," Rebecca said. "I'm getting into this, it makes sense."

"Answer it," I said, "or he'll lose his mind."

CHAPTER 14

It took us a couple of hours to collect the modern computing devices. I had made a call with my private smartphone from the coffee shop to the CEO of the company; he called me back in ten minutes with an exact address and a contact person. We drove to a sprawling outdoor mall that wasn't far from a good starting point for Route 66, in Pasadena. We collected Amy's provisions from a grocery store. The CEO had taken the same sojourn, so he knew where to go, and he recommended the best, most powerful product they made.

"Dude, why'd you pay for this stuff?" Amy asked. She had taken a quick tutorial inside the store from a savant-like Asian man. "That girl thought you'd lost your mind."

"I hate freebies," I said. I watched a group of shoppers walk into a specialty market. "I invest based on earnings; a clear, objective mind. I don't know, free stuff messes with my thinking, no thanks."

"It must be cool," Amy said. She gripped the tablet.

"Sorry," Rebecca said. She was playing with her own new tablet. "This is so much fun."

"Make a call, walk into a store," Amy said. She looked at me. "Get whatever you want, and they had no idea who you were."

"I know, it is cool," I said. I grinned at Amy. I had restarted our vintage automobile. We sat together, allowing the engine to warm. "It's been said before: fame is a fool's paradise."

"Your grandfather really had an effect on you," Amy said. She scratched the back of her neck. "He's why you're sort of humble. I think you like being hidden."

"I guess," I said. I watched the shoppers move in and out of the glass doors along the stretch of popular retail stores. "Once you see the world, meet famous people, eat fancy food, it all becomes nonsense."

"But still," Amy said.

"If you are kind to everyone you meet, treat them with respect..." I said. I tapped along the thick barrier between the chauffeur's compartment and the wealthy owner.

"Don't be fooled," Rebecca said. "He does have another side that's not this pleasant, fair warning."

"Stop," I said. I messed with the gear-shift knob. "That side comes from my father."

"What was he like?" Amy asked.

"Cold-blooded," I said. I stared back at Amy, making her uncomfortable. "Anyway, I found out people plan trips across Route 66 for years in advance, like it's a big deal. I don't get it."

"Dude, that's why I'm in," Amy said. She scooted forward. "Route 66, 'The Mother Road'. Dude, it's Americana!"

"How are you so clueless?" Rebecca asked. She kept playing with her new toy.

"Where to, then?" I asked, shrugging. "I was just following my grandparents' path."

"Fair Oaks Avenue," Rebecca said. She looked up and pointed at the tablet screen. "They would have driven along that road, right over there. Amy, we're right here."

"Way cool; that dude sent us to the right spot," Amy said. She started to bounce and nod. "I recommend we drive past that sign, the sign for sure, and then go look at the Colorado Street Bridge."

"Got it," I said, shifting into second gear. I drove across a busy parking lot and turned right onto Fair Oaks Avenue. We drove together down the double-lane concrete road, which was segmented down the center by a thick, yellow, reflective stripe. We coasted past single-story, red-brick shops that faced across the narrow street at Spanish-style buildings with flat roofs.

"Maybe up there?" Amy said.

"What am I supposed to see?" I asked. I waved over at a passerby who liked our antique transportation.

"Ah, never mind," Rebecca said.

"Well, that blows," Amy said. "That storage building was here when they drove past. It would have had a big, neon sign. Wait, that's the sign, it's just for a different company."

Amy tapped me on the shoulder.

"I see it," I said. "They would've looked up there?"

"Yes, that's where the sign they drove past was. It's one of the few signs that are pre-WWII," Amy said. She looked down at her tablet.

"Still up there, wow," Rebecca said. She tried to snap a photo.

"Well, that's interesting, sort of," I said. I pressed down on the steering wheel throttle, and I felt the engine cycle faster. "Next?"

"Yeah, go to the Colorado Street Bridge," Amy said. She pointed her forefinger forward, just past my face. Her hair fluttered in the breeze. "Make the next right and, in one block, make a right onto Orange Grove. When we get there, park on the side. I have a section from his diary; it's hilarious, you'll love it."

I followed Amy's instructions, finding a parking spot along the side of the old freeway that was parallel to the busy, modern version.

"We just drove up a section of the Arroyo Seco Parkway; it

was the first freeway out here, in the West," Amy said. She pushed her eyeglasses back against her eyes. "When they went across this bridge, he was terrified of it. They must have gone to Griffith Park one last time, before they came across this bridge. It was the only way."

"The lampposts are a lot like the ones near the LA Public Library," Rebecca said. She leaned over, closer to Amy.

"It *is* narrow," I said. I stared at the dusty, two-lane bridge, which had a metal fence bolted into the ornate concrete barriers. I suspected it was to keep sad souls from ending their lives.

"Okay, here goes," Amy said. She read, "We got our start. It was hard to leave. Hazel cried. I'm getting better at driving the A. The manual shift was tricky, at first – I was all hands and feet – but I squeezed down on the throttle, and off we went. The steering wheel shakes. It was all fine and dandy, until we got to a narrow bridge. It was a busy circus. I death-gripped the steering wheel and kept my eyes forward on the next auto. Hazel smiled. She thought it was fun. I did not."

"His writing style has changed," I said. I gripped the steering wheel, which was from the same time period. I could hear Amy and Rebecca conferring about our next destination. "Where to, next?"

"Aztec Hotel. We'll just do a drive-by," Amy said. She handed me her tablet, with the directions highlighted. "Follow that."

We stayed off the modern freeway, opting for city streets. Mount Wilson loomed to our left as we began to drive at the base of the San Gabriel Mountains. We drove along East Colorado Street, past the boutique shops and skinny palm trees that leaned forward. It was a slow-moving drive, from street light to street light, but it was also beautiful to notice the different architectural blends, from the Spanish influences to the hard-glass-and-steel modernists. I enjoyed the unique drive, because it reminded me of how nothing here looked like every other street corner, as it did across the country. We stayed off the Foothill Freeway and drove past Santa Anita Park toward Monrovia, along oak-and-palm-lined streets. The streets transformed from upscale Pasadena to modest buildings and homes, and then we drove near the old hotel.

"Mayan?" I asked. I had to stop the car to take a closer look at the odd architecture. We all got out and stood at the street corner. "What on earth is that?"

"I know, it's super cool," Amy said. She pointed at the Mayan patterns along the stucco exterior of the hotel. Back in my grandparents' time, it had been a hip location. "They likely drove past it. He made no reference to it, but it was here, then."

"It looks like it has a nasty rash," I said. We got back into the car.

"Behave," Rebecca said. She tapped on the compartment barrier. "We saw it, that's off our bucket list."

Amy stood next to the car with her hands on her hips. She stared out across the flat, natural scrub.

"Next, I would go to the Wigwam Villages," Amy said. She laughed as she got back into the car. "But that came after them, so it's just weird. Instead, we go to Barstow. This spot has a lot of interest for you, in a couple of different ways. It has a railroad connection."

"Yeah, I get it, Grandpa came out on a train," I said. "But I still want to see the Wigwam Village, can we?"

"You are so weird," Rebecca said. She pointed forward. "Daylight's burning!"

"Dude," Amy said. She leaned over the passenger compartment barrier to point at a digital map. "I think we can make it to this museum, good place to stop."

"Rebecca," I said. "Can you call ahead?"

Amy turned and handed her smartphone to Rebecca.

"I can make this happen," Rebecca said. "Keep driving."

CHAPTER 15

Los Angeles' thin angel haze was long behind us. It would have been fun to drive through San Bernardino and check out the Wigwam Village. I was tempted to stay overnight in one of the concrete teepees, but we had plenty of clear daylight and a long, open road in front of us. Rebecca thought I had ulterior motives. She was right. I'd learned at my age to never be wasteful, and I felt that raw urge that you take for granted when you're sixteen. I glanced back at Rebecca and wondered where all the time had gone since we'd been smacked down by the hand of God. A truck horn brought me back to reality.

I loved the challenge of cruising up the busy, twisting, modern road between the San Gabriel and the San Bernardino Mountains in my fancy 1929 status symbol. It was the same pass that the famous and the not-so-famous would have traveled through to move down into Hollywood, but my grandparents had driven in the other direction, toward what they defined as their 'call from God', and their path had been much less certain and much less reliable.

"This is kind of dangerous. It's loud," Rebecca said. She glanced down at the ever-present train tracks as the commercial trucks hurdled past us, their horns blaring. I responded with our bugle-like horn.

"I'm being careful," I said. I kept a close watch on the dense traffic in front of us.

"And this is not my idea of cool; wind in my hair," Rebecca said. She smacked the back of my head. "This is nuts."

"I'll be careful," I said. I drove up the gradual incline that was married to the nearby constant train traffic, which moved coal, supplies, and commerce in the opposite direction; down into the LA Basin. We drove across the other side and then descended from the windy Cajon Pass, surrounded by the hulking, sun-bleached boulders. The wrinkled, tan mountainsides were littered with rocks and thorny, green bushes. It occurred to me that my grandparents had ventured across the same pass and the flat Mojave Desert in a Model A Ford with a four-cylinder, forty-horsepower engine. Alone. They were all alone.

Their car had a ten-gallon gas tank, placed above the engine, and they could drive at a comfortable speed of about fifty miles per hour. 'The A', as my grandfather called it, got about twenty miles per gallon.

We had an attractive, 125-horsepower beast from the same era with plenty of storage room, meaning we could drive over 300 miles before we needed to refuel. But where had they refueled or found food on their journey? Our worst case scenario involved a mobile satellite smartphone call and the appearance of my security detail. The only shocker would have been Amy's expression, wondering where those dark suits and the helicopter had come from. If they'd had an empty gas tank, a mechanical problem, or a nasty backfire, it might have meant death under the intense desert heat, stranded along a heartless road with the realization that no help was nearby. They had a faith that I didn't understood. I guess, to leave us so fearless, faith and love must be intertwined.

At least they would have died together; that sort of made it all right.

"The Wigwam Village might have been romantic," I said. "Maybe we should have gone."

"Who are you?" Rebecca asked. She gripped the top of my head. "You don't *seem* to have a temperature."

"You have to admit it," I said. "A teepee can be romantic; they even had a cement pond that Jethro Bodine would have loved."

"Romantic? Maybe in 1950," Rebecca said. "You been popping those happy pills?"

"No, but I'm having fun," I said. I turned and stuck my tongue out at her. "I don't even have a prescription for that stuff, but we do own a stake in the company. Sex sells."

"You sure about that?" Rebecca asked. She glided her left hand along the barrier. "Do I need to drive?"

"Careful," I said. "I might have to pull over."

"Get a room," Amy said. She was lying on the bench seat, reading a diary. "At your age, I'm surprised."

"By what?" I asked. "I'm not dead."

"He's just a big talker," Rebecca said.

"Your grandparents were all over each other," Amy said. She moved forward and held out the open diary. "Want me to read? He's really quite sweet."

"Ah, I'll pass," I said. I pushed the diary away.

"Let me see," Rebecca said.

We had driven into the Mojave Desert, heading toward Barstow along sparse roads that the sands were constantly trying to recapture. The landscape was populated by rusty bridges, old gas stations, and crumbling, abandoned roadside bars and hotels that appeared to have survived a nuclear winter. I thought that, if you wanted to get off the modern electrical grid or hide from the mob, selling worthless souvenirs, these haunts would be the perfect destination.

We kept the gas tank full and, from time to time, we stopped, ate cheeseburgers, and drank Coke at an appropriately pre-1930s destination. In those moments, I was entertained when our journey would cross paths with European and Asian tourists who were attempting to discover America's 'Mother Road'. The America of endless optimism that they were searching for had long since been trampled by its government. I thought Americans had become sheep, and the one thing I held certain was that sheep either get sheered or slaughtered. The America that these tourists were searching for was a propaganda myth, concocted after the destruction of World War II had left an untouched United States the task of gluing back together those parts of the free world not hidden behind the Iron Curtain. History had one constant: if you won the war, you wrote the history and reaped the rewards. The Mother Road that John Steinbeck had written about was from long before WWII, during manmade hard times when nothing would grow in the dry dirt and massive dust storms enveloped as far east as New York City. But where was *my* Mother Road? My birth mother was dead, and I couldn't go back in time; all I had left was in front of me.

My grandparents had driven into the heart of a land in financial ruin – a land that had eked out a centrally planned existence before World War II, when the Japanese naval fleet had left us with no place to hide. We forget that, at the time, over seventy percent of the United States population wanted nothing to do with WWII. We wanted to remain hidden. Standing next to a car that tourists had taken paparazzi-like pictures of, I wondered what they dreamed about America, living in their countries. I suspected we all searched for the same feeling: that life had a meaning and purpose. I shrugged and smirked at them; I thought life was as random and cruel as the stars.

As we'd driven along, the shops and old buildings had given way to a pristine land that had become silent, forgetting humanity's touch. For miles and miles, the road waved us forward, along the low, desert plain, past yucca plants and Joshua trees, but then I saw an old, wooden windmill, surrounded by yellow, dead brush and green bushes. The railroad tracks appeared, and then the implements for farming. It was intimidating and fascinating to think about traveling along the two-lane road in a Model A Ford. It wouldn't have been the smooth, concrete road bisected by a bright-yellow line, with convenient reflective signage that you were near civilization, but what I had seen, they had seen. I kept the throttle down, heading into Barstow. The old car thrusted forward.

"Amy, that's the train station?" I asked. I stopped the car and pointed toward a long, brick building with a line of archways on the first and second decks.

"Yeah, super cool, it's from their time," Amy said. She tapped on my shoulder. "But it looks closed."

"Let's go find a concrete teepee alternative," I said. I turned the automobile around and we drove back into Barstow.

"I don't think there are any serious hotels out here, but I tried," Rebecca said. She frowned at the modest streets, buildings, and homes. "I guess we'll make do, right?"

"My grandparents did, it's not fancy, but it does look well maintained. That means they have pride," I said, spotting a hotel. Its lights were on, and it seemed in a safe area, not far from a police station and our next morning's destination. "I think this will work, and I'm sure you two won't mind helping me put the car cover over our transportation. It even has a lock."

"Dude," Amy said. "You must have been a boy scout."

"Not me," I said. I parked near the hotels front doors. "I didn't have time for it."

CHAPTER 16

"June 17th, '30. I showed Hazel the train station. It was busy and loud today. It was the last stop I got off at before I made it to Los Angeles. I told her I didn't have enough money to eat here. She smiled up at me. I love her. We had a good lunch. I wonder what my parents will think."

Amy stopped reading and closed the diary. She took off her reading glasses and stared up the wide, grand staircase.

"What's wrong?" I asked. I stood on the original terrazzo flooring for the train station and hotel.

"He read a newspaper; he wrote another entry just before they left the next morning," Amy said. She took in a deep breath and opened the diary. "I read the news; we are in a heap of trouble. Has God sent us a lesson? Nobody was smiling. I understand now. I am scared. I hope I can find work. I am ashamed; I have been so blind to what I want. I'm afraid our mission might end before we even get started. We have just enough money to get along for now. I pray. I must be strong."

"What did I miss?" Rebecca asked. She was examining a postcard rack.

"Stock market crashed, 1929," I said. I walked over and

studied the old black-and-white photos of the station and the black-tie restaurant that was now an empty room. It still had the original copper fixtures. "He finally realized what was happening to the country. Smoot-Hawley was enacted, and it edged us further into a depression. This railroad depot was a major crossroads, right?"

"For sure," Amy said, nodding. She walked out the back doors and under the brick arches and the tall colonnades that would have shaded waiting passengers from the desert heat. I followed her and stood on the sand-swept, brick-and-concrete platform. It overlooked two sets of train tracks.

"How'd you know about that... What did you call it?" she asked.

"The Smoot-Hawley Tariff. It was a dumb act. I've studied business history, that's my world. I suspect he sensed bad things were coming. The stock market continued to fall. This must have been quite a place," I said. I stared over at a hulking train engine. "They spent a lot of money here, with all the hand-crafted moldings and this building. What is it?"

"They say it's influenced by Spanish and Southwest Indian architecture, with Moorish elements," Amy said. She put her hands on her hips. "I guess; if what I read is correct."

She stared down the side of the long, brick building and out at the remaining train tracks, which were crossed over by a steel-and-concrete bridge. A desert mountain blocked the Western horizon.

"What are you thinking?" I asked. I stared up at one of the tall towers topped with a square, clay roof.

"This place would have been extremely busy, in their day," Amy said. She strolled along under the original signage for Barstow. "Your grandfather could have been standing where you are, right now."

"Amazing, that train," I said. I watched a well-used train

pulling freight cars full of black coal through the station. "That would have reminded him of Kentucky, can you smell it?"

"Smell what?" Rebecca asked. She had walked out and behind us. "It smells industrial, to me."

"Yeah, sulfur," I said. "Remember being in China?"

"Oh, yeah, yeah," Rebecca said. She put on her sunglasses. "What do you think, historian?"

Amy waved away Rebecca's comment. She walked back toward us and pointed at a historical marker.

"This place was one of the first chains; it consisted of a restaurant, a hotel, and a railroad depot. It was a really big deal, back then," Amy said. She smiled and pushed her palms against the building's bricks. "I'm glad I came along. This was America; it holds so many memories. Your grandfather was here, and then he ended up at the LA station. Remember being downtown at that joint you called a dive?"

"Yeah," I said. It chilled me to think about him in this building. First, as a young man scared about what he would see in Los Angeles, and then as a married man with responsibilities and a deeper fear of the future.

"Let me read another entry," Amy said. She opened one of his diaries she had marked with a thick LA Public Library bookmark. "Nervous. I am not sure driving was a good idea. The train would have been safer. What have I done? I prayed. I prayed and prayed. I need to be strong. She depends on me. What have I done?"

"Wow," I said. "That ain't Norman Rockwell, that's real-life stuff."

"These places were important," Amy said. "These were safe places, to sleep, get gas, you know."

"I was curious, where they got gas and whatnot," I said. I crossed my arms. "What's next?"

"Let's take a walk through the museums," Amy said. She

closed the diary. "We have some time, then we head toward Needles and another train depot. It was their next stop."

"Cool," I said. Amy waved for us to follow.

We walked into a large museum dedicated to trains and the coal-powered engines that had stoked the United States economy. We walked around, checking out reminders of the Mother Road – all the colorful metal and porcelain with neon gas station signs that reminded me that oil, gas, and coal were the energy sources that built the open road.

"That was actually cool," Rebecca said. She was checking her lipstick in one of the car's rearview mirrors. "How far?"

"I think just under 150 miles," Amy said. She was examining a road map on a mobile computing device my grandparents couldn't have imagined.

"Well, I do know one thing," I said. I grinned over at Rebecca. "We have no cigarettes, and we are not headed to Chicago."

"You are so weird," Rebecca said. She pointed at the road. "Drive. We can get to at least Kingman, Arizona before it gets dark, right?"

"For sure," Amy said. "No worries."

CHAPTER 17

We drove along the two-lane freeway toward Needles. Eighteen-wheeler after eighteen-wheeler passed us, transporting cargo containers across the flat, scruffy desert. I thought I needed to get our antique girl a good bath, soon; her metal curves were getting pelted with sand, but she was still getting all the drivers' looks and their honked well wishes.

After we left the safe freeway, and with Amy's encouragement, we investigated original Route 66 segments that told a very different story about my grandparents' time. Our modern road was like running a straight line of hardened concrete glue across the country, gobbling tracts of land with the benefit of eminent domain. In contrast, my grandparents' road had been full of potholes; a patchwork of bituminous dirt-and-pebble segments that wove a winding path, connecting American towns. Over time, the road had created a unified self-confidence for children born to the farm, tempting them to venture out and seek new lives and destinations. It told them that there was a big world for them to see, beyond the farms, yellow wheat, and cornfields.

"I've never seen you like this," Rebecca said. She sat next to me in the chauffeur compartment, gripping my forearm. "You've got a late-'80s, *Miami Vice* sort of beard growing, but most of all, you seem content to drive along and hardly say a word."

"They were so brave," I said. I shook my head. "I was clueless to this and who they were."

"This has been so cool," Amy said. She sprang forward from behind. "Let's just do a drive-by for the next train depot at Needles. Cool, for sure, but I really want to get into Arizona; it's got some super-cool stuff."

"You've really gotten into this." I said.

"For sure; history comes alive for me," Amy said. She leaned back. "I think I might really write the historical book about our trip."

"Terrific," Rebecca said. She took a picture of the side of my face. "It'll have terrific photographs."

"You should post the scans on your Facebook page; his diaries are amazing historical documents," Amy said, holding one up. "He wrote short statements first, but then his writing opens up. He's growing older, it's just so cool. He was so nervous until they got to St. Louis. I've skipped ahead, want me to read from after they got to Kentucky?"

"Sure, I guess this has been good exploration," I said. I gripped the steering wheel at ten and two o'clock, like a teenager. "Don't post anything to the Internet just yet."

"I know," Rebecca said. She grinned down at her camera.

"This is a different type of exploration," Amy said. She put on her reading glasses. "I had forgotten how green and hilly Kentucky is. I have missed home. I was not sure what Hazel thought. We had driven from Lexington, which she liked. We continued to Kentucky, where she met my parents. The family was quiet, she was quiet.

"My father hugged me. My mother is not the hugging type, but she was glad we had made it back. She stared at Hazel. She can be mean."

"*Shreni Belle, Mize,*" I said. I pushed the throttle down.

"Great-Grandma and -Grandpa."

"You know," Rebecca said, "we shouldn't make fun of other cultures and what they call each other."

"True that," Amy said.

We drove along the freeway and paid our respects to the railroad depot at Needles. It was interesting to drive across the California-Arizona border because, like every state-to-state intersection I'd ever driven across, the color of the roads and the maintenance pattern changed. We maneuvered down I-40 but drove off the interstate to investigate the Old Trails Bridge that my grandparents had used to drive over the Colorado River. Amy had informed us that it was a historic bridge, because a daring cantilever system had been used to create the 600-foot span that supported the steel arches. I imagined my grandparents driving across the bridge, along the then-National Old Trails Road toward St. Louis. I smiled, and then we returned to I-40 and made our way to Kingman.

"They were happy to get to Kingman," Amy said. She started to laugh. "This is funny, in a way, now that we've made it." She kept smiling as she read, "We made it to Kingman; we have a place to stay. We are happy to be alive. We both agreed we would never drive across the desert again. At the bridge, we looked back and just shook our heads. The A has been dependable. Hazel kissed me. I'll sleep good. Just happy to be alive."

"Ha," I said. I could almost hear his voice. "He could make me laugh; he had the best deadpan humor."

"Wish I'd met him," Rebecca said. "Your stories really make him come alive."

"See?" Amy asked. "History isn't just looking backward."

"I think you're right," Rebecca said.

"Yeah, yeah," I said.

I parked in front of an old hotel within Kingman's Historic

District. Rebecca had called ahead and booked us two rooms at a nearby hotel with an indoor pool. The old hotel, which no longer hosted guests, faced the brown desert and railroad tracks. We strolled along the streets behind the hotel.

"Amy, let's go shopping!" Rebecca said. She stood near a large window, looking inside at a vintage clothing shop.

"Cool," Amy said. As Rebecca opened the thick, wooden door, a bell rang, and they entered a shop stuffed with flapper-style clothes, vintage hats, and dust. "By the way, it's not part of their story, but we're only about an hour away from the Hoover Dam."

I had my hands in my pants pockets. I nodded at Amy.

"It's not like I'm on the clock. Also, I've never seen the Grand Canyon," I said.

"I'd recommend we drive to Flagstaff," Amy said. She grinned. "It'll keep us on their journey."

"Good idea," Rebecca said. She gripped Amy's hand.

"Fine with me, but I'll let you all go have fun," I said. I shrugged. "I'll find something to do."

I walked down the street and found a quiet visitor's center. Inside the air-conditioned building, all the information was in front of me. As a people, we had gone from the horse and wagon to the railway, and then to cars and airplanes. Now, the Internet allowed us to travel without ever leaving the house. It was about speed and efficiency. It told the story of how, over time, modern interstate systems had starved old downtowns of the vibrant foot traffic that originally helped the hopeful communities on Route 66. It was a process I saw repeating with online retailers and brick-and-mortar shops. I thought we'd sped up so fast that we'd forgotten the uniqueness of our cultural melting pot. Instead, we'd blended into the same vanilla of prefabricated strip centers, fast food chains, and stucco housing developments. It bored me.

During their day, my grandparents had been on a mission to start their missionary lives, but what were all the other Route 66 tourists searching for? I guessed we'd all lost our way as we searched for innocence. I walked back to retrieve my Pierce-Arrow and then went and found a carwash for a good bath. Afterward, I hand-toweled her dry. The carwash attendants thought I was crazy to give them all a handsome tip for watching me work, but it was about love.

CHAPTER 18

The Hoover Dam was much bigger than I'd imagined. We walked along the curved, sun-bleached observation deck, watching groups and couples take a variety of different-angled selfies like a swarm of tourist-ants overcoming a centipede. It sounded, and felt, like an angry beast was trapped beneath my feet, spanning the border between Arizona and Nevada and generating 4.2 billion kilowatt hours each year. It was finished in 1936, a tax-payer-funded, make-work project that cost many innocent lives and almost a billion in US dollars. It was an odd sensation to realize I could afford it.

"Progress," I said. I stared over the side at the smooth-surfaced, arched-gravity dam. "It looks like something a pharaoh would have had built."

"It's like staring at Mount Rushmore for more than a minute," Rebecca said. She sat down on a hot, concrete bench and glanced back at the vast Lake Meade. It looked like a protective blue mote snaking through the brown mountains and splashing against the dam. "It's not going anywhere. Boring, unless we had a boat. Now *that* might be fun."

"I guess we can say we saw it," Amy said. She shrugged.

"A lot of people died here," I said. It had been much easier being a distant investor for most of my life. To have driven those unemployed men to their deaths during the Depression wasn't how I rolled. "Without energy, we don't exist. We need electricity."

We drove back down toward Kingman; it was just us and the warm breeze, driving across I-40 toward Flagstaff.

Five hours later, we stood together at the southern rim of the Grand Canyon.

"I don't have the words," Amy said. She sat down near the cliff edge and stared down at the upside-down mountain range trapped beneath the flat, desert scape. "It's like God swept out the dirt and left the cliffs and a place for the water to flow." She walked to us, wiping a tear from her eyes. "I don't know why this place..." she said. "It's like I'm expecting a Native American to appear — you know, colorful feathers everywhere, his handprints on the horse's chest — riding up to the summit. His horse making a dust cloud, spear in hand, shrieking up to the sky."

"You really should write," Rebecca said. She adjusted the flapper-style hat they had found back in Kingman. "You look great, let me get a close-up."

She strolled behind me and took a photo of me and Amy staring across a golden horizon – deep, jagged channels carved into the earth below.

"What happened to the stalactites?" I said, grinning. "Get it, from the ceiling?"

"What?" Rebecca asked. She waved me away. "You okay?"

"I get it," Amy said. She strolled away. "I'm really... I don't know how to say this..."

I scratched my brown-and-gray beard. I thought it strange that my thick head of brown hair hadn't been matched by the scruff across my face. It was sad, but I guessed God likes to create uniqueness with every living creature. If we all looked like Elvis, there wouldn't have been an Elvis.

"What's that?" I asked. Amy held her forehead in her hands. She had started to pace along the side of our now bathed and shiny Pierce-Arrow. I was proud of my manual labor; the car sparkled. Amy walked over to me and encouraged me to sit down. She had one of my grandfather's diaries in her hands. She stared at Rebecca who, by instinct, walked over and sat down next to me.

"I need to just read this," Amy said. She glossed tears from her eyes and opened the diary. "Just let me read this aloud."

"All right," Rebecca said. She stuffed her camera into her purse and gripped my right hand.

"We are here. It has been some days. I took her for a walk into the mountains. I had to go there. It was something I had to do. I took her there. I told her everything."

Amy stopped reading.

"Ruby?" I asked. I squeezed Rebecca's hand.

"Yeah?" Amy said. "How'd you know?"

"Family stories," I said. I shifted my shoes in the sand. "I guess I have a good memory."

"Yeah," Amy said. She hugged the diary. "I'm glad I came along. You can have all your money, it's not about that; this is a historical treasure."

"I'm lost," Rebecca said.

"Go on," I said. I felt a tear leave my eye. "I've never heard him tell it."

Amy stared down at me. She wiped her face and put on her eyeglasses.

"I walked her to the spot. It was quiet. The birds were gone. I took off my coat, I sat her at the spot. The rocks and the trees looked the same. I told her. The leaves that day were dark green. Green, moist from rain. I remember, that day, feeling raindrops hit my face. They would not stop after, like they were pestering me to stay awake. I remember looking up at the sun between the tree limbs. It smelled like spring. It was the birds. We had gone into the mountains to chase the birds. To shoot some stupid birds."

Amy stopped reading. She wiped her face with several tissues. She handed me the open diary.

"I can't," she said, and she walked away, toward a cluster of redbud trees waiting to bloom again.

I held the diary. It felt ancient to my fingertips. I encouraged Rebecca to follow Amy. I wasn't certain I would read what was left. I took in a deep breath and then stared down at the page, reading under my breath.

"Brother and I, we had been talking, about this or that, I don't remember. We had been walking in the mountains behind home. It was a nice day. We had been shooting stupid birds. He wanted to be a preacher. He liked Reuben, the circuit rider, thought he was a mystery man, with his white beard and horse. And then we had sat down. I remember I felt the gunshot blast. My right ear burned. My neck was hot. He had set the barrel down and it went off. He was dead before I could move. He didn't say anything. I grabbed him. I hugged him until he stopped shaking. I heard him stop breathing. I stared at the ground. I screamed. I hugged him. I carried him back. None of us talked much, we just buried him. I miss him. I still miss him."

I closed the diary and hugged it close. I walked over towards the canyon's edge. I hated being near heights, but that day, I didn't care. Everybody had their phobias; mine were heights and confined spaces. If I were honest, it had to do with my childhood. It's not pleasant to be locked in a closet, to have your innocence taken, to wake up afraid each morning, to feel afraid day after day after day. I know there are scars hidden inside our minds. Everyone has them; scars deep enough in all of us that just a thought can take you back to the exact moment, but I couldn't imagine having been next to a brother as they shot their own head off.

I acknowledged an Asian couple that walked past me then stared down at the grains of dirt. I wondered how my grandfather had told my grandmother about the day his teenage brother had died in his arms. It was probably the moment that Kansas girl had sat in the Eastern Kentucky forest and felt he loved her beyond any rational reason. It was an invisible bond. If you know someone long enough, you begin to understand their hopes and dreams, and then they share what's really going on behind their eyeballs. As I gazed across the Grand Canyon, at brown and gray rock veins in the distance, it became a moment where I felt what it meant to be alive. I stared back toward the parking lot, watching Rebecca hug Amy. I had noticed her mobile phone hadn't rung in a while.

I thought Rebecca saw something in Amy that had died many years ago.

CHAPTER 19

I stood at a windswept street corner in Winslow, Arizona, watching modern traffic cycle across a large, white 'Route 66' sign stenciled onto the outbound lane. My antique girl was parked at an angle in front of me. Next to her was an old, dark-blue Ford truck with more dents than a greasy teenager has pimples. I hadn't been in a mood to stop at Canyon Diablo. It wasn't something I wanted to see; the asteroid that had crashed into the planet was from before humanity, much less my grandparents' time, and after Hoover Dam and the Grand Canyon, I wanted to get back on their schedule. It was all I cared about; all I thought about was them. Why had I felt so connected to them and not my own parents?

After we drove from the Grand Canyon, my job was to find a late lunch spot, but I had heard the brakes squeak, and I wasn't comfortable with any squeaks. Amy and Rebecca had ventured off and spotted another vintage shop to plunder for real and not-so-real relics. I reflected that my grandmother had needed to scrimp and save to afford a simple hat, or a pretty dress, or anything. It hadn't allowed for much. I sat down on a wooden bench.

"Hey there," I said. An old man with thinning, gray hair waved at me and pointed at my fancy car.

"Now that's a car," he said. He wobbled against his wooden cane as he went further down the sidewalk and into a barber shop with a red, white, and blue barber pole out front.

It was Hazel. It had taken me most of my life to realize she was the driving force behind my grandfather. She had been his purpose; God was just along for the ride. But I remembered how hard she had worked. It was because she had believed in him that she'd carried out her missionary work. I guessed that each had provided what the other lacked. I had always thought that Hazel had a tough mind; she had an assassin's calm. On the other hand, Stephen had never met a stranger. It must have been beautiful. But, like all things, it had come to a tragic end. It was part of the reason I questioned the existence of a higher power. As I sat there, I watched random couples. Some walked their dogs, others held hands and strolled in and out of the shops. It was the security of their love that had most mattered to my grandfather; I was certain of that. I had seen it in his eyes. After his wife's death from breast cancer, he'd had a sadness that would appear from time to time, but it had been there even before that. I thought about the old family photos, and his eyes told me something was always missing. It was his brother. He had always searched for someone who should have been there; his brother's sudden death marked him deep inside, at his core. Like a veteran struggling with trauma, he'd never spoken of the accident, but then I read from his diary, and his entire life made perfect sense to me. He appeared a strong, resolute preacher, but I suspected that, inside, he was as fragile as the old man who had just moved past me. It was Hazel. In the same way, Rebecca made me strong; even though she endured my fits of depression, my lack of attention, my nasty fits of rage. She was my red-tailed hawk.

It wasn't long until the old man emerged from the barbershop with a fresh haircut. He trudged toward me like a Charlie Chaplin character sans mustache.

He sat down next to me, wheezing and wiping his face with a white handkerchief.

"Girl trouble?" he asked. He grinned at me with yellow teeth. "Let me catch my breath."

"Which one?" I asked.

"The metal one," he said. He gripped the oval top of the cane. "She looks to be in good working order."

"She is," I said.

"Shopping?" he asked. "The human one?"

"Yeah, across the street," I said. I pointed past the metal parking meter at the red-brick, indicating a line of two-story shops Rebecca and Amy had disappeared into.

"Don't mind me sayin', you look a bit scruffy to be drivin' that," he said. He touched his smooth chin and nudged me. "Just kiddin'. Let me guess; you're on a Route 66 sojourn."

"Yeah," I said. I chuckled. "You're right."

"Back in the old days, that was a rich buck's car," he said. He blinked as he inspected the Pierce-Arrow. Several tourists walked between us and the car. "I guess you're doin' all right."

"Yeah, we get by, stay busy," I said. "You retired?"

He nodded and re-gripped the cane with both wrinkled hands.

"I hate it," he said. He spat on the ground. "But my body don't agree; it decided to retire me."

I patted him on his bony shoulder.

"Don't matter how much you got in the bank," I said. I leaned forward with my elbows atop my knees. "Happy, healthy, and wise, right?"

He rolled his well-worn shirt sleeves up to his elbows and sighed.

"I miss my girl, too," he said. He cleared his throat.

"Sorry," I said. His eyes reminded me of my grandfather's after Hazel died. "What was her name?"

"Oh, ah, Daun," he said. "Korean; I met her while I was wearing an army uniform. You know..."

"Sorry that I'm pestering you with questions," I said. I sat back and inspected the busy Historic District. "Where's a good lunch?"

He gripped my left forearm and pointed down toward a modest, one-story, adobe-walled diner with his cane.

"Good coffee, black," he said. "It smells real; the Naugahyde's original, not too touristy. We never missed a Sunday morning."

"Sorry, can I ask you something personal?" I asked. I interlocked my fingers.

"I got nothing to hide, at my age," he said with a sniffle.

"True," I said. "What's it like now? At your age?"

He stared down at the sidewalk. He thought for several moments as he covered his mouth with his hand.

"You have a quick brain," he said. He tapped the cane against the weathered, concrete sidewalk. "She came here, just trusted me, we had a good life, but I'm glad she went first. I wouldn't want her to be here alone, not like this. I've seen death up close, I'm not afraid, but bein' alone—"

"Sucks?" I asked.

"Sucks," he agreed. He stared up into the sky. "It just never occurred to me that, one day, I'd be old."

"I see," I said. "I'll tell you something: I didn't plan this. My grandparents drove through here in the 1930s, on the way to Kentucky. My wife found my grandfather's diaries recently. My grandparents met in LA and, the next thing I know, I'm sitting here, with you. It's funny what you learn along the way."

"I was here, back then, when they came through. I bet they stopped over at La Posada, maybe one of the old gas stations," he said. His smile reappeared. "But I was in a baby crib, I bet me and her are the same age."

"1929?" I asked.

"Ah," he said. "I always liked them a bit older."

We silently enjoyed the warm sunshine, but then he nodded past me.

"Well, hello," Rebecca said. She had wrapped a colorful, cape-like, vintage scarf around her shoulders. "Look what I found."

"Ah, you're lovely," I said. I turned to my new friend, embarrassed that we hadn't shared our names. "Sorry, this is?"

"Stu," he said. He reached up to shake Rebecca's hand. He pointed up at Amy. "And is this lovely creature your daughter?"

"No," Amy said. She blushed. "I'm a historian, just tagging along to help them."

"Historian?" Stu asked. He looked back over at me. "Well, you must be doin' alright to bring along a historian and that car. First time you forgot to shave?"

I hesitated for a moment.

"She's a new friend," Rebecca said. She glanced down at her new scarf.

"Stu recommended we go over there, for lunch," I said. I scooted forward. "Stu, you want to get lunch with us, my treat?"

"I'll take a rain check," Stu said. He grinned. "I've got to get back home; I have a date tonight."

"Date?" Rebecca asked.

"Met me a young one, my rehab nurse," Stu said. "We hit it off, thought I'd get a haircut and a clean shave. She's cookin' for me tonight, at my place."

"You salty dog," I said. I encouraged them to head toward the diner.

"I ain't dead yet," Stu said. "I think she'd be all right with it."

"Yeah, I think so," I said. I leaned down and shook his hand. "I have no doubt. You kids have fun tonight."

"Modern medicine," he said. He patted his shirt pocket. "Got me some of them magic pills."

"Yeah?" I said. "I hope Grandpa bought a rubber?"

"This ain't this grandpa's first rodeo," Stu said.

CHAPTER 20

As we drove along Steinbeck's Mother Road toward Albuquerque, the pale-blue sky seemed to dome over the flat, desert plain. It was as if it were painted, with dabs of blurred clouds made from white cake frosting. I bypassed another concrete Wigwam Village; I wasn't quite as interested in it this time as I had been back in California. Perhaps I was feeling my age, but Stu had sure seemed confident. After Amy had done some trip planning, I called my master mechanic, Wylie, who would be waiting for us at the Hotel Albuquerque. As we drove along a preserved section of Route 66 within the Petrified Forest, Amy found an entry in my grandfather's diary. She read the entry, and it triggered my curiosity.

"We drove quite far and, luckily, we made it to a safe place. The desert doesn't end. There was a good amount of gas and food. It was a good spot to rest. We had stopped along the road. It was like heaven appeared. I had, at first, just seen the desert, but the sun was maybe playing tricks. The tall mountains were painted with lines of red, orange, and even yellow. It wasn't just brown. It was silent. We prayed. We said nothing. We held hands and just wondered about God and the beauty we had never seen."

As the clear evening overtook the day, we stood together at a round observation deck on a mesa that overlooked the orange desert. I stared up at a round, gray moon. It was from a different time, but it was the same trapped orb that my grandparents had stared up at from their time, wondering what it all meant. It was the same moon that Jesus, the Caesars, Da Vinci, Newton, and every other famous name that had roamed the earth had stared up at and wondered if their Gods were in their favor. I realized, standing near Rebecca, how unimportant I was. I had all the money, I had all the access a man could want, but I would die as a private person. It was my choice. My grandparents hadn't cared what anyone thought; they had only cared what their God wanted. I admitted, though only to myself, that I had cared what humanity thought. I had always defied nature; I was more than prepared to fight the current and forge upstream, but I was clueless as to why I hadn't shaved.

"I don't know what to say," Rebecca said. She squeezed my hand, kissed my cheek, and let go as she walked down a path toward the far side of the inn's rear seating area. She stood still and took photos of the irregular, jagged badlands.

"This is cool," Amy said. "Like a US cavalry outpost from a John Wayne movie. Even though it has a flag, this is apparently Navajo land. I think Geronimo was an Apache, right?"

"I have no idea," I said. I smiled down at Amy. "But I know one thing; I'm getting chilly."

"For sure," Amy said. She crossed her arms.

"I guess we should expect a covered wagon to appear between those clumps of bushes and the hills," I said. "I understand why they call it 'the Painted Desert'; it's majestic, in its own way."

"Yeah, I was reading," Amy said. She took off her glasses. "This is part of the Petrified Forest National Park; this stuff is way before your grandparents."

"True, that," I said. I clapped my hands and stared up as a red-tailed hawk circled above the old inn. It seemed unconcerned with us, but I knew that out there, among the greenish bushes, was the early evening meal it was tracking.

I closed my eyes and thought of my hawk friend from home. Home? It occurred to me that it *was* my home; not the old chapel my grandparents had built and missioned from, which we were headed toward. Our home was the place I had felt the safest, because it was where Rebecca and I had built our life together. It wasn't about the fancy neighborhood – we could be happy anywhere – it was about our relationship. A home was for happiness, not hate, not what I had experienced.

"How did you get so rich?" Amy asked.

"Hedge fund," I said. I crossed my arms. "It's about the math. If you control the math, your emotions, you can control everything."

"Dude, dude, what does that even mean?" Amy asked.

"I can explain," I said.

"Will I understand?" Amy asked. She hugged her tablet.

"Understand this," I said. "Math tells us outcomes, we make our decisions based on cold reality."

"Do you exploit people?" Amy asked.

"I don't mean to," I said. "But, sometimes, yes. They'd hurt me too, though."

"I have a hard time making decisions," Amy said. She stared past me.

"Anything I can help with?" I asked.

"I don't think so," Amy said. She walked away. "Thanks, I needed a break from life."

I stared across the desert plain. It looked like a collection of hulking, fire-breathing dragons had been frozen in time after they had blasted the petrified wood. Now, they slept blanketed with sand and desert bushes. The sky I had stared up into had become like sheer curtains, sweeping away the dying sunlight. It was as if

God had decided it was time for sleep, but man had discovered the secrets of the light. We would head to bed at a time of our choosing.

I had resisted the urge to shave off my beard that night, but I was starting to become impatient with it. Why had Jesus had a beard? At least, the Anglophile pictures of Jesus had him with a long, flowing beard. My ancestor Reuben, a circuit rider according to family photos, had a long, white, Moses-like beard. At that moment, I wanted to ask my grandfather. He had always had common-sense answers to my questions. As I stood in a place he might have stood, I felt what it was like to miss someone enough to simply cry. I loved Rebecca, I assumed, but I wondered what love felt like.

"Be ye kind," I whispered to the desert. I wiped away a tear.

CHAPTER 21

Before the sun had fully awoken, I took the early morning to wipe the desert off my horseless carriage. I took my time to make sure she was appreciated. Then, her silver headlamps and archer led us along the concrete road toward the endless, flat, brown horizon. I thought I could have almost taken my hands off the steering wheel, given how the road was a straight line all the way to Albuquerque. I was in awe of the thought that my grandparents had driven across the empty desert in a black Model A Ford in 1930. I guessed they had loaded up with extra gas, water, and provisions, like they were on a camping trip. If the A had broken down along the Mother Road, they would have needed a lot of luck to survive out in this wilderness. It was a road no mother would allow her child to drive along, but they had lived to tell the tale. I couldn't get their courage out of my mind as we drove into Albuquerque.

"I'm told we should order fiesta burgers," Rebecca said. After we had checked into our comfortable, Spanish-style-architecture hotel, she had asked the hotel concierge for a classic New Mexico lunch recommendation. "It's sort of what we should do; a local thing."

"I do know that I'm hungry. The college kids probably think

I'm a wacky professor," I said as I zipped up my tan jacket. "And I'm thankful we stopped for gas."

"No kidding," Rebecca said. She unloosened her scarf. "I'm glad I bought some Navajo blankets. If you drove that road at night, you would have gone mad. Now I know why Native Americans used peyote."

"Peyote? Whoa," Amy said. "Makes me respect them more. Is that how they survived?"

"No kidding, now I know why they call it 'the Land of Enchantment'," I said. We moved across the brown-tile floor to the restaurant's busy front counter, above which hung a vast menu. "I've never been so happy to see a billboard for gas."

"Amy, after we feast, where to next?" Rebecca asked.

"First, I need to track down Wylie," I said. We ordered our food. "Let's hang here for a few days and recharge. My girl needs some attention: oil, lube, you know."

"I'm finding several spots," Amy said. She tapped her fingers along the smooth surface. "He wrote about a couple of places here. They stayed here, too."

"Maybe some sweet rolls?" Rebecca asked. She sat next to me, watching a college kid devour a large sweet roll. "I have to do that."

"That's a serious funeral roll," I said.

"What?" Rebecca asked.

"At funerals," I said, "they always made sweet rolls. I don't know why. Called them 'funeral rolls'."

Amy sat down on a slick, red, Naugahyde bench in front of Rebecca. She opened her burger wrapper.

"He wrote about a cemetery," Amy said, "but they went north at Oklahoma City."

"Why would they do that?" Rebecca asked. She bit into her burger. "Any ideas, Evil Bob?"

"Kansas?" I asked. My mobile phone started to vibrate.

"Yeah," Amy said. "I'm curious as to why. Um, 'Evil Bob'?"

I put my hand up, and then I answered my mobile phone.

"Great, Wylie's here," I said. I stuffed the mobile phone back into my jacket pocket.

"Evil Bob," Rebecca said. She nudged me with her elbow.

"It's not a compliment," I said.

"Go ahead, tell her," Rebecca said. "We don't want her to freak out."

I took a good, healthy sip of my carbonated drink.

"I guess I got lucky," I said, sighing. "'Evil Bob' is a nickname that I unfortunately earned."

"But it allows us to own fancy cars," Rebecca said.

"Know what a hedge fund is?" I asked.

"Not really," Amy said. "I'm a history junkie."

"Well, they've been around since the 1920s," I said. I stared up at the ceiling. "I operate a large fund. I have investors that trust my judgment to make them money, and I'm really good at it."

"Move over, Bacon," Rebecca said. She leaned into me. "I'm going to get a to-go order."

I stood up to let Rebecca escape to the front counter.

"Why 'Evil Bob'?" Amy asked. She studied my face. She whispered. "Are you in the mob?"

"No," I laughed. "We're much worse."

"Don't scare me," Amy said.

"I kid. We conduct business in a variety of ways. We don't have a lot of regulations to slow us down," I said. I glossed my fingers over my beard. "See, we take large positions in companies. Stocks, you know? The industry is known for shorting the market, when we think it's wise. For the most part, we act as contrarians, when the math works."

"Yeah." Amy nodded. "I don't understand."

"We hedge our bets by playing both sides of the market," I said. I watched a giggling young couple sit down near us. "In other words, we sometimes bet against a stock; we short it. Our thinking is that it'll go down in price. A brokerage loans us the stock, we sell at a determined price, profit with the difference. Got it?"

Amy shook her head 'no'.

"We also take positions in currencies," I said. I reached forward for Amy's hand. "Get this. Let's say, with the Russian ruble, we take a leveraged position with another currency."

"Why?" Amy asked.

"Good question. We think some countries are manipulating their currency to make their exports cheaper. For example, to get more dollars," I said. I held my hands open. "It artificially props up their economy, and it creates uncertainty in the markets. I don't like that. I like certainty and the real profits that come from it."

"I'm not into gambling," Amy said.

"Oh, we're not gambling," I said. "We have mathematical models and algorithms that guide our decisions. It's a game, but a game with mathematical rules."

She just stared at me.

"Game? I have no idea what you just said," Amy said. "But it must be super cool to be 'Evil Bob'."

"Not really," I said. I turned to search the windows, to see if my friends in the black SUV had appeared.

"What are you looking for?" Amy asked. She pointed toward the front. "Rebecca's over there."

"I know," I said. I turned back around and tapped on the table-top. "I'm no humble billionaire, that's an act. What would a prime minister, a king, or a president think if you blew up their economy by hitting their currency hard?"

"Man, that's crazy," Amy said.

"Sort of. Some have issued warrants for my arrest," I said. "Just so you know, I have a security detail. They're always nearby. I'm so used to them, now, that I forget they're even out there."

"Whoa," Amy said. "So, you're like really famous?"

"No," I said. "I'm rich. I'm powerful. I cause problems."

"That's harsh," Amy said. "Cold-hearted, man?"

"Not really, just cold reality," I said as Rebecca returned to the restaurant booth. "You've probably never heard of the richest people. You probably don't have any idea what they look like, right?"

"Yeah, I guess so," Amy said. She sat pondering my question.

"Which would you choose?" I asked. I held out my right hand and then my left. "To be rich or be on the cover of a supermarket gossip magazine?"

"Success," Rebecca said. She clutched a box that had a distinct brown-sugar smell. "Where to, Amy?"

Amy sat back. She studied Rebecca. She considered my question.

"Don't worry," I said. I pointed my thumb behind me. "They're a precaution. If someone does something, we have mechanisms to destroy their economy. I think they're more scared of me than I am of them."

"Rich," Amy said. She nodded at me. "Rich for sure; I could roam about unnoticed... like you."

"Thus, 'Evil Bob'," Rebecca said. She folded her colorful scarf around her neck. "Let's go be tourists."

"Amy, I can have you home before the sun goes down," I said. I stared at her. "I hope you stay, you have nothing to fear, but let me know if you're worried."

"Have you ever heard the term 'wolf in sheep's clothing'?" Rebecca asked. She nudged me to move.

"All right." I stood up. "Let's go find Wylie, my car needs love."

"Yeah," Amy said. She grabbed her computer as she scooted across the red Naugahyde. "I'll hang."

"Evil Bob," Rebecca said. "He's the wolf, I don't want you to meet him."

"And she loves you?" Amy asked.

"Tough love," I said.

"He has qualities," Rebecca said. "He just needs to find them again, right?"

"I'm trying," I said.

We walked together toward my curvy, antique status symbol, which a couple of college boys were gawking at.

"I'm not evil," I said. I blinked, as the bright sunlight had overtaken the day. I gave Rebecca a disappointed glance. "I'm just cautious and honest."

"I'll hang," Amy said. "I've never known peeps like you."

"Good," I said. "Let's go find Wylie."

"Awesome," Rebecca said. She got into the back passenger section, next to Amy. "Please, drive us."

I shut the car door and primed the pressure of the gas pump.

"Yes, madam," I said.

"Awesome ride," a boy said. They nodded as they stood on the sidewalk in front of the campus entrance.

"Thanks," I said. I put on sunglasses. "Study hard, take some risks, and maybe you can get one of your own, one day."

"Sweet," another boy said. He pulled on the nylon strap of his knapsack.

"Later." I turned to look back at Amy. "That cemetery in Kansas, you have an address?"

"Not yet," Amy said. She looked down at her computer.

I drove back to our hotel and steered up near the valet station. A pure-gray-haired man with a thick, Old West style mustache waved the valets away. He opened the back passenger door.

"Hi, Mr. Wylie," Rebecca said.

"Hey, good to see you," Wylie said. He had a wide-toothed

grin set in a tanned, weathered face. "I like those blankets; I bet they work well in this weather."

"It was a stroke of genius," Amy said.

"Hi," Wylie said to Amy.

"Hey," Amy said. "I'm Amy."

"She's a historian," I said. I hugged her. "We lucked out and got her employer at the LA Public Library to let us borrow her for a few weeks."

"Oh, impressive," Wylie said. He walked to the front bumper and inspected the headlamps, the archer, and then along the curved artillery wheel well. "She looks good. How's she driving?"

"It's like a mobile couch," Amy said.

Wylie laughed as he folded back the side hood. He stared down at the hulking straight-eight.

"She's a beast, for her time," I said. I stood next to Wylie. "I just want to be careful; the brakes have squeaked a bit. Can you take her to get a checkup? I don't have any major concerns, but we just drove across the desert."

"I'll get the dust out of her," Wylie said. He put on his reading glasses. "I've never seen you with hair on your face."

"I'm letting my inner Walt Whitman out," I said. I handed Wylie the key.

CHAPTER 22

We had rented a black SUV with thick tires to drive around Albuquerque. We checked out the art deco, pueblo-style KiMo Theatre and hoped the ghosts would leave us alone. We investigated the Barelas South 4th Street Historic District that my grandparents had driven along in 1930. We went in and out of the quaint shops, appreciating the colorful pueblo architecture and the interesting people in their turquoise jewelry. The city was full of green trees that shaded the modest, Western-style adobe homes built along thin city streets. I wondered which ancient gas station my grandparents had stopped at and where they had stayed. Amy hadn't found an exact location.

"Tired. We found a hotel," she read.

"That's it?" I asked.

"Totally," Amy said. "It's like he was so tired, he didn't have the energy left to write."

"Well, let's make the best of it," I said. I wasn't surprised by the influence the railroads had had back in their day – the now empty train stations had once been the crossroads for millions, before I had been born – but I was surprised to learn there had been a Civil War battle near Albuquerque. We enjoyed the neighborhood of Nob Hill, but it had been developed long after my grandparents had passed through. What passed as history now, my grandparents wouldn't have seen.

On the second day, we ate at the Pig & Calf Lunch building that my grandparents had visited. Amy had encouraged us to find the *Madonna of the Trail* statue. I parked across the street near a large parking structure, and we walked over to the street corner.

"I found an interesting diary entry," Amy said. "It's about their life in Kentucky."

"Go on," I said. I looked back at her.

Rebecca sat down on a concrete bench. I stood looking up at the eighteen-foot-tall granite monument of a bonnet-covered pioneer woman holding a baby in one arm and facing west with a Daniel Boone-like shotgun in her other hand. Her older child gripped her long dress. Amy moved closer to us.

"God has blessed us. The friends and family helped build our chapel. It's strong, well built. We gathered. The women made a meal. We held hands. It was my first service. Hazel is with child. I am thunderstruck. I am a grown man. I wonder what Brother would think."

"He never forgot his brother," Amy said. "Ever."

"He never spoke to me about his brother," I said. I stared up at the granite *Madonna*. Future president Harry Truman had attended the dedication in 1928, when he was chair of the National Old Trails Road Committee. The twelve statues traced the transcontinental dirt road that had stretched from New York to California years before Route 66.

"One of those things we keep closest to the heart," Amy said. She held the diary open with her thumb.

"Daughters of the American Revolution," I said. I read the dedication to the bravery of pioneer woman. "I won the citizenship award from the Daughters of the American Revolution, I was in the ninth grade."

"Oh, super cool," Amy said. She loped around the tall monument. "There are more of these. I'd never heard of them before."

"It's weird, but it makes me think of my grandmother," I said. I backed up and stared at the monument's strong face. "They lost the farm in Kansas, she ends up in LA, only to drive back across the country in a Model A. Amazing."

"I feel like I know so little about my own country," Amy said. She crossed her thin arms. "Why didn't I learn about this in school – the creation of the highway system, after the railroads?"

"Yeah," Rebecca said. She snapped a photo.

"Good news," I said. I had read a text from Wylie. "'Our mobile couch', as you call it, Amy, has been inspected stem to stern. We are good to go."

"Yay, I fancy our couch," Amy said. She stuffed the diary into her bag.

"What's next?" Rebecca asked.

"Texas; we've got to visit Glenrio, on the border," Amy said. She hopped over toward me. "Can I ask a favor?"

"Sure," I said, grinning.

"Can I get a ten-gallon hat?" Amy asked. She clasped her hands together like she was praying to me. "I've always dreamed of a big cowboy hat, like Tom Mix."

"I always dreamed of a big cowboy," Rebecca said. She examined the back of her camera, rolling through the digital photos. "But I'll settle for something tasteful."

"If you get one," I said, "we all get one. I guess mine should be black."

"Super cool. They filmed part of *The Grapes of Wrath* there," Amy said. She scampered past me and hopped into the SUV. "Let's go."

"Well, I guess we're headed to Texas," I said. I glanced up at the *Madonna* and blew her a kiss. "A Texas cowboy hat? I guess it's about time."

***

It had been a spontaneous decision, on my part. I was used to making investment decisions based on a lot of data, and thinking through scenario analysis models, but I had a team that provided me with the information and gave me their recommendations. Then, I would argue with them before I made my decision; we weren't a spontaneous dictatorship. My hedge fund was a calculated, money-hunting, profit-making machine, and I lusted for big wins.

I was standing at the valet station of our busy hotel, out in the cool air, when I realized Wylie needed to ride along with us. I didn't know why, I just knew he needed to come along. I don't think he was pleased. It was his crumpled, sandpaper facial expression; he fake-smiled at us. But I was the big boss, and the only cars that the master mechanic meticulously cared for were mine. I had old and rare Ferraris, Bugattis, and Aston Martins, as well as new models. I owned old, American-made muscle cars. I loved cars that were unique, and Wylie loved them all, but I loved my 1929 Pierce-Arrow most of all.

She was the first classic car I'd been able to afford, and she was mine only after I'd outbid a competitor at an auction. I'd wanted her. Now, she had the lowest value of all the cars in my collection. It was about the car market, competition, and uniqueness. I guessed it was because she was my first, and you always remember your first love.

"You want me to *what?*" Wylie asked. He looked over at Rebecca for help. "Really?"

"You heard him," Rebecca said. "This is his version of *Jonny Quest*, we're just along for the ride."

"But, ah, but," Wylie said. He clasped his hands together. "But what about the other cars?"

"They'll be just fine," I said. I walked past a few guests,

heading toward the front doors, and slapped him on the back. "They're like cats; they have plenty of food and shelter, they'll be there when we get back, waiting for us."

"You know I hate to travel," Wylie said. "I didn't pack much."

"I know," I said. "But you know I can buy anything you need, right?"

"I guess I'm coming," Wylie said.

"Good," I said. "Who knows, maybe we'll make a barn find."

"That's a good point," Wylie said, nodding.

"Amy, where to?" I handed the key to Wylie. "You're driving; I need a break."

"Texas-New Mexico border," Amy said. "Glenrio; they stopped there for gas."

Wylie tested the metal throttle.

"Which direction is Glenrio?"

"Remember," Amy said, tapping me on the shoulder. "Ten-gallon hat: I want a ten-gallon hat."

I put my hand up in the air. I was eager to get a cowboy hat, too.

"Agreed. I get a black hat," I said. I pointed forward. "Amy, please navigate. Wylie, Route 66 beckons. Remember, I get car sick."

CHAPTER 23

Back inside our fancy ride, we left Albuquerque well behind us with a full tank of gas. Along the way, Wylie purchased a fresh pack of cigarettes and hid them in the pocket of his white, long-sleeved shirt. He intended to smoke them as we headed toward the border ghost town of Glenrio, Texas. I had encouraged him to stop the addiction long ago, but I knew he'd protect the antique car from any ashes or burns at all costs. Amy had discovered my grandparents had camped out in Glenrio.

"Camped out?" Rebecca asked. "Why would they do that?"

"Money," I said. I looked back at Amy. "Right?"

"Yeah, totally," Amy said. She tapped the diary page. "They had limited funds for hotel stays, and he decided it would be fun to sleep under the stars."

"Youth," I said. "Of course, they were in their twenties and not afraid of much."

"Your grandparents? I'd be afraid of snakes under all the brush and rocks," Wylie said. He gripped the steering wheel as he investigated the dashboard gauges. "Model A would be simple, a good choice from then, but a '32 would have been better."

"She primed?" I asked. "Why a '32?"

"She's primed. Ford upgraded the cars; Model B, Model 18, added the Flathead and a lot more power, like this beauty," Wylie said. He grinned as he shifted the car into third gear. "Now, we can get this machine moving."

He drove us along the modern I-40 concrete, which made a more direct route than the nearby, meandering old Route 66 as we traversed the Sandia Mountains. I wondered if my grandparents had seen the same clear, blue sky, painted as it was with Salvador Dali-like white clouds above high rock formations that, at sunset, the Spaniards had thought resembled a red-to-green watermelon rind.

"Sorry," I said. I smirked. "I whiffed on that."

"It's what I do," Wylie said. He coughed. "Cars have always been my mistress, wife, and lover."

"Dude," Amy said. She patted me on the shoulder. "We should stop in Santa Rosa, they went swimming there."

"Swimming?" Wylie asked. "How? It's all sand and rock out here."

We made a diversion and paid homage to Santa Rosa, which Amy told us meant 'Holy Rose'. There, we located waters called 'the Blue Hole'. I wasn't into swimming, and it seemed an odd attraction, hidden within the arid, Southwestern desert where, for centuries before the white man took the land by force, Native American tribes had tracked massive bison herds that provided them a livelihood. Amy read to us about my grandfather swimming in it.

"It was a blessing. The blue water cooled us off. Amazing what God gave us. We needed it. Got gas, food, and we drove on to stay in Glenrio. Hazel's tired from driving, but we are making good progress. There are others headed to California: farm speculators. Hazel understood, I did not. We prayed for them to have a safe journey; to turn to God and not the evil of drink and money."

It was an odd moment, looking into the dark, blue waters and remembering my grandparents had driven through Santa Rosa before John Steinbeck had written *The Grapes of Wrath*. As it turned out, they'd even filmed part of the film version in Santa Rosa, but we were headed in the opposite direction from the Joad family's literary destination. My grandparents had driven the road when the wheat fields to the northeast of us were still spinning gold.

Wylie perked up as we stopped to stare at the Blue Hole; we were amazed to imagine cowboys and desert travelers had intersected at its edge. We stared down at the round pool that was now a popular diving site.

"Interesting," I said. I read a sign about the waters. "There's interconnected water underneath the desert, all under our feet."

"I always liked the quiet ones, liked the church girls," Wylie said. He took a big drag from his lit cigarette and pointed at some young women. "Like your water; it's always what's hidden beneath the surface."

"You old dog," I said. I laughed as I winked at him.

"Like what's hidden in your lungs," Amy said. She covered her face with her hands.

"Good," I said. I hugged Amy. "Shame him into stopping."

"Simmer," Rebecca said. "Okay, enough Mount Rushmore; we can stare at this all day, it's not going anywhere. So, where do we head to next?"

"I found a car museum," Amy said. "Interested?"

"Absolutely," Wylie said. He turned his head to blow smoke away from Amy. "Well, Boss, if you want to?"

"Why not," I asked, nodding.

We drove toward the museum, which had a yellow, *Munsters*-style hotrod out front. I was into purity, so I wasn't a big hot-rodding fan, but I respected the passion. I suspected there would be a few pure muscle cars inside that would interest me. Rebecca wasn't pleased, but it would have been a sin to old Detroit to just drive past, and I knew Wylie would enjoy himself; he might even find me a new toy.

"I wanted a ghost town," Rebecca said. She frowned. "Well, boys, I guess it's cars, cars, cars."

"Oh, come on," I said. I poked her. "It's a peace offering for Wylie, he bleeds motor oil."

Before I moved any further, Wylie had turned off my vintage automobile and paid his five bucks to go inside. He even paid for Amy to follow him. I negotiated with Rebecca to get her out of the car. After I paid our entry fee, I stood on the checkerboard floor and stood watching Wylie and Amy investigate the collection of shiny, American-made hotrods hidden within the simple, metal shed.

There were souped-up Camaros, Mustangs, and a 1966 candy-apple-red Corvette. All the cars appeared to have been well maintained. The metal walls were adorned with numerous filling station signs like 'Phillips 66' and 'Texaco', Route 66 road signs, and a James Dean cardboard cutout. Wylie stared back over at me, standing near a hotrod Model A, but I wasn't impressed. He gave me thumbs-up as he examined the car engines. I shrugged, thinking it was high-quality auto mechanic porn.

"Hey, this one's got a Ford Flathead Six," Wylie said. He waved me over and then almost dove into the engine. Amy stared at him. She looked back at me. I shrugged. He backed up and pointed across the room, which was lit by bright, florescent lights, at a Chevy pickup. "Buick Nailhead V8, awesome. This is a treat; you tricked me."

"I didn't," I said. I stared over at Amy. "Tell him."

"It's totally random," Amy said. Rebecca snapped a photo. "Remember, when we get to Texas..." Amy added, pointing at me. "Cowboy hat."

"I know," I said. I walked further inside and around a modified, dark-blue '49 Woody with side wood panels. "It's beautiful. Where's the surfboard?"

"It screams 'California'," Rebecca said. She snapped another photo of me standing next to the classic car. "Work with me, work with me, I'll make you a star."

"You're troubled," I said. I examined the door jambs; they had been aligned in a time when craftsmanship made Detroit every man's motor city. "I wonder if the numbers match up?"

"I'm not the one with a beard," Rebecca said. She walked over and sat down on a cushioned bench that was seat-rigged between the tail fins of a 1959 Cadillac Eldorado. Red signal lamps were on either side of her as she sat where the trunk should have been. I watched her examine her camera's screen as she flipped through her saved photographs. It would be easy for her to email them home for later use. To my grandparents, it would have been an unimaginable digital device. I remembered how, when I was a child, my grandfather thought his black-and-white Kodak Instamatic camera was cool, until he got a Polaroid with instant film. Polaroid cameras always fascinated me. I loved how, after the flash went off, the photos were spit out the bottom of the camera. If I were in the photo, I always got blue floaters in my eyesight, and the chemical smell was unique. As the computer age overtook the nuclear age, man was inventing a microchip world that stored our beings, from snapshots in time to our genetic code.

As long as none of the images made their way into social media, she could take all the photos she liked. She knew I couldn't risk having my exact whereabouts shared with the planet. Just then, one of the cars got my attention. It was almost hidden near the back garage door, parked between a pale-green Pinto and a baby-blue California Special. It appeared to have gone untouched for decades: a black, two-door 1930 Ford Deluxe Tudor. It even had a sand-and-dirt patina. I signaled for Wylie.

"What do ya think?" I asked. I kneeled down to look underneath the car for any rust and then gripped the spare tire near the driver-side door. "It looks like someone just pulled it inside and parked it."

"She looks solid," Wylie said. He unhooked the vented side hood to show the modest L-head inline-four engine and clicked on his mobile phone flashlight.

"The numbers all seem to match. It looks original; it even has the original safety glass. It's near-impossible to find them with those. With all the rocks, crap, you'd think the car would look like it was shot up by a machine gun."

"I want it," I said. I stood back and looked at an almost exact copy of my grandparents' Model A Ford. It was as if the time capsule had been waiting all these years for me to find it and bring it home. I had a perfect spot for her inside my spotless garage. "Let's find the owner."

"Stay here. I'll find him," Wylie said.

Typically, Wylie would play the role of innocent mechanic when searching for the car owner. We'd pulled off our 'good cop, bad cop' routine many times before. I hated auto auctions. I had an oversized competitive gene that tended to cloud my judgment, and I'd end up overpaying. After the fight, I would feel like a post-high drug addict, so I preferred to acquire my new girls via direct negotiation. That, or I sent Wylie out with my checkbook and the instruction to use his best judgment.

After about ten minutes, Wylie returned with an old lady who had dyed-red hair and matching cowboy boots. She was wearing more than the appropriate amount of turquoise jewelry, and I glanced over at Rebecca, who was quite amused.

"This is Mildred," Wylie said. He winked at me. I assumed the gray-haired fox was hitting on her just enough to make her think she'd be getting her juices flowing again.

"Well, hey there," Mildred said. She shook my hand like she could pull it off.

"Hello, Mildred," I said. I pointed over at the A. "I love her, might she be available?"

Mildred walked over and kicked the front passenger-side tire.

"Oh, she's something else," Mildred said, but she kept shaking her head side to side. "Can't let her go, she was my granddad's. It's not about the money; I got others we might bargain about, but this one's kinda special. She's like family."

"1930?" Wylie asked. He had known it was a 1930 the instant he saw the classic American car; he was just playing go-between as I calculated my next move. I was going to get the car, it was just a matter of how cooperative Mildred would be. "Original safety glass?"

"Oh, honey," Mildred said. She smiled at a grinning Wylie. "You've got a good eye for hot girls; we're both all original."

"I have no doubt," Wylie said.

"Whoa, get a room," Amy said. She put on her reading glasses and inspected her computer. "I feel ill."

"Mildred." I crossed my arms. "We'll promise to take great care of her, we'll not even touch her. I think that would be a mortal sin. Her patina, she's perfect."

"Oh, now I know I'm talking to some genuine gearheads," Mildred said. "That's why I have her parked over here, out of the way. I should put a 'do not touch' sign on her, don't you think?"

"Yeah," Wylie said. He walked behind the A to examine the back bumper, knowing I was about to go in for the kill. "I love her curves. So simple yet so perfectly dependable."

"I like you, Wylie Coyote," Mildred said. She winked at me.

"Tell you what," I said. I glossed my fingers through my beard. "You have a family attachment, and that I can respect, so I'll offer you twenty-five thousand, US, plus you can come visit her in my garage in California. She'll be out of the elements, inside a big garage, low humidity, and to put a cherry on top, Wylie will be there to take care of her. Do we have a deal?"

I put my right hand out to encourage her to shake on it and get the deal done. I knew I was overpaying, but I wanted the car.

"Oh, you're good," Mildred said. She pointed at me.

"He likes cars," Rebecca said. "I like it because I know where to find him."

"Sorry, honey," Mildred said. She shook my hand. "Not for sale. I even have her in my will, going to my grandkid. He had to promise not to harm her."

"That's cool," Amy said.

"Yeah," I said. "Cool."

Rebecca noticed the look in my eye. She whispered over at Amy, who walked over and sat next to her. I wanted the car, and I was going to acquire it. Mildred would only be a temporary challenge.

"I think you're going to meet Evil Bob," Rebecca said. She shook her head at me to behave. Mildred glanced over at Rebecca.

"Sorry, Bob," Mildred said. She put her hands on her hips. "Like I said, I have others."

"You sure?" I asked. "I'll even make arrangements for your grandchild."

"You're a real pisser," Mildred said. She waved me away.

"Man, you're relentless," Amy said. She sat back.

Wylie coughed to get Mildred's attention.

"I'd recommend you make a deal," Wylie said. He was no longer grinning. "He's my boss; I do think he's offering you a premium price for the car."

"No," Mildred said. She crossed her arms. "I think you all need to head on out of my garage."

"Okay," I said, but I stopped for a moment. "Mildred, you have a nice place here, you know. But I bet the community tax base could really benefit from a new big-box store, or maybe a nice, new resort convention center, you know, right here."

"What's he doing?" Amy asked Rebecca.

"He's just being himself," Rebecca said. She frowned at me. "He has a vindictive streak."

"Who do you think you are?" Mildred asked. She waggled her head. "Get out of here, boy."

"Boy?" Wylie said.

I nodded at Mildred, putting my hands in my pants pockets.

"Ever heard of a thing called 'eminent domain'?" I asked Mildred. "I'll offer you thirty thousand, but that's my final offer."

"Leave," Mildred said.

"Very well. Sell me the car," I said, turning to face Mildred, "or I promise you that, in about six months, give or take, a nice man will show up at those glass front doors. He'll make you an offer for your property, you'll tell him 'no', right?"

"You bet your sweet ass," Mildred laughed.

"Good girl," I said. I death-grinned at her. "But then your friendly city government will take you to court. They'll go before a judge, who will consent for them to expropriate your property for the common good. Fifth amendment to the Constitution. Of course, they'll pay you a fair value."

"You're crazy," Mildred said. She pointed toward the front doors. "Out! I'll never sell and there ain't no way. I know everyone, they ain't going to take what's mine."

"Mildred..." Wylie said. He handed her a business card. "He's not kidding. Take my card. I love your place; it's like a car oasis."

"You can stay," Mildred said. "Wylie Coyote."

"I suspected," I said. I winked at Mildred. "But what makes politicians happy? Tax dollars for them to spend, it's as easy as that. I hope you'll change your mind."

"Man, you're cold-hearted," Amy said.

"You have two days to consider my offer," I said. I opened the front door and looked back at Mildred. "Maybe you should look me up, do a Google search. My name's on that business card."

Mildred watched us leave and locked the front door behind

us. I escorted Amy and Rebecca back into our vintage, gas-powered chariot. Wylie skipped to the other side of the car and throttled her up.

"What do you think?" I asked him.

"She'll sell," Wylie said.

"I don't like being mean," I said. I looked at Amy. "She irritated me; it made me want the car even more."

"Why were you so mean?" Amy asked, slumping back.

"I'm a businessman," I said. I glanced over at Rebecca. "I prefer to encourage, but sometimes I have to push. It's about control. The old girl thought she was in control. I do want the car, but she needed a lesson in life. I will win."

Amy got out of the car. She started to walk down the dusty road.

"I'm leaving."

"I'll go get her," Rebecca said.

CHAPTER 24

"Women," Wylie said. He sucked in a drag of his cigarette and blew the smoke from his nose. "*No* clue."

"You're old-school," I said. From behind the locked front door of her museum, Mildred watched us.

"How so?" Wylie asked. "You know you have her."

"Yeah, she's easy," I said. I shrugged. "A real smoker blows the smoke all the way through the lungs and out the nose, that's what I meant."

"Oh, I see," Wylie said. He flicked ash off the burning cigarette tip. "Yeah, well, what's up with the kiddo?"

"Not sure," I said. "Emotional type, but she's a good kid. I'm twice her age, I could've been her father."

"We have your cars," Wylie said. "Those are our kiddos."

"Yeah, good point," I said. "Better-behaved."

We watched Rebecca hug Amy. She held Amy close – mother close. Slowly, they walked back toward us. If life had been different, Rebecca would have been a great mother. She had all the maternal instincts but, in her youth, she had yearned for business success; to build a legal practice. She had a fire in her, an ambition you cannot teach. But then our paths crossed, her destiny changed, and a stillborn child's ashes were hidden away in one of her dressing closets. It was an injury we both bore as best we could but, given my childhood, I had decided God had insulted me for the last time.

"Sorry," I said. "I didn't mean to scare you."

"Why are you so mean?" Amy said as she wiped tears from her face.

"It's business," I said, but Rebecca told me all I needed to know without a single word. I nodded. "Promise me you'll stay, I'll promise to behave."

"I want my cowboy hat," Amy said.

"Yes, you'll get it," I said. "That, I will make happen."

It was quiet as we drove together under darkening skies toward Glenrio, Texas. I glanced back at Amy. Wylie and Rebecca were used to me, but Amy was different. She was young, and she hadn't been baptized in emotional scar tissue. Like my grandparents at the time they had driven along Route 66, her choices were in front of her. Her idealistic sunrise had barely emerged above the horizon, and she was unaware what life would be like at dusk. I was at my journey's midpoint, or at least that's what the law of averages told me. I wasn't looking forward to being an old man. I knew death waited patiently for me, and it would enjoy taking me into total darkness. It was the one outcome I had zero control over; staying alive was only a delaying mechanism, and I had the financial means to fight it off with modern healthcare, but I remembered watching my grandmother fight the cancer that would take her life and watching my grandfather pray and pray. He'd had no money to pay for fancy healthcare; he told me he'd left the decision up to God. But if mercy from God was death, then God had taken his time as my grandmother's body was ravaged one cell at a time. For that indignity, I had not understood their supposed loving God. She had given her life to mission to the sick, to worship God, but God had repaid her by slowly roasted her in chemotherapy and radiation. I always wondered why God didn't simply let her go to sleep and not wake up. Thankfully, the one gift my grandfather had given me within my abused DNA was the ability to read people. I knew a ten-gallon cowboy hat wouldn't make Amy completely happy. There was something else eating at her, it bewildered her mind, and she was terrified.

My grandfather had been a close observer of people, and he had loved to walk along the city streets in his black, mud-covered dress shoes. In the summers, I would stay with them. When we went into town to get groceries, I would walk along with him. I'd watch him talk to the old men in bibbed overalls who were whittling away in the afternoon sun. He had to be a good observer, because he was called to save souls, and a big part of that was rallying the membership to support his church. A church operated like any business; without human and financial resources, it would die.

Now, I sat in my fancy car, driving across the flat desert plain and wondering what ailed me. It was that old feeling that had returned; I had felt it growing, even as it hid in the pit of my stomach. I could numb it with alcohol or devotion to making more money for my fund, but it was always lurking, I was always afraid. I was afraid to lose control over my life. My instinct was to crush my competition, to never show weakness, but dealing with a younger person who didn't care about my business left me at a disadvantage. I wasn't sure what to say to Amy.

"Sorry," I said. I turned to look back at Amy. "Sorry you had to see that, I'm not proud of that."

Amy stared past me at the scraggly bushes that held the desert together.

"Why are you so mean?" she asked again.

I tapped the thick barrier between us. Amy sat next to Rebecca, and Wylie ignored us and focused on the road. It was a fair question, a question to which Rebecca already knew the answer. Wylie waved back at a happy passerby in a minivan and then another in a four-door sedan who honked their horn.

"I think they like the car," Wylie said. He tapped on the steering wheel. "This is a treat."

"When we get to Glenrio," I said, "I'll answer your question. It's a fair question. But I am sorry, and I hope you will forgive me."

I knew what Glenrio was about, because I understood what a ghost town represented.

"Let it go," Rebecca said. She reached forward to massage my arm. "It'll be all right."

Wylie drove past a big, yellow sign: 'You are now leaving New Mexico, Land of Enchantment'. As we entered the Central Time Zone, the interstate's surface changed from a sandy brown to a hard gray. Wylie steered the car off at exit zero; he was amused, as he had never seen an 'exit zero'. The old Route 66 road was infested with long fault lines that wiggled across the pavement, patched with black tar. He parked in front of an old diner that hadn't had a customer or a cook in decades. As I got out of the car, the loose dirt crunched under the weight of my shoes. I noticed that the oak tree limbs on the other side of the road looked sparse, as they'd lived most of their days next to empty buildings. I thought the tree trunks needed a good hug.

"This is a ghost town, for sure," Rebecca said. She took a photo of the withered, white-painted café. "When we get to Amarillo, I want to get a heavier coat. It's getting a lot colder. I hate being cold."

"Yeah, my fingers are frozen," Wylie said. He flicked open his lighter and lit a cigarette. "Sorry, Amy, old people have bad habits."

"Whatever," Amy said. She wouldn't look me in the eye.

I stood next to her and zipped up my jacket.

"I'll answer your question about why I come across as mean."

Amy stared at the vacant property: the long-forgotten cars

rusting back into the dirt and gravel surface, the metal signage frame that now lacked a purpose.

"Not much here," Amy said. "Just old stuff from a long time ago, but it's important, because it's part of the Route 66 legacy. It's about America, I guess."

"I see reality," I said. I pointed at the abandoned post office, which had a long, overhanging roof supported by cast-iron poles. "The government paid to put that there, and then they just walked away. Why?"

"I don't know," Amy said. "But that's not an answer; you were mean to that old lady."

"I was doing her a service," I said. I stared into Amy's brown eyes. "She was holding onto the past. You don't live in the past. You live for now."

"If that helps you sleep at night," Amy said. "You're nothing but a bully."

"I offered her an above-market price to benefit her present. I doubt her sweet grandchild would have appreciated that car," I said. "He'd sell it for cash before she was buried."

"But it was her choice, it's her stuff," Amy said. She tilted her head at an angle. "Not yours."

"True," I said. I shifted back on my heels. "We make choices every day, what to buy or sell. It can be a product or a service. It's a constant battle."

"Do you always talk in circles?" Amy asked.

"Yes, I was 'mean', as you call it. She thought she had control," I said. "I have control. I was teaching her a lesson. If that makes me a bully, so be it."

"There he is again," Amy said. She shook her hands in front of me. "Evil Bob, woohoo."

"I like you," I said. I scratched my beard. "You have a gift few have; you're able to be honest."

"So what?" Amy asked.

"Fair enough," I said. I exhaled. "I'm brutally honest. It might seem that I'm mean, I'll give you that, but I'm competitive. She pushed my buttons, and I pushed back. It's called 'competition'."

"But why?" Amy asked. "Why be mean?"

I stared down at the dirt and clumps of yellow grass.

"Okay, I'll tell you: it was how I learned to survive," I said. "My father was a pathological liar. He beat and intimidated my mother. He tried to grind her into the dirt." I pushed forward onto my toes. "I do not back up, ever. Either I'll fight or I'll die."

"Don't take this the wrong way," Amy said, "but you're the one holding onto the past."

"What's up with your phone?" I asked. "It's gone silent."

"I turned it off," Amy said.

"The air has been cleared," Rebecca said. She walked between us. "Mount Rushmore has spoken; I need a coat. Let's get out of here."

Wylie continued on the I-40, and I slept most of the way to Amarillo covered in a colorful Navajo blanket. It was cold, and my face felt numb, so it wasn't long before I walked up to the concierge desk of the fanciest hotel Rebecca could find. I paid for three rooms on the Cattle Baron's Concierge level.

"I'm going to bed," I said. I wiped my stinging eyes. "Go back home, Amy. I'm not a nice man, like my grandfather, I'm Evil Bob. I have no intention of changing."

Rebecca walked over and hugged me.

"Go to bed," she said, nudging me onto the elevator. "I'll be up soon enough. Go shower and shave off that silly beard. We'll sort this out in the morning."

"I want my cowboy hat," Amy said. She started to cry. "I don't want to go."

"You sure?" Wylie asked. He hugged her. "It's okay, he's mean to everybody he likes."

"Yeah," Amy said. She whispered, "I found the cemetery."

CHAPTER 25

The drive to Oklahoma City would only take us five hours; maybe a few moments more or less. My grandparents had driven across the Texas and Oklahoma plains at a time when they were blanketed with homesteaders' golden wheat fields, well before the Dust Bowl storms that would consume anything living. It was the spot where we would leave Route 66. We would drive north, toward Kansas. It had started to make sense; my grandmother was a Kansas girl. When she was a teenager, her father had died from polio. It must have been an agonizing death for a farmer. Back then, a farm couldn't operate without a strong back, and the dry land wouldn't always cooperate. A line of credit kept the farm operating until a bountiful season paid down the debt. For her family, the bountiful season never came.

Modern commercial farms are about vast acreage supported by huge implements connected to satellites that monitor the soil's moisture, not to mention the secret to preventing more dust storms; the crop rotation that allows the topsoil to be reborn. The commodities markets had given me my start. At the time, I had tried to learn every aspect of farming, so my educated bets would pay off. But to lose your spine, like my great-grandfather, would be like taking away a writer's fingers.

After her husband's death, my great-grandmother had lost the farm to a swindler who bought her debt and then foreclosed on the farm. Eventually, the suitcase farmer had slithered back to the big city, but not before killing the soil with over-farming, a lack of rain, and, in truth, the federal government's intervention, which triggered the Dust Bowl. His departure also came too late for my grandmother. Her family legacy was lost to history, and they had to move to California, the only place that offered them the opportunity to start over.

I shaved and went to bed. I slept past seven. It felt good to feel the chilly, Amarillo air blow across my clean face. Amy had spent a sleepless night reading ahead in my grandfather's diaries. I'm sure she was conflicted by who I really was, but she found entries that I would never forget. They described his true nature, in his own words.

"Given a pig by Mr. Landrum. It squeals, it eats, the children love it. It gets into my garden; the girls chase it into my corn stalks. I wish it did not have a name. 'Bessie'. I know it will feed our children, next winter. It is a blessing, but I am afraid. I pray for the strength to do the deed."

It was pure luck that my grandmother had ended up on a Los Angeles street corner to come across my grandfather. They should never have met. He chose to escape Eastern Kentucky for Bible school after his brother's death, but my grandmother had been a refugee of fate. I suspected she had entered the nursing profession because she'd felt helpless, unable to save her father. But at her core, she was a hardened farm girl.

It's always what motivates us that drives us forward, and what motivated me was amassing wealth. Perhaps that was how God, or a much more sinister entity, whispered to us. I remembered her as quite bright, a lot like my sister. Either could have been a physician, but in the 1920s there were no females accepted into the medical schools. It wouldn't have mattered; she lacked what I now had: money and influence. I thought that was all institutions for higher learning really cared about, then and now. I hated the fact that I thought that, and that I thought it was all organized religions cared about, too.

"Bacon, bacon," Wylie said, later. He hummed a happy tune. "That's a Rebecca-ism."

"Thank you, Mr. Wylie," Rebecca said.

"Grandma didn't play," I said. I watched the busy, downtown Amarillo intersection traffic cycle in front of us. "Where to?"

"I think it's not far," Rebecca said. She pointed her forefinger past my head. "Just off 6th Street, right there."

"Got it," Wylie said. He parked along the busy city street. A passerby waved at us, giving our classic car a thumbs-up.

"Do you know what the word 'bespoke' means?" I asked.

"No," Wylie said as he checked the car's dials.

"I'm talking to Amy," I said.

"No," Amy said. She rubbed her eyes to help focus on me after she took off her eyeglasses.

I turned to look at her.

"'Just for you'." I turned to look at Amy. "I looked this place up all on my own. I called ahead. It'll be made from beaver fur, not cheap felt, and it will be sized to your head. In other words, it's bespoke for you."

"A real cowboy hat?" Amy asked. She started to bounce on the cushioned back seat.

"And everybody has to get one," Rebecca said. She sat up. "Even you."

"Whoa," Amy said. "This is a dream."

"No, this is no dream," I said. I stared down the street at people walking to work. The one thing I had noticed: it was a workers' town. "The cemetery – it's in El Dorado, out in the middle of nowhere?"

"Yeah," Amy said. She held the diary in her hands. "It's for locals, family plots."

"Read the next entry," I said. "I know what happens. Then, let's go have fun, get some hats, agreed?"

"Agreed," Wylie said. He put the car key in his pocket. Amy opened the diary. She slipped on her eyeglasses.

"Today. I dreaded it. Bessie was fat. Mr. Landrum asked me after service if I wanted him to slaughter it. I stupidly said no. His son, Ernie, looked at me. Ernie's a good child. I wanted to assure him I was a strong man. I got up early, I got the shotgun, I prayed for courage, but all I did was pray. Bessie looked at me, she knew it was coming. Hazel came. She took the shotgun and shooed me to take the girls into the mountains. I took them to the place. I heard the shotgun blast. I sucked in all the air I could. The girls looked at me. I told them all would be all right, God had a plan. It was all I could think to say. I am numb. Why, Brother?"

"You mean your grandma shot that pig?" Wylie asked. He looked at me in disbelief. "My kind a' woman... ah... sorry, sorry. Whatever."

"No worries," I said. I waved for Amy to close the green-dyed, leather diary. "You don't know, Wylie; his brother died next to him. Shotgun blast. It was a hunting accident. I guess it's the reason I don't hunt, either, but I understand him and her. Even more so, now. Thanks, Amy."

"Sorry," Wylie muttered.

"Thanks. She was a farm girl, so she knew how to put down a pig. I bet she skinned it, butchered it, all that," I said. I clapped my hands. "She was tough, but in a good way. Man, she wasn't scared of anything. Anyway, who wants a cowboy hat? I know I do."

"I do," Amy said. She stuffed the diary back into her bag.

"Yes," Rebecca said. "But tasteful; understated. I don't want to look, you know, rodeo. I remember, I went to a rodeo wearing a belt buckle my friend had loaned me for the night. Maybe I was twenty? It was bad. Apparently, you have to earn those. I didn't know."

"I never knew that," Wylie said. He got out of the driver's side and closed the door. "Like a trophy?"

"Exactly," Rebecca said. She frowned as she undid her scarf. "I just thought I looked cool."

"Ah, enough," I said. I waved for them to follow me into the shop.

The first thought that I had, as we all walked into the Western wear shop, was about the smell. It was leather blended with a cigarette-smoke scent that reminded me of the odor of a tack and leather shop in Kentucky. The strong, oak, tongue-and-groove floorboards creaked with age, and the dark, wooden displays were covered with various cowboy hats, boots, and shiny belt buckles. The displays had decades of dust; this store was for the serious buyer. It was quite obvious that there had never been any sale signs or big discounts to attract customers. A tall, lanky, balding man wearing well-worn, black, ostrich-skin boots stood near a curtain that covered the entrance to the back stock room.

"Hey there," he said. As he sauntered toward us, he waved us further into his shop. "Bet you're the fella that called."

"Yes," I said. He had a firm grip, with long fingers. "You're Shorty?"

"That's me," Shorty said. "Been goin' by 'Shorty' since I was a teenager. Ya'll here to get ten-gallon hats, right?"

"Amy, our friend," I said. I nodded toward Amy. "It's really a gift for her, but we'd all like one. Mine needs to be black; it's sort of a little running joke."

"Tom Mix-style," Shorty said. He stared over at Amy as he put his hands up above his head. "Right?"

"Exactly, from the old cowboy movies," Amy said. She smiled and looked at Shorty as if he were a magician.

"Well, young lady, I'm your man," Shorty said. He held his hand out and proceeded to escort her over to the back counter. He measured her head and brought back several options that he thought would fit well.

"This is serious," Amy said. She felt the soft, velvety fur with her thumb and forefinger.

"Oh, now, this is it," Shorty said. He had a pair of readers pushed to the tip of his nose. "See, here? This is double-stitched. Inside, the headband is goat leather. But, most importantly, how does it feel in your hands?"

Amy held the white cowgirl hat. She glided her fingertips along the bent-up edge.

"You won't break it," Shorty said. "Give it go."

"If you break it," I said, "I'm still buying it."

"Quiet," Rebecca said. She leaned in front of Amy. "Put it on, Miss Bacon Bacon."

"It's really lightweight," Amy said. She stood tall as Shorty maneuvered the hat onto her head. Her hair bent up where the hat came down to above her ears. "It feels weird."

"Looks a bit tight," Shorty said. He observed the hat and pushed down on the side of the crown. "I can fix all that; make sure it keeps its shape."

"You look like a real cowgirl," Wylie said. He stood to the side of us, leaning against a leather belt display.

"You ever heard the term 'mad as a hatter'?" Shorty asked.

"What *does* that mean?" I asked. "I've heard that expression a thousand times."

"Used to use mercury, making felt," Shorty said. He patted Amy on the shoulder. "Made the cowboys go *loco en la cabeza*. You know: crazy in the head. But they don't do that anymore, so you'll be just fine."

"That's terrible," Rebecca said.

Shorty smirked. He had a machine that blew hot steam inside the hat. He pushed the head band out, making minor adjustments to improve the fit. After three tries, he placed the cowgirl hat onto Amy's head.

"How's that feel, now?" Shorty asked. He winked over at me like a proud father. "Look over into that mirror, cock it a bit to give your look some attitude. If need be, I can bend the sides in more, if you like, but I think you look like you need a six-shooter holstered near your right hand."

Amy looked at her reflection wearing a classic cowgirl hat. She started to cry. She looked like a newly crowned Western wear beauty queen. She smiled back at me.

"You're welcome," I said. I crossed my arms. "I'm not always mean."

"Cowboy boots," Rebecca said. She clapped her hands. "Yes, you need cowboy boots."

"Shorty, she'll take it," I said. I shrugged at him. "I think you're going to be busy for the rest of the morning."

"Fine with me," Shorty said. He waved Amy toward a boot display and repeated his sales process. This time, with a little encouragement from Rebecca, Amy picked a tall, bright-red leather boot with a white-stitched daisy pattern.

"Super cool," Amy said as she pulled them on. She stared down at her new boots, walking in a circle like a third-grader showing off at school.

"You look ready for the rodeo," Shorty said. "Who's next?"

For the next two hours, we all got our bespoke cowboy hats. Mine was black, while Wylie stayed traditional with a more cattlemen style and Rebecca chose a bone-colored hat with the sides bent sharply up. Of course, Rebecca was not to be denied, and we all got cowboy boots. I went with a French toe, black-dyed ostrich-skin, Wylie went with a brown, caiman-skin option, and

Rebecca had to have brown ostrich-skin with a pointy tip rumored to have been created to kill cockroaches. I paid Shorty without reading the bill. It would have made Amy's colorful hair fall out, but we had something to talk about as we traveled toward Oklahoma City. My foot felt strange nestled inside the cowboy boot, pushing down on the metal floorboard accelerator. I shifted into third gear as I turned onto the I-40 entrance ramp, and Wylie answered his mobile phone. He said 'thank you' and turned off his phone. He glanced back at Amy and then over at me.

"What's up?" I asked. I had my cowboy hat on my lap.

"You're the proud owner of a Model A Ford," Wylie said.

"Dude," Amy said. She hid her face with her cowboy hat as she studied her tablet. "Not cool, not cool."

"I know," I said. "I guess you have work to do; we'll get you squared away in Oklahoma City."

"Sounds good," Wylie said. He brushed his thick mustache with his mechanic's hands. "It won't be easy to get back to no man's land."

"Welcome to Route 66," I said.

CHAPTER 26

After we'd resisted the temptation to check out the American Quarter Horse Hall of Fame & Museum, I kept the throttle down to keep our speed up near sixty miles per hour. She was old, but she had a big, eight-cylinder heart. Wylie had made certain her oil flowed free as each piston was ignited by a clean gas mixture. Thanks to his hard work, I was confident she was in good working order. It wasn't like we could stop at an auto shop to get a part, if need be.

The only constants I had noticed, driving across the flat plain, were the breeze and the railroads and trucks transporting cargo across the interconnected tracks. Scraggly buffalo grass covered the roadside right down to the drainage line between the opposing lanes and over to the wire fences that were held together by large, wooden toothpicks that leaned away from the wind. Long irrigation systems were pivoted at the center of the idle working fields, and some fields were covered in blown-down yellow and green buffalo grass that resembled a van Gogh painting, waiting for their next turn to feel the plow open their brown, fertile soil. The occasional rickety windmill stood tall near collections of metal farm buildings, and white-painted, wooden-planked main houses. The scene had repeated itself time after time along the road. As we crossed the Texas state line without incident, the I-40 road changed from gray concrete to a blacktop surface. We sped past a marble sign that read 'Oklahoma'.

"What's that?" Amy asked. She pointed across an empty field at a massive concrete structure.

"Grain elevator," I said. "It's a fancy silo that stores grain. Farmers sell the grain to them, they sell futures contracts and whatnot, they profit from the difference. You know farmers spend their off-season tracking commodity prices? They gamble all year."

Wylie and Amy just stared at me. They stared back over at the grain elevator, and then back at me. It was a conversation I wasn't going to have with them.

"Never mind," I said.

"Pull off, here," Amy said. She pointed intently to my left, across the interstate. "That's it, they stopped there."

"Where?" Rebecca asked.

"The service station," Amy said. She tapped her hands behind me. "Here, here..."

We didn't need gas. I had stopped to get gas at a major trucking complex, earning my vintage, gas-powered girl multiple horn honks. It had been a proud moment for Wylie. I turned the steering wheel and we exited the interstate, turned left, and drove underneath a thick, concrete overpass, then left again along the original Route 66. As I pulled up near a two-pump station that no longer offered gas, it began to sprinkle, so I parked in the service bay, beneath a second-story apartment that was supported by two tapered, white-painted, concrete piers. The intensity of the rain picked up; dark-gray clouds released a shower that painted the landscape with a clear liquid. It sounded like well-done bacon sizzling on a hot, cast-iron skillet, and it smelled as if an earthy aroma had been sprayed across the interstate.

"That was good timing," Wylie said. "Looks like Lucille's Gas Station was Johnny-on-the-spot."

"No kidding. We've been lucky so far," I said. I got the car tarp out. "Let's put this over it, to keep the moisture out. This won't last long, I hope."

Wylie and I covered the car with the long, custom-made tarp. The front door to the narrow station was locked, and all we could do was spy inside the windows and wonder what it had been like in 1930. I could almost imagine my grandfather standing on the wooden floorboards, making conversation with the gas station attendant as my grandmother shopped.

"Stopped in Hydro, Oklahoma," Amy read. "Got gas, food. We lucked out and found a place to stay called 'the Provine Service Station'. It is flat. Dry. Tired. The nice man said they rarely get rain. He gave us a good road map. Hazel knows the way back home to Eldorado. We prayed about it. God will show us the way." She pushed her reading glasses back closer to her eyes, adding, "This is where I found it."

"My God," Rebecca said. She stared across the moist interstate. "Out here, alone, with a few trees, it must have been a hard life."

"For sure," Amy said. "'Will Rogers Highway'? Who was he?"

"I'm not sure," I said. I wiped away rain from the front of the car and inspected the tarp.

"Funny man, a long time ago," Wylie said. He inspected underneath the car and pulled the tarp down. "There..."

"Sure," Amy said. She tapped at her tablet. "I need to know who he was. 'Route 66', 'the Mother Road', and now 'Will Rogers Highway'. Why couldn't they make up their minds?"

I leaned back against the building, between the front door and window, with my hands in my pockets. It must have been an exciting but stressful time for my grandparents. Each day, they got closer to Kentucky. I wondered how my grandmother had dealt with the experience. My grandfather had known where they were headed, he had known what to expect, but it would have been all new for her. She had made a conscious decision to leave everything behind.

It was like looking at what was left of Route 66. It was easy to look back into history, but to have lived in the moment, to have considered your future prospects, and then to have forged ahead with the one you loved, trusting that some divine force had prepared safe passage for you; all of these things took real courage.

In a sense, I could feel her presence, that day. It wasn't just that I knew they'd been here, like George Washington had slept in every bed and breakfast across the original thirteen colonies. I had the same feelings she'd had when she decided to cut people out of her life. All that was familiar was gone except for the hope that a better, happier life was before you. I wondered what it really felt like to be happy. She had made her decision, and I thought it had paid off for her.

"I'm wondering if I can make a suggestion?" Wylie asked. He walked over and stood next to me. He had his cowboy hat on. "I'm heading out on my own in Oklahoma City, right?"

"Well, I guess that's the plan," I said. I watched drips fall from the edge of the roof line. "But I've got no timetable; that A isn't going anywhere. I had the money sent to her, the situation is under control."

"You can stay, Tex," Rebecca said. She came over and put her arm on Wylie's shoulder. She tipped his cowboy hat back. "I'm getting cold, need to get back inside."

"Thank ya, ma'am," Wylie said. He hugged her.

"Yeah," Amy said. She stood nearby. "Stay. You're super cool and all."

"I'm happy to get the car," Wylie said. He coughed. "I know this isn't part of your plan, but when we get to Oklahoma City, mind if we check out where the Murrah Building was?"

I leaned my head back against the cold concrete and stared up at the center of the old ceiling.

"I totally forgot," I said. "Absolutely. How quickly we forget."

"That was so, so sad," Rebecca said.

Amy stared at us. She patted the tarp in a low spot.

"I feel like I should know what you're talking about," she said. "But I'm not remembering."

"Homegrown terrorist attack," I said.

"Blew up a building," Wylie said. He covered his mouth with his fist. "Killed a bunch of people, but I remember the faces of those babies. They were innocents. It still bugs me."

"Did you know some of them?" Amy asked.

"Not a soul, but those children," Wylie said as he sucked in a deep breath. "It sticks with me, you know? I watched it live on TV and just felt helpless."

"It's like the day Elvis died, but much worse," I said. I dug my hands into my pants pockets. "You're so traumatized by the event, you never forget it. When you remember it, you go right back to the exact spot where you were when it happened."

"We do," Wylie said. He pushed his cowboy hat down.

"And that's the shame," Rebecca said. "I guess it'll be good to experience, to remember."

"I think you should write about it," Rebecca said. She looked back at Amy.

"They killed babies?" Amy asked. She smoothed her hand across her face.

It was an overpowering moment. I remembered, after 9/11, a cold winter day when I had walked alone down from Wall Street. I stood within a quiet crowd at Ground Zero and stared down at the deep hole left in the heart of Manhattan and the rest of America.

That senseless tragedy was from foreign-born terrorists. What we had in front of us now was the work of some homegrown American terrorists.

I had failed to understand. I never feared a fight, but I had always remembered the advice that I was given by an old business mentor. He had said to never pick on someone that cannot defend themselves. I thought that was wise, and it jelled with my grandparents reminder to 'be ye kind'. But I wasn't always kind. I wasn't kind to Mildred, because she could defend herself. I was more concerned with fairness, and so I paid her a fair price. But it was beyond my mind to understand how terrorists operated. They took advantage of the weak. Of all the people I had ever met who I was certain wouldn't have been afraid, it was my grandmother. She wouldn't have said a word. If they had appeared at her doorstep, a well-maintained shotgun would have awaited them.

"It's always the weak." I closed my eyes after I had stared at the framed photos of faces set behind a long, glass display. They wore the clothes of the mid-1990s. It was a cross-section of humanity; even the little babies, black, white, and other, weren't spared. "It's pure evil. Nazi evil."

"Whoa," Amy said. "I don't really remember learning about any of this, sad. Glad I came."

"Good, I'm glad you think that," Wylie said. He wiped tears from his wrinkled face. "Sorry, it just comes back to life for me. The photos of those little kids get at me. I don't know why. I was working at a high-end garage; we had a little TV in the shop. We all just stood there, watching the news. Man, it was terrible. Helpless. You know? But then 9/11 came along, and I guess this became small potatoes."

"Did you have kids?" Amy asked. She hugged Wylie.

"Wanted to," Wylie said. He leaned forward in his cowboy boots. "But the wife at the time had other plans. I guess cars are my kids."

"And you're a good father," I said. I patted him on the shoulder. "But you'd have been a good father."

"Ah," Wylie said. "It's just how these babies never got to live. Just seems unfair."

We stood near each other. I felt my knees ache and a lump rise in my throat.

"It always scares me," Rebecca said. She tightly gripped my hand. "Being at the wrong place, at the wrong time... the things that can happen."

"I know," I said. I hugged Rebecca, I felt her warmth. "But you have to live."

"I suppose," Rebecca said.

"The place reminds me why I'm lucky to be American," Wylie said. He tapped on the glass. "We can take a good punch, but we get up, and we keep going, you know?"

"My grandfather would be proud of me for saying this," I said. I scratched my forehead. "But that's what Jesus did, right?"

"Who are you?" Rebecca asked.

"Stop, you know," I said. The wall of photos spoke to me. "You're right, Wylie. They would expect nothing less. Remember us, but keep going. *Illegitimum non carborundum,* 'don't let the bastards grind you down'. I think that defines us all."

"Be quiet," Rebecca said. "This makes me sad."

"I just feel stupid that I never learned about this," Amy said. She loped along the display. "All the other displays are cool. Historical, broken stuff, don't get me wrong, but these faces, whoa, of murdered babies, a bunch of dead babies."

"Yes," I said. I sensed Rebecca needed air, so I led her outside.

We walked outside into the cool November afternoon and over to the flat, rectangular, black reflective pond that was the footprint from where the Murrah Building had once stood. I thought the upright chairs on the grass hillside made an impression, as if the fallen sat watching us. The chairs were even more affecting for me after looking at the actual photos of the victims; some of the chairs were small, as if for children. The monument had been master-crafted to cause an emotional response, and it had worked. It was within a city that I had flown over many times, but it was more than a Route 66 stop. I thought it represented the inside of America, the guts, not the pretty edges along the coastlines. It would be easy to think of it as the soul of America, a cliché without feelings, but that would be too simple, too non-specific. I thought it was the farmers' lungs that, with each collective breath, cleansed our spirit. It was their strong backs that built the railroad tracks or that turned the soil into something that fed us. It was for the farmer to have stood in a field with a new crop, dirt on his hands, leaning defiantly back into the breeze, his only hope to feed his family the possibility of rain. It was so simple yet so complex of a calculation. It wasn't about being pretty; it was about being authentic. My grandmother had come from the soil.

We stood between the two marble walls and looked up into the sky. I realized my grandmother had accepted her fate. It was the one thing she had done all her life; she had taken action and she had never looked back. Standing near the tall, double-doored front entrance to the monument, I could see the Gates of Time, one marked with the last moment of peace and the other with the first moment of recovery. To my eye, each seemed to be protecting the other. My grandmother had been my grandfather's protective wall, all across his lifetime. If Route 66 were the Mother Road, my grandmother had simply been an American who defended her claim to freedom. My grandfather, Stephen, had been her freedom. She had understood him; she hadn't left her family behind on a whim. As they had driven across America, she had embodied the silent pilgrim spirit. At that moment, I wondered why my own mother hadn't protected me. I thought she was the victim of a tyrant's rule, but her mother would never have accepted the 'victim' label. I guessed we all have our own destiny; we just have to live with the decision to follow it.

"What are you thinking about?" Amy asked. She stood near the corner of the pond.

"It's all a myth," I said. I stared up at the gap between the tall walls, and then over to the matching walls from across the reflective pond that embodied time. "After World War II, we were all just happy to be alive, I guess. Happy to drive down Route 66 and create these weird oddities. It must have been great fun. But when my grandparents drove it, they just wanted to start life. To them, it was just a road. We forget how hard life was, then. There was no nearby Walmart; all the money they had, it had to last."

"They were good savers?" Amy asked.

"They had no choice," I said. I wiped my eyes.

"Why are you crying?" Amy asked.

"I don't know, happy memories," I said. "They're the only people I truly miss. I guess those photos, the children, they make me wonder, remember the 'what if's."

"That's super cool," Amy said. She loped toward me.

"How so?" I asked as Amy handed me her tablet.

"It just means you love them," Amy said. She tapped on the tablet's smooth surface. "That them?"

I stared down at my sister's Facebook page. The picture was of my grandparents. They stood next to their black Model A Ford. The spare tire was lashed to the back. My grandmother wore a white dress and a simple, flapper-style hat. My grandfather confidently stood behind her, his left hand on his narrow hip. He wore a thin tie, his shirt sleeves rolled up past his elbows.

"Weird," I said. "They're in Kentucky, I can tell: the trees, the dirt road."

"Handsome couple," Wylie said. He leaned in from behind me. "Nothing stays hidden, these days."

"Yeah?" Amy asked. "Your sister's page was a goldmine. Can I tell you all something?"

"Sure," I said.

"Looking at those babies..." Amy said. She crossed her arms. She started to cry as she covered her face with her hands.

"What's wrong, kiddo?" Wylie asked. He hugged her.

"I'm pregnant," Amy said.

"You're not alone," Rebecca said. "You're not alone."

I pushed my left hand against the cold monument.

"I'd like to say congratulations," Wylie said.

"I'm not sure what to do," Amy said.

"Me neither," I said. Amy looked lost, her eyes unfocused. "Maybe I should call my sister; it's been a long time."

"I think that's a great idea," Rebecca said. She reached for Amy. "Let's go for a walk."

CHAPTER 27

The twin-engine Gulfstream G650 defied gravity as it descended from a cloudless, blue, Oklahoma sky. I heard the powerful engines throttle down as it taxied along the blacktop surface toward the executive hanger and past the commercial airliners. It looked like a musclebound bird that could barely support its own wingspan.

"You own a plane?" Amy asked. She covered her ears as the jet taxied closer.

"No, they're terrible investments," I yelled over the plane. It had eight passenger-side portholes and a pointy nose that led the way into a tall hangar. "I buy into a service; it's less of a hassle. It's sort of like a lawn service; does what I don't want to do. Make sense?"

Amy had taken her hands off her ears.

"Will Rogers, again?" Amy asked. She scowled up at the sign. "They even named an airport after the dude. I need to research him. I do have an advanced degree in history, I think."

"It bugs you?" Rebecca asked.

"Yeah, like, I should know who he was," Amy said. She put on her reading glasses. "I have to find out..."

The jet's cabin door opened like a curved, white-painted tongue to reveal the metal steps. After a few moments, my sister hesitantly emerged from inside. Her blonde hair was beginning to gray, but she had the same doe eyes and straight nose as my grandmother.

"Hello, Brother," Ruth said. She hugged me. "And Miss Rebecca, you're always so put together. I love your fancy boots."

"Sister," I said. "This is our friend, Amy, and Wylie's taking your seat on the plane."

Wylie walked over to shake Ruth's hand. He gripped her hand with both of his.

"Are you a cowboy?" Ruth asked.

"Master mechanic," Wylie said. He tipped his cowboy hat. "Your brother's my boss; he got me the hat and cowboy boots. I have a car like your grandparents' to go collect."

"Oh, really?" Ruth asked.

"Hey, it was my idea, but not the car," Amy said. She waved over at Ruth. "Hey there..."

"That's a great idea," Rebecca said. She clapped her hands. "If you're on for the journey, you have to have cowboy boots and a hat, too. It would be rude not to get you some."

"I'm not sure what to say," Ruth said. She blinked. "I guess..."

"I don't want to be rude," Wylie said, taking off his cowboy hat, "but I have a plane to catch."

"Thanks, Wylie," I said. "Keep me in the loop, like you wouldn't anyway."

"Roger that. Stay positive, kiddo," Wylie said. He hugged Amy and then Rebecca, and then he walked with purpose across the concrete pad to the plane. He waved back at us and disappeared inside the passenger cabin.

"Later, dude," Amy said. She tipped her cowboy hat.

Ruth's suitcase had been offloaded and placed near the hangar offices. We walked over and retrieved it as the plane began to back out of the hangar. Once we moved inside the office, the seal on the glass doors muffled the noise of the plane.

"Well, Brother," Ruth said. "What's this all about?"

"I found your grandfather's diaries," Rebecca said. Amy pulled one out of her bag. "Amy's a historian. We snagged her from the LA Public Library, and she's been guiding us."

"Not really," Amy said. She held up a diary. "He's been guiding us."

"Well, I didn't expect that," Ruth said. She closely examined the diary in Amy's hand. "I'm glad I brought a coat; it's that time of year."

We exited the executive hangar and found my car parked near the front doors. She was shiny and proud. Thankfully, Wylie had taken some time to monitor her vital signs. My sister stared at the vintage automobile, knowing it was from a time when both Charlie Chaplin and my grandparents had lived in Los Angeles.

"This is your car?" Ruth asked. She just stared at the ruby-red Pierce-Arrow.

"Aw, she's just pretty," I said. "Like you."

"Aren't you the charmer?" Ruth said. She pointed at me. "But I know you, so what's up?"

Rebecca opened the passenger door and waved for Ruth to sit in the back, between her and Amy.

"I've got some blankets," Rebecca said as I secured Ruth's suitcase to the trunk rack.

"Where to?" I asked Amy.

Rebecca put her arms up and waved at me.

"These are beautiful," Ruth said.

"Cowboy boots, driver, these Navajo blankets," Rebecca said. "First things first..."

After a brief Internet search, Amy located a quality Western wear shop. The attendant wasn't as smooth as Shorty, but, all in all, he was a well-qualified person to attend to my sister. She had

Rebecca choose the cowboy boots: soft ostrich leather with pink stitching everywhere. After, Ruth just stared down at her boots. They agreed on a fitted cowboy hat. Rebecca bought her a big belt buckle with a thick leather belt and told her to wear it with pride.

"What am I to think?" Ruth asked. She took off her cowboy hat and examined it. "Finally snapped?"

"Maybe Amy should read from his diary," I said. I looked over at Amy. "Where to?"

"Oh, I've got this," she said. She pulled out a green-leather diary and opened it at the marker. "It's called 'the Milk Bottle Grocery', here are the directions."

"Got it," I said. We all got back into the car and drove out of the parking lot.

"We made it to Oklahoma City," Amy read. "My hands are tingling from gripping the steering wheel so much. Hazel just smiles at me. We found a grocery, we got some food, we found a road map. Hazel knew the rest. She knew where he was buried."

"That's my grandfather?" Ruth asked. She stared at the diary. Amy handed it to her. She held the diary in her hands, examining it. "Where has this been?"

"In the basement," I said. "They were hidden down there; Rebecca found them."

"Why?" Ruth asked. She read the pages. She turned to the front page. "Why? That's him, he's young."

"I don't know," I said. I shifted into second gear as we drove away from the Western wear shop. "After Amy read some of the diary, I just felt like I needed to follow them. This wasn't planned. I'm busy, very busy, but here we are, out here in the middle of it all."

"I know," Ruth said. She closed the diary and handed it back to Amy. "I know, but I just feel robbed sometimes, like I had everything robbed from me. I should have known about these, it's all we have."

"Me too," I said. I waved back at her. "I'm glad you're here. We're about to drive north, like I said on the phone. There's something I want you to see."

"What's north?" Ruth asked. "You were rather vague, as usual, but you were quite convincing. My husband thinks you've lost your mind."

"Cemetery," I said. I scratched my chin.

"You found it?" Ruth asked. "You found him? The farm?"

"Amy did," I said. I pointed back at her.

"I can read for you," Amy said. "I've found several entries, he's really interesting."

Ruth glossed her fingers along the pages that Amy had within her thin hands.

"I never knew," Ruth said. "What'd he say?"

"He wrote about everything," I said. "He wrote about Ruby's death, driving out here. Our grandmother was amazing. She was the real deal; I miss her even more, now."

"Really?" Ruth said. "Why? What was wrong with our mother? I don't understand, why'd she just stuff this into that moldy basement?"

"I know, but maybe we got lucky this time," I said. I shifted into third gear and accelerated down a two-lane road, past downtown Oklahoma City. "Amy, maybe the death of his brother? And the story about the pig, yeah, the pig..."

"Oh, yeah," Amy said. She searched through the diaries and found the page marker. She read the entries again. My sister started to cry. She covered her face with her hands.

"So, I guess you know what's up?" I asked. I glanced at her through the rearview mirror.

"Yes," Ruth said. "I never felt afraid with them."

"I know," I said. "I know."

"What do we do, Brother?" Ruth asked. She wiped her eyes with the back of her hands. "What are you searching for?"

"That's a good question," Rebecca said. She held Ruth's hand. "I just wanted to go down to LA, for the fun of it, but then your brother got on one of his wild-haired ideas. And, well, we went for it."

"That dude was really famous," Amy said. She held her tablet close to her face. "Will Rogers was from Oklahoma, he was born Cherokee and grew up to be a cowboy and actor. He was into all sorts of stuff."

"I've heard of him," Ruth said. She nodded. "Grandpa was part Cherokee."

"I studied US history," Amy said. "I don't remember reading about him, it kind of ticks me off. Hey, think about it, he was *the* dude from when your grandparents were still in LA. I bet they used to listen to him on the radio. Not cool; not cool not to know about him."

"Well, now you know why everything here is named after him," Rebecca said.

As we approached the address, I stared up at a large, white-painted milk bottle atop a tiny, triangular brick building.

"Can't miss this place," I said as I parked the car. We got out and walked toward the odd structure.

"This was on the original Route 66," Amy said. She pointed up at the milk bottle. "That thing came later, but it's a historic site."

"You know what that is?" Ruth asked.

"Milk," Amy said. She stared up at the large, sheet-metal milk bottle.

"Milk used to be delivered," Ruth said. "After you used it, you left the empty on your front porch and the milkman would stop by and trade it for a full milk bottle. Before we had supermarkets..."

"Funny, but my grandparents came here," I said. I felt the weathered brick beneath my fingertips. "I bet even Will Rogers was inside this place at some point; it's too convenient."

"Yeah," Amy said. "Super-cool to think about."

"I say we stay here one more night," I said. I walked toward the car. "Definitely need to find a steak house and a good night's sleep. In the morning, we drive north and find that cemetery."

Rebecca looked over at a colorful mural of a woman riding a buffalo painted on the side of the building.

"Oklahoma City, where the thunder rolls," Rebecca said. She shut the passenger-side door. "Let's hope not."

CHAPTER 28

Interstate 35 was a straight-line ride toward Wichita, Kansas. We had driven almost halfway toward our next destination. It was a cool morning, the clouds lingered above us, and the sun splashed its rays everywhere within the visual spectrum. Along the gray concrete road, with its wiggly, black-tar repairs, it was comforting to see all the trees that lined the road and hid the fenced-in farmland. But, further along the road, the flat plain returned, along with the wind. I could see into the distance at the clusters of metal farm buildings, which housed the hard, metal implements that waited for another spring, but it was the black SUV that got my attention. It appeared from behind us, coming up close to our back bumper and flashing its large headlamps.

"Were you speeding, Brother?" Ruth asked. She turned to peek behind through the rear window at the hulking SUV. "Talk yourself out of this speeding ticket, they look serious."

"No, that's not the police," I said. I put my hand up out of the driver-side window to acknowledge them. "I think they want to chat."

"It's them?" Rebecca asked. She covered her mouth with her hand.

"Dude," Amy said. "You weren't kidding."

"Yeah, told you," I said. I pulled off the highway and parked as the SUV pulled in close in front of us. A sturdy-looking African-American man with a flat-top haircut sprang out of the passenger side of the SUV. He pointed to his left as he ran toward me.

"Look, out there," He said. He kept pointing. "Look, to your right, at the clouds."

I stopped and turned as freeway traffic sped past us, a whoosh of air pushing me back on the gravel roadside. I scanned the horizon but only saw dark clouds.

"Thunderstorm?" I asked. I looked up at the man, who was breathing heavy. "Why are you bothering—"

"No, dust clouds. We have to get out of here, right now," He said. He nudged me back toward my car. "Get back in your car, take the next exit, park on the east side of the first building you see, we'll follow."

I slammed the car door shut.

"What'd they want?" Rebecca asked.

"A dust storm is coming," I said. I zipped up my jacket. "We have to get off the highway, now."

"No way," Amy said. "This really is the Dust Bowl, whoa."

It was surreal to look at the oncoming dust clouds. They looked like grainy, black smoke billowing a mile high, as if from a campfire full of water-logged wood. They were thick, dense, and fast charging. I could hear the storm's growl and feel its thunder under my shiny, new cowboy boots. The one thing that struck me, and tricked me, was the clear, blue sky at the top of the expanding dust wave. It was impossible to outrun it. As my hands shook, I got the car back into gear. I smashed down on the accelerator, slammed into second gear, and squeezed hard on the metal throttle.

"Who was that?" Ruth asked. Her hair blew across her face.

"Our security detail," Rebecca said. She rolled up the passenger-side window. "Are we in trouble?"

"Security detail?" Ruth asked. She scooted forward.

"Ask Evil Bob," Amy said. She took off her reading glasses and stared out. "This is weird. It's, like, biblical over there."

"Yes, not now, I have to get us off the road," I said. I kept glancing west and then forward for an exit sign as the storm approached.

The strong winds blew across the concrete interstate like a dead-of-winter black blizzard. It reminded me of driving to school during a snowstorm, but it was dark brown, not winter-snowflake white. My heart was beating hard rhythms, and I gulped for air. The car creaked with the wind as it tipped my silver archer up and draped it in a hazy brown. Rebecca screamed. It was less than a mile before we would reach the next exit, but it felt like eternity. I finally saw the exit and maneuvered off Interstate 35. I couldn't see much except for a restaurant sign. I turned right, drove up in near-blindness, parked, and shooed the ladies into the restaurant. The security detail parked behind my car and helped me cover it with the tarp. I locked it and they grabbed me, pulling me inside past the wooden door.

"Welcome, want some steak and eggs for breakfast?" a balding, middle-aged man asked. He took off his glasses and waved us over to the lacquered, oak-front counter. "It'll blow over in an hour or so; you're all safe here. I turned up the air-conditioning."

"That was scary, don't need air," I said. I wiped dirt off my face. The four security guards huddled behind me, dusting themselves off.

"Not from here?" he asked. He leaned on his thick hands and examined us for any lost limbs.

"No," Rebecca said. She brushed dirt from her hair.

"Well, welcome to the Great Plains. Air-conditioning keeps the dust out," he said. "We get tornadoes and dust storms. Florida and their hurricanes got nothin' on us."

"You're funny," I said. Outside of the restaurant, I saw that everything was draped in a grainy brown, like we were inside a dirty washing machine. The street light flicked on to illuminate a pale blaze.

"Now I know why they say, 'Oklahoma, where the wind goes blowin' down the plain'," Ruth said. She wiped dirt from her eyes. "What have you gotten me into, Brother?"

"No kidding, dude," Amy said. "Feel like I went to the beach. I hate the beach."

"This happen much?" I asked. I walked toward the front counter.

"Dry spring, ever so often we get droughts, it's just the nature of things," he said. He pulled out a menu from underneath the counter. "You all go have a seat, I'll come out there."

Our security detail moved around a sturdy rectangular table. They encouraged us to find another.

"They always this friendly?" Ruth asked. She sat down on a wooden bench near another rectangular table. We stayed closer to the center of the open-floor-plan restaurant and away from the wide, glass windows that flanked the front.

"Well, they don't like to mingle with the target," I said. I sat across from my sister. "It's about their protocol; I just play along and try to behave."

The restaurant man took the security detail's drink order. They ordered coffee and water. He strolled over to our table. He had a chain-smoker's laugh.

"Sounds like we're being sandblasted, out there," I said. I gripped the plastic menu holder.

"We call those things 'black blizzards'," he said. He dabbed his forefinger with his tongue and peeled over an order ticket. "You know what the three most important words are in Oklahoma?"

"No idea," I said. I looked up at his happy face.

"'Will it rain'," he said. He pressed his ink pen against the menu pad. "What can I get ya?"

"Tea," Rebecca said. We all agreed with her, and he walked back toward a side kitchen door.

"Why do you need security?" Ruth asked. She stared at me, turning her head like an inquisitive dog.

"Whoa, my fingers sparked," Amy said. She held her hands in front of her.

"Static electricity," I said. I guessed it was an abnormally dry climate.

"That was cool," Amy said, "but I don't want that to happen again. Freaky! I'm preggo, after all."

"I have some hand lotion," Rebecca said. She pursed her lips after she'd inspected her purse. "But in the back seat of the car."

"No worries," Amy said. "I've got my own."

"Congratulations," Ruth said.

"Thanks," Amy said. "I guess."

"'Evil Bob'?" asked Ruth, remembering.

"I've made a few people mad at me," I said. I crossed my arms. "I—"

"Your brother has a warrant out for his arrest," Rebecca said. She kept reading the menu.

"Brother?" Ruth asked.

"We made some currency bets that, well, let's just say we did a little better than expected," I said. I stared down at the tabletop, examining the growth rings of the sacrificed tree. "Destabilized a currency, in fact. Thus, my people made me get the football team."

"Thus, the nickname," Amy said. I frowned at her.

Ruth sat back and stared at me. I had a pretty good idea what was coming next. I looked up at the exposed timber beams that held the roof in place.

"You should pray for forgiveness," Ruth said. She leaned

across and gripped my hands.

I refused to look into her blue, puppy-dog eyes; eyes that were trying to guilt me into becoming an improvised minister, like my grandfather. I liked being wealthy, I thought it was fun, and this was, in part, the reason I remained distant from her. She didn't approve of what little she already knew about my lifestyle and career.

"Thank you, dear," I said. I was thankful when the restaurant man returned with our drink order.

"Where ya all headed?" he asked. He placed our drinks in front of us.

"Wichita, and then on over to El Dorado," I said. I picked up the hard, plastic glass full of ice and tea. "Grandmother's from there."

He nodded and stared out the window.

"I know it," he said. He stuffed the service tray under his armpit. "Oil; up there, they got a big oil refinery. I think you'll see those grasshoppers."

"What's that?" Amy asked.

"Oil pumps," he said. He made a seesaw motion, moving his forearm up and down.

"I thought it was all farms?" Rebecca asked. She sipped her drink.

"Oh, sure: wheat, cattle," he said. He buttoned his shirt sleeves. "You'll get there in no time. This thing be gone soon enough. Still have family there? Nice people."

"Grandma's father's buried there."

I looked over at my sister.

"Never been, it's not like it's on my bucket list, but I guess I'm just looking for what connects me to me."

"I love you, Brother," Ruth said. She almost cried, but, if there was anything our childhoods had taught us, it was how to make the feelings go away.

CHAPTER 29

As the restaurant man had predicted, with an ease learned from hard experiences, the storm came and went quickly. We dug our cars out from the dry dirt and continued past Wichita under a cloudless sky, then on into my grandmother's hometown, El Dorado. Our none-too-pleased security detail continued to follow us from a safe distance, but there wasn't enough traffic for them to hide behind us. My sister thought they were an odd group of hulking men.

I spied on her through the rearview mirror. I thought she had a whole Hemingway novel full of questions for me, but she remained quiet, though she dutifully wore her new cowboy hat. I thought that was progress; maybe she would leave behind her questions and judgements, but I didn't think she would. Her questions would come in a quiet moment. She had the patience and the dignity to wait for that moment; it was her way. I guess the singular, worldwide constant is that time only gives up its secrets as we age, until we pass into an eternal memory. Our memories are shared from person to person, each experiencing the same process. I thought time had been kind to my sister. I had known her from my very beginning; we had survived growing up under constant domestic stress. We used to hide inside our bedroom closets with all our worldly possessions in paper grocery sacks, wishing it was just a bad dream. But it was our reality. So I had a good idea what she was thinking, behind her blue eyes. I suspected it wouldn't be too far from what our grandparents would have thought about my rather complicated existence. She had a quality I had never possessed; she trusted that the ethereal God would provide for her. I wished I had her faith. I had tried, growing up, but I never thought any of what I was told at church was true, and I couldn't understand how people acted one way on Sunday, for church, but were very different people in their daily lives. It was all a big hoax, I thought, a fable to give people false hope that their lives mattered. I couldn't reconcile why a loving God would allow an innocent child to be murdered, or die from a genetic defect, or why a mentally ill, homeless man could be beaten to death for his last nickel, or why an entire country could be held under a tyrant's grip, or how a race of human beings could be sold into slavery.

As I pondered and struggled, we made it to El Dorado.

"I guess we might want to think about getting a place to stay," I said. I kept driving along the small town's quaint Main Street, which was fronted by two-story, red-brick buildings constructed during the turn of the last century. I thought Norman Rockwell might have found the street a useful inspiration for a painting of a fabled Fourth of July parade.

"And food," Rebecca said. She was behind me, searching for a hotel using her tablet. "I'll find a place, I hope. We might be sleeping in the car..."

"'El Dorado' means 'golden land' in Spanish," Amy said. "I love this tablet; even out here in the middle of nowhere, I still have a great connection. Super cool."

"Where's the cemetery located?" I asked. "I guess we should go there first thing in the morning."

"That diner is open," Ruth said. She tapped my shoulder. "Grandpa loved diners, remember?"

As I parked the car along the cleanly swept street, I smiled, remembering how he had loved to work the room at the cigarette-infested White Flash diner. It was at a time when you understood what having Prince Albert in a can meant, and all the dusty men seemed to have dark, burnt spots at the tips of their forefingers.

"He would have been an honest politician, that soapbox preacher," I said. I glanced back at Ruth as I switched off the car and stuffed the key in my coat pocket. "Loved those White Flash sliders."

"Never," Ruth said. "He had too much class for that."

"Remember his shoes?" I asked.

"They were always black dress shoes," Ruth said. She smiled at me. "With mud all over them—"

"Exactly," I said.

"You all really miss them?" Amy asked. "I don't get it, what up with the shoes?"

"They were the only sanity we had," Ruth said. She scooted behind Amy as they got out of the car.

We stepped up the concrete steps, into which concave bruises had been carved by merciless time and foot traffic, and into the bright, open diner with its name stenciled in black letters across the tall, glass front door: 'El Dorado's Finest Home Cookin''. It had a pale, blue-and-white checkerboard tiled floor; a long Formica bar with charcoal-colored, Naugahyde-covered metal stools; and several square, wooden tables surrounded by simple, wooden chairs. It smelled like a county fair.

"This place is right out of central casting," Rebecca said. She strolled up to the middle-aged woman behind the bar. "Where should we sit?"

"Not from here?" she asked. Her readers dangled from a silver chain atop her white blouse.

"No," Rebecca said. We followed her to a table near the front, next to the wide windows that overlooked the quiet street. A young girl with long, flowing, brown hair held together with a yellow, elastic ponytail holder served us four ice waters in Ball Mason jars.

"Hi, welcome," she said. She had a clean complexion.

"Menu?" I asked. I sipped the cold water.

"Oh, not from here," she said. She pointed above the counter at a chalkboard with the menu written in white chalk.

"There's a theme brewing," I said.

"I see, sort of," Rebecca said. She squinted. "I forgot my glasses."

"My grandmother was from here," I said. I looked up at her. "Does that get us a locals' discount?"

"Who's your grandmother?" she asked.

"Well, she's dead, she's a 'was'," I said. I glossed my fingers across the cold glass. "They left here a long, long time ago."

"Oh, so why'd you come here?" she asked. She pointed out of the window at my curvy antique. "That yours?"

"That's one of his favorite girls," Rebecca said.

"We're looking for a cemetery," I said. "From my grandfather's diary; they drove through here in 1930. We're out having a trip, following their journey from LA, California. We're just nuts, nothing special."

"You're retracing their steps?" she asked. She looked at me, standing in tennis shoes that had never left Kansas.

I smiled at her.

"You're a Kansas girl?"

"I am," she said. She looked at me like I was some mystical character that Dorothy had met along the yellow brick road. "What's California like?"

"Amy's from LA, it's down south from us," I said. I pointed at

Amy. "We hide up north, near Carmel. It's a colder climate. We move about at a much slower pace."

"It's chill," Amy said, nodding.

"My grandparents met there," I said. "My grandmother moved out there after they lost the farm here in El Dorado. My great-grandfather is buried here, somewhere." I turned to look over at Amy. "You mind reading?"

"Oh, for sure," Amy said. She put on her reading glasses and opened the diary.

"Oh wow," said the waitress. "That looks really old."

"We knocked on the farmhouse door. We are blessed; they let us stay. We went over to her dad's spot. It was near a bend in what Hazel called 'the Walnut River'. I expected her to cry. She did not. She is much stronger than me. She has a spirit that I love. She's a Kansas girl. She has a tough soul. I have never loved someone like I love her. I want to protect her, but I think it might be the other way around."

"So, where's the Walnut River?" Amy asked.

"How sweet, he must have been a kind man," said the waitress. She looked up at the ornate, tin ceiling, which was nailed to wooden ceiling joists set in place in my grandparents' time. "That's not where the cemetery is, though." She waved over at the middle-aged woman, who acknowledged her, set down the newspaper, and walked toward us.

"What's the matter?" she asked. She had a concerned expression, like we were out-of-town troublemakers.

"Grandma, do you know where a cemetery is, near the river?" she asked.

"Looking for my great-grandfather's grave," I said. I pointed up at the girl. "I didn't get your name?"

"Sorry, sorry," she said. "I'm Ruth, you know, from the Bible."

"I'm a Ruth, too," Ruth said.

"Really?" I said. I smiled over at the older lady. "Any ideas, Grandma?"

"Behave," Rebecca said.

"There are a lot of bends in that river, and my name's 'Hattie', if you're curious," she said. She looked down at her grease-splattered shoes and then pointed east with her left hand. "I think the only place it could be is off 54. There's an old family cemetery out there. It's on good land; it's in the park, not far from here. Take Old Mill Road, but you'll need to park and walk back toward 54. I reckon that's the place, but not for sure."

"Okay, I understand," I said. "'Hattie' is a beautiful name."

"I think it's just back in there, toward the river," Hattie said. She smirked. "You're cute, but so was the devil."

"You have no idea," Rebecca said. She didn't look over from scanning the chalkboard menu.

"Terrific, you got me," I said. I clasped my hands together. "So, what's for dinner?"

"Oh, honey," Hattie said. "We still got some hickory-smoked ribs. Our fried chicken would make the Colonel envious, okra, collard greens."

"You sold me on the chicken," Rebecca said. "I'm starving."

"Ribs," Ruth said. She appeared pleased. "Collard greens, I love collard greens. They're good for you."

"Yeah, collard greens," I said. "Grandma could make some serious collard greens... for a white girl."

CHAPTER 30

The barbecue ribs I'd had the night before had owned me. After, Hattie had directed us to a chain hotel not far from Central Avenue and near the road to the next morning's destination. The people who operated the hotel were kind, and they hadn't asked many questions. I was certain they hadn't thought much about my curvy vintage car. I suspected they thought it was showy, but they didn't say a word. It was a nod, a masked expression. I understood their riddle; my sister and I had a similar riddle we had used, growing up. It had reminded me why I liked Midwesterners; they were honest, the hardworking spine of America, but they had a remarkable gift. They weren't about showing off that spine. If one was to ever seek an authentic American, I thought they should start there, along the Kansas plains, where my grandmother had been born into this uncertain world. In truth, she was always a Kansas girl, she just happened to love a Kentucky boy.

All I had the next morning was a mug of black coffee. I suspected I had an oversupply of dead calories that would take a month to disappear. I drove along the two-lane, blacktop road on East 54, which was fronted by modest, two-story, brick buildings and tiny homes. We headed away from El Dorado under clouds that looked like shredded, gray cotton balls and coasted toward the southeast in hopes of finding a warmer climate. We crossed under a thick railroad bridge and over a two-lane, white-painted concrete bridge with ornamental side rails.

"Man, I don't want any part of January," Rebecca said. She had snuggled up with a thick blanket.

"It's getting that time of year," Ruth said. "Thanks, Brother, the cowboy hat keeps my head warm."

"This girl did have an air heater, under the seat, behind your ankles," I said. I worked my fingers into my driving gloves. "But I haven't used it since I bought the car, and I think Wylie would advise not to."

"We'll stick with the blankets," Rebecca said.

I turned the car left and off the road, then left again down a narrow, gravel path. As Hattie had instructed, I parked in an empty lot for the Riverside Park. Together, we walked back toward a red-painted, arched bridge with a wooden-planked surface, past a sturdy, yellow oak jungle gym and metal picnic tables. As we strolled forward, I saw a flat clearing atop a high point above the flowing river. Within it was a triangular, fenced line surrounded by ancient oaks and maples, as well as the outlines of marble monuments.

"You'd never find this in the summer," I said. Fallen acorns crunched under my shoes as I ducked beneath a thorny oak branch.

"It's beautiful. I bet it's magical on a sunny day, like a green fairyland," Amy said. She stood reading the names on the monuments; some were set into the soil, others positioned upright, but none of the monuments were there to draw attention to the deceased. They were simple markers only for those already interested. "It's so peaceful here, the river sounds tranquil."

"It is peaceful," Rebecca said. She hugged me from behind

and then walked along a line of monuments. "We could build a fire, roast marshmallows."

"Not likely," I said. "But you are a pyro…"

"Here," Ruth said. She kneeled down and pulled out clumps of grass that surrounded the rectangular monument. "There he is…"

"He had a cool entry from being here," Amy said. She had already opened the diary.

"I thought the one from last night was cool," I said. I walked over and stood next to my sister. "But go for it."

"Hazel spent the day cleaning up around the cemetery. The farmer helped us. He was a nice man. His children were helpful. His wife was buried here. Hazel wanted me to perform my first funeral service for her father. I prayed hard. She told me to be strong. The children watched me.

"The farmer took off his hat, but I did as I was taught. I did my best, even though I was nervous. Hazel hugged me after. I thought of my dead brother. Why? I let Hazel be, she was quiet for a long time."

"Thank you, Amy, I know that was him," Ruth said. She stood up and hugged me. "Why are we *really* here?"

I nodded at her as I backed up.

"I don't know," I said. I stared down the steep-sloped river bank as the constant water traffic frothed over the mud and stones. I glanced back at Ruth as Amy and Rebecca strolled back toward the car. "I guess the diaries give me hope. I feel like after they left us, we lost everything, you know?"

"I know," Ruth said. She stood next to me. "You have more money than you could spend in ten lifetimes, but you're still my unhappy little brother. Why?"

"Are you happy?" I asked.

"For the most part," Ruth said. A soft breeze caused the trees to sway into each other. "You can't live in the past, let it go."

"I'll tell you something," I said as I watched driftwood bounce off smooth boulders and zig-zag wherever the river flowed. "I don't really care about the money, cars, houses. I never have."

"Why'd you call me?" Ruth asked. She stared at me. "You rarely communicate, stay hidden away, and then this? That car? Have you gone mental on me?"

"I haven't lost my mind," I said. I sighed. "When Rebecca found his diaries, at first, I wanted to ignore them, you know. But then we started reading them, we found Amy, and for the first time in my life, I just went for it."

"Well, that's a first," Ruth said. She smirked. "You always have a scheme."

"I love you, Sister," I said. I held her cold hand. "Can I ask you something, just between us?" She nodded. "Do you remember when we used to hide in your closet?"

"Of course, it was our hiding place," Ruth said. She gripped my hand. "All they did was scream at each other."

"I've always felt afraid. It's like I go back there, it's like a fight I can't fight," I said. "I'm mean, sometimes, and I think it's because I feel afraid. I don't like that part of me, but it made me rich."

"I know, you've always been competitive," Ruth said. "Try to love yourself, Brother."

"I learned to always listen to my instinct, Grandpa taught me that," I said. I turned to face her. "I never make a bet I don't trust, almost by instinct, I see it in my head."

"I'm not sure what you're saying," Ruth said. She stepped back and studied my face. "But I know you're serious."

"Dad beat the crap out of me, or he'd play mind games," I said. I clenched my jaw. "I realized he hated me for having more potential than he ever had. I always thought they hated me, but for different reasons."

"Let it go," Ruth said. "Let God deal with him."

"I know," I said. I stared down at gravestone. "But now, I feel like I'm being pulled along by them, for some odd reason. I sense they're talking to me. Am I crazy?"

"I don't think so, I guess," Ruth said. She brushed her hair back under her cowboy hat. "I trust you with my life, so I'll play along. I'll pray for you."

"I wonder what it would have been like to be a kid," I said. "You know?"

"I do," Ruth said. "Keep things simple now, have a simple faith."

CHAPTER 31

As I drove the car away from the cemetery, we passed under the leafless tree canopy, which stoically waited for winter to blow across the bumpy Kansas heartland. I was happy to have found the grave. It was an odd sensation to have stood near a calm bend in a random river, in the November cold, watching clouds of my warm breath as I stared down at a simple gravestone. It was nothing special to the passerby, but it was special to me. I read the name. I noted the beginning and ending dates. I had never met the occupant below the headstone, but I had known his daughter; she had influenced my life. Without her, I wouldn't have existed.

And I was here with my sister. It was a place my grandparents had made a special trip to visit. For them, it must have been a financial sacrifice to stop. It cost them extra gas, extra food, extra time, and they had to seek a place to sleep. My grandfather had made a special note within his diary. I could almost imagine my grandmother in her youth, kneeling down, picking away weeds, and crying as my tall, dignified grandfather expressed his first funeral homily for his father-in-law, a man he had never met. It gave me a certain wholeness that I hadn't felt for many years. The thought that I had ancestors who would have loved me unconditionally. The thought that they would seek out my last resting place, for no other reason than 'just because'. There are words that directly connect to feelings and emotions, but then there are feelings that cannot be expressed by words, only felt, or only shown by a single tear that's quietly wiped away.

It was as if I had been peering into a snow globe, coldly admiring the same pretty weather, the same pretty house, the same pretty landscape, the same pretty friends, and the same pretty wife. But I had always felt alone, wondering what it would be like to live there – to be inside. Now, I realized I owned the snow globe.

"Amy, have you read anything interesting?" I asked. I took off my cowboy hat as I started to encourage the vintage car to accelerate within the Interstate 35 traffic. "You feel okay?"

"Yeah," Amy said. She nodded. "I was holding some back; it's like I have these intimate snapshots from their life, so I'm not sure when—"

"Read them, tater, tater," Rebecca said. She wrapped the blanket tighter around her legs. "Help me think about something other than the weather."

"The accident, I just want to…" Ruth said as she wiped a tear from her eyes. "My great-uncle… I never met—"

"Yeah," I said. I nodded. "Me too, me too… Any idea where they might have stayed in Kansas City?"

We drove past the quiet farmland, where clusters of round hay bales waited to be shared like unwound sweet rolls. Amy re-read the moment my grandfather's life had changed. It was full of survivor's guilt. Next, she read about their daily life as they built their ministry and their family. The day the community came together to build their simple, wooden chapel where they held services for forty-two years. The days that his sermons were well received, his thankfulness to God to have saved another soul, and when he wore a white smock as they waded as a community of believers into the Troublesome Creek to baptize another sinner.

I had never understood the rituals, but, driving along the open road, I missed them. The rituals were the strong tree roots hidden deep within my DNA. They had been my missing center, but then Amy's discoveries caused me to realize my grandfather had been the glue that kept the community together – it was what his job had meant to the community – but my grandmother was the glue that kept my grandfather together.

"This one I think is so valuable," Amy said. She sounded a little professorial. "From a historical perspective, I found it useful to understanding daily life during World War II."

"Yeah?" Rebecca asked.

"It was a boy he had baptized," Amy said. She stared down at the diary. The page edges waved back and away from Amy as a soft breeze flooded the passenger compartment. "His name was 'Ernie'. He was in the family that gave them the pig."

"I loved that one," Ruth said. "My grandma was strong."

"No kidding," Rebecca said. She leaned forward to tap me on the shoulder. "I wish I'd met her."

"It's always the quiet ones," I said. "Go on, Amy." I waved at a passerby who had honked at our fancy car.

"You're still waving at strangers," Ruth said. "He would wave at people as we drove to school, he's so odd."

Amy pointed her forefinger at the diary page to keep it still.

"Sad day," she read. "I am heartbroken. Ben Turner called me at the house. He had two military men at his store. They were lost. Ben asked me to speak with them. He said it was important. I went. Colonel Nahrgang and a Captain Palmer had a folded flag. They looked impressive, medals and whatnot. Ernie had been killed. I had to act strong. I felt punched in the stomach. I thought he was safe on a general's staff. They were searching for the Landrums. They were lost in the hills. I took them home. I got the girls cleaned up, and Hazel drove behind us. My stomach was sour as we drove into their holler. Mr. Landrum was on the porch, drinking coffee, smoking. He stood up, looked dead at me, and he went inside. We stood on the porch as Mrs. Landrum came."

Amy stopped reading. She looked over at Ruth. I caught her look in the rearview mirror.

"What does he mean 'holler'?" Amy asked. "Is that like a subdivision?"

"No, it's a valley, a flat spot in the mountains," Ruth said. She stared up into the darkening sky. "A sort of area in the mountains where you could build a house, that sort of thing. Does that make sense?"

"Oh, yeah, I see," Amy said. "I've never read that before, interesting." She nodded and then started to read. "We took off our hats. Colonel Nahrgang told them Ernie died a hero. He leaped onto a grenade thrown at the general. He had saved lives. Ernie was buried in France. The flag had been draped on his coffin. Mrs. Landrum hugged the flag. She cried. Hazel nudged me, and I straightened up. We held hands and I said a prayer. It was quiet. I have never heard the mountains so silent, the animals were sad, too. The girls stared at the Landrums and at us. I explained later."

Amy took off her reading glasses. As she reflected, I exited the interstate and stopped to fill up the tank at a massive, well-lit truck stop. We had numerous loud honks of approval; my vintage girl was old, but she still stood out without any effort. There was a modest breeze, there was always a breeze in the Midwest, but the place still smelled and sounded like every gas station in the United States.

"Those must have been hard times," Amy said. She shook her head and propped open the passenger-side door. "To live through a world war..."

"No kidding," I said. I leaned against the car.

"How far to Kansas City?" Ruth asked. She had all the markings: the cold, flushed cheeks, the watery eyes, but most of all it was the dank soldier's frown from constant exposure.

"An hour, maybe less," I said. I pointed at Amy. "Any idea where they stayed?"

"Sort of," Amy said. Her face was contorted into an odd, crinkled expression. "I think they stayed with a friend on 18th Street. He wrote something I'm uncomfortable with; not sure I want to read it out loud."

"Hand it over," I said. Amy opened his diary to the page. It was an odd sensation to adjust to my grandfather's handwriting, but the gas station light was bright enough that I didn't need my readers. It was written as if he wasn't confident in his writing, but I managed to read the passage, and I understood what she had meant. He wasn't being racist: he was writing from his time. It was like any business, I thought. History worked like a balance sheet; it was a snapshot in time, just the facts, just the numbers as they are at that exact date. But, as I had learned in my adult age: as with the Bible, people liked to manipulate truths that seemed inconvenient in present day. I guessed it made them feel better.

"I bet you've never read anything like that," I said to Amy. I tapped her knee, which was poking out from the open side door. "He was far from a racist; he was being respectful, in his own way."

"That's hard to read," Amy said. She shook her head.

"Well, read it for me, too," Ruth said. She took off her cowboy hat like she had been bucked off a bull.

"Hurry up, Bacon, I'm getting hungry," Rebecca said. She waved over at me as I coughed to clear my throat.

"We made it to Kansas City," I read. "We stayed with Grace Mary on 18th Street. Hazel's friend. They also lost their farm. Sad. Hazel's not blue. Grace Mary perked her. We are blessed to stay for a few days, to rest. Grace Mary took us for food, barbecue for the first time. It had a molasses taste, reminded me of home. She took us to listen to Negro music. It sounded like they were not happy. They are believers. Grace Mary liked the Negro food. It reminded me of home. I would like the barbecue again. I would like to attend a Negro church," I closed the diary and turned to Amy. "'Negro'? That bothers you?"

"Yeah," Amy said.

"It's not the N-word," Ruth said. She looked over at me. "We grew up hearing a lot worse. I just think it's stupid."

"I used to get called 'hoogie'," I said. I wiped my face with my cold hand. "Oh, check out my nose..."

"Robert," Ruth said. She gave me the 'please don't go there' look. "That's not nice..."

"What?" Amy asked. She looked at me, then at my nose, and then back over at Ruth. "What am I missing?"

"My nose," I said. I grinned. "When I was in junior high, they called me 'nigger-nose'."

"Dude, not cool," Amy said. She pushed back into the bench seat.

"Seriously," I said. "My black buddies on the football team called me 'super-hoogie'. They liked me, I liked them; they were just giving me a hard time."

"I remember that," Ruth said. She covered her mouth with her hand as if to filter her words.

"'Hoogie'? What does that mean?" Rebecca asked. "I'm from Nebraska, we don't talk like that."

"Means 'punk-ass whitey'," I said. I replaced the gas pump and paid for the gas with a credit card, then I walked back toward Amy. "I know one thing: back then, the one thing I always respected about my black friends, you didn't say anything about their mother, not even in a kidding way. Good way to get your butt kicked. Now, these days, I don't understand—"

"Let's get some food," Rebecca said. She hugged in close to

Ruth. "We need food. And warmth. You and Amy can discuss the PC police crap another time."

"All right, all right," I said. I walked around the car, got inside, and started her up. "On to Kansas City. 18th Street?"

"Yeah," Amy said. "I think that would be cool, but did you ever call someone... you know?"

"Oh, never," I said. I sucked in a deep breath. I pumped the gas pressure up and switched on the engine. "I remember I heard it, many times. The difference was, they meant it. I didn't get it. Crazy people scare me."

"You two need to behave," Rebecca said.

"But I never heard the mountain people say it, not once," I said. My fingertips fiddled with the throttle as I watched the red tail lights from interstate traffic cycle toward Kansas City. "We never learned hate from our grandparents."

CHAPTER 32

I decided to stop for a few days to allow a nasty weather pattern to pass, and so we took in Kansas City and waited for warmer weather to return. We all needed to rest and enjoy the city. We stayed at an old, art deco hotel near downtown and toured the National World War I Museum and Memorial. It was a symbol from when my grandparents had visited Kansas City. At the time, they'd had no clue another world war awaited them. We toured the Negro Leagues Baseball Museum and Amy's mind was blown. We had a variety of barbecues, as much as we could, we toured museums, and we roamed 18th Street and Vine Street like a pack of teenagers until my custom cowboy boots were broken in.

I could almost hear Shorty say, "Well now, there you go."

"I never knew about Negro League baseball," Amy said. We waited for my antique girl to emerge from the valet parking. "They have so much culture here, it's really artsy. In Kansas City? Negro baseball? I'm not sure... can I say that?"

"There's more to the country than what you see on the television. Ask me about 'Negro' when we enter a slave state," I said. I patted her on the shoulder. "Weird to think our hotel here was finished after my grandparents drove through Kansas City."

"This place was a piece of art," Ruth said. "This is a real treat. I'd never been in a jazz club. That was a lot more fun than I would have imagined. I admit it!"

"Ruth, you need to get out more," Rebecca said. She hugged me around my growing waist. "What's next, frisky man? Amy, you feel okay?"

"St. Louis," I said. My car was parked in front of us. "I told you: at my age, I'm not to be wasteful."

"I'm good, but keep that to yourself," Amy said. She shrugged. "Don't worry about me."

The valet, who was wearing a green vest, had taken extra care to ensure my girl wasn't scratched or dinged and assured me so as he opened the driver-side door. Another valet opened the back passenger section. Wylie had checked back in and advised me he'd delivered the Model A Ford to my garage. He hadn't touched the dusty patina, but he'd made sure it was in good running order and encouraged me to tool about Carmel-by-the-Sea in it, once I returned home. I looked forward to that moment, perhaps it would remind me of my grandparents.

"I was told we have to compare the great barbecue we had to the offerings in St. Louis," I said.

"I liked Kansas City. Nice people. It's bigger than I expected," Amy said. She was reading her tablet. "Can we do the Arch?"

"Arch?" Rebecca asked. She snuggled her cowboy hat onto her head. "Not me, I've been in those pods once."

"I'll do it," Ruth said. "I ain't scared."

"Who are you?" I said. I glanced back at my sister. "You've turned into a real cowgirl?"

"I've always wanted to do it," Ruth said. She grinned, but I could also see tears in her eyes. "Now I will; my kids are grown."

"I love you, Sister," I said.

"Who are *you*?" Rebecca asked. "You can't be going soft."

It was a magnificent November morning with a modest chill

in the air to remind us winter approached, but there were no gray clouds along the horizon as I drove onto Interstate 70 toward Kansas City's barbecue competitor, St. Louis. Beyond the lanes of concrete were vast clusters of oak trees. Some of the trees had given up their leaves, while others resisted with orange and red colors. The sheer, carved limestone rock walls reminded me that the terrain was no longer desert, but full of roaming hills, meandering forests, and fresh air. Steel and concrete bridges crisscrossed the interstate at upward and downward angles. We had dark-blue, metal signs that told us there was fast food just beyond the next exit at a roadside hotel. Meanwhile, large, green, metal signs above us assured me St. Louis waited for us on the other side of Missouri. For the most part, it was a straight drive along the concrete interstate as we drove past everyday life within America's breadbasket. But within the center of Missouri, the flat farmlands reappeared along with the other signs of the Great Plains: metal buildings, grain silos, and the wind.

"Amy, does my grandfather have anything to say?" I asked. "I miss him."

"Where'd the trees go?" Rebecca asked. "I could even go for a Route 66 concrete teepee."

"I've sparked something," I said. I smirked back at Rebecca. "I've allowed my inner Evil Bob to infect you."

"Hush," Rebecca said.

"This drive makes me sleepy," Ruth said.

"How do these truckers do it?" Rebecca asked. She stared up at a hulking eighteen-wheeler with a wind deflector atop the cab. Of course, the trucker gave us an approving honk for our curvy chariot. "I'd wreck from boredom."

I exited off Interstate 70 at the college town of Columbia, Missouri. We had driven for several hours, and it was time for an early lunch. Just to be safe, I refueled the car. We found a coffee shop with the ubiquitous double-tailed mermaid on its sign.

"I feel human again," Rebecca said. She sipped her double expresso. "Amy, got anything?"

"Yeah, I just need to find it," Amy said. She tapped her hand on the tabletop. "I found an entry for here, someplace called 'Stephens College'."

"Sweet," I said. I sipped my double-espresso black eye coffee. "Read away."

"We decided to camp in Columbia but were blessed that a kind lady allowed us to stay at the Stephens College dormitory. It was all women. I had to sleep alone. We were blessed, but I did not like to sleep without her."

"Is he pouting?" I asked. I drank more coffee.

"I think so," Amy said. She tapped her tablet. "It's nearby, maybe five minutes from here."

"Let's go," I said. "I have to see this place."

We got back in the car and cruised through Columbia and past the old Stephens College dormitory. It was comforting to know that Stephen and Hazel had slept here. It was a quiet campus in Middle America that time had blessed with an aged, ivied texture and patina.

"They were here," Ruth said. "Somewhere here."

"Yeah," I said. "When they were young."

"Thank you, Brother," Ruth said. She sank back into the back seat as she contemplated the moment. "It's fun to think of them being young, adventurous. I love it."

I shifted the car into third gear as we drove back onto Interstate 70. We drove several more hours as the trees and rolling hills returned, the quiet farmlands disappearing and the trucks returning. Then came the cars, with numerous roadside billboards and more white-stripped, concrete lanes. We were within a busy city, but just as we passed underneath another crossing bridge, we saw the distinct downward oval shape of the Gateway Arch.

"Amy," I said. I pointed forward. "See that?"

Amy pushed forward on the bench seat.

"Super cool," she said. She gripped the car barrier. "What do you think?"

"Sure, it's not even two o'clock," I said. "I bet it's still open for business."

"Get food," Rebecca said. "I didn't sleep much, thanks to you."

"Don't be wasteful," I said.

CHAPTER 33

Twin-engine jets left the unmistakable white-plume swirls of their vapor trails along the clear, late-afternoon Missouri sky. It wasn't unusual for me to ride in such speedy, modern machines. Often, I would set my computer aside and gaze down at the earth, wondering about the what and who below. What was their life like? What was their journey? Were they happy?

I stared up the side of the gleaming Gateway Arch and leaned against the curve. The smooth stainless steel felt cold. It was tapered upwards like I had shot a thick, silver arrow into the sky. The band got thinner and thinner until the apex and then got bigger and bigger as it fell to earth. I thought it odd I was standing next to a symbol celebrating Western expansion as I drove back east along my grandparents' trail, but I was happy to have been the contrarian. I loved the hedge.

"I'm not getting in that thing," Rebecca said. She crossed her arms as she watched the descending line of humanity disappear underneath the concrete deck beneath the Arch. Meanwhile, Amy and Ruth were queuing to take the elevator ride up to the top of the Gateway Arch. "One fat, smelly person, and you're dead."

"It looks like it sways back and forth," I said. I reached over and gripped Rebecca's hand. "Don't cross your arms, it closes you off to your handsome husband."

"That's my line, buster," Rebecca said. "At least you got me a hotdog to tide me over. You wore me out, last night."

"Complaints?" I asked. I put my hands on my hips.

"No," Rebecca said. "I've missed that horny, midnight man."

"Save yourself for barbecue," I said. I pulled Rebecca closer to me. "Does it smell like fish?"

"I never knew how nice your sister was," Rebecca said. "She's lovely, but the Mississippi River, I think that's where the fish smell is coming from."

"Good point," I said.

I turned around to look down the green-grass west bank at the cream-in-my-coffee-colored Mississippi River. It flowed south, toward the Gulf of Mexico. I glanced across the fabled river at the Illinois side with its smoke stacks, steel, and industry. The river traffic was quiet but for an occasional rusty tugboat or long cargo vessel. A fisherman at the muddy bank was casting a line for fish I wouldn't have wanted to eat. I wondered what it would have been like during Mark Twain's time, aboard a steamboat, imagining the sounds of deep-bass horns and high-pitched whistles as the paddle wheels' wake frothed them toward their destination. Minneapolis was to the north, Memphis and then New Orleans were to the south. I stood there among the international tourists, wondering which bridge my grandparents had used to cross the wide river.

"She looks a lot like my grandmother, my sister," I said. I turned around and looked under the Arch at a domed, Greek Revival building and into the active St. Louis downtown. "We caught back up with Route 66."

"Great. I take full blame! Your grandmother must have been quite pretty," Rebecca said. She gripped my cheek and kissed me.

"This was my idea, but where did this spontaneous man come from?"

"I don't know. I'm not worried about anything, right now," I said. I smiled. "Instinct, I guess. I'm having fun."

"You never have fun, you know," Rebecca said. "Fun... that's my job."

We walked along the sidewalk and down the stairs into the monument. As Amy and Ruth were risking their lives inside the elevator pod lifting them up to the top of the Gateway Arch, we were underneath the soil, learning about westward expansion and thankful we were on the winning team. There was a nice bronze bust of Thomas Jefferson, credited with his vision to expand the country west and our American Manifest Destiny.

"It wasn't our fault; blame divine providence," I said.

"Not pleasant if you were a nomadic Native American," Rebecca said. "Or an African slave who got to know Tom Jefferson in a carnal way..."

"Nobody's perfect," I said. I shook my head.

"I found some historic hotels," Rebecca said. She stood near me, inspecting postcards and other tourist-cash-liquidating items that would end up in a late-summer garage sale. "But not where they stayed. I wonder what Amy found."

"Yeah," I said. "But let's go ahead and get some rooms in one of those old places, we'll sort the rest out over dinner."

"You mean barbecue?" Rebecca asked. She blinked her eyelids at me with a faint grin. "I'll need to detox the swine from my system after we eat, you know."

"You are not a Miss Piggy," I said. "Where did all the Germans come from? Tour bus?"

"Funny! Be nice. There are lots of them roaming about today," Rebecca said. She picked out a box of notecards with an understated Gateway Arch etching. "But you'll need to send me to the fat farm."

About an hour later, an excited Amy and Ruth stepped behind us. Their eyes were full of wonder after surviving their journey inside the egg-like compartment with two tourists from Berlin. The foreign visitors were headed west along Route 66 toward California. They had rented a cherry-red 1971 Cadillac Fleetwood Eldorado convertible in Chicago, and they were full of questions about where to go and what to do along the Mother Road. Ruth thought they were odd in a certain 'Mike Myers as Dieter from *Saturday Night Live*' way. In fact, she thought the one who wore wire-rimmed glasses was named 'Gunter', but she hadn't heard the other person's name – she wasn't even certain if they were male or female. Amy had informed them of the historical significance that awaited them: John Steinbeck, the Dust Bowl, Will Rogers, and my grandparents' journey in a Model A Ford. She'd told them about our journey, explaining where and why we had stopped. She'd even told them she'd thought the concrete teepees were overrated for an overnight stop but a must-see. After they had ogled Ruth and Amy's custom-crafted gear, they'd wanted exact directions to Shorty's for cowboy hats and boots. I prayed for Shorty's safety, but he was a real Texan, so I suspected he would be packing his friends Smith & Wesson.

"Just chasing that American dream," I said. I nodded at the notion of roaming a foreign country along a mythical road. "Not sure I'd do it."

"But you are," Ruth said. "Right now."

We chose a hotel that had once been called 'Roberts Mayfair Hotel'. Amy was amazed that we'd found another art deco hotel that was really a time capsule back to the Roaring Twenties. During the time period known for bathtub gin, jazz, and dancing, my grandparents hadn't been much for roaring, though they'd been crazy about humbly praying. We asked the concierge to recommend a St. Louis-style barbecue joint. The concierge explained that there was a significant dispute between warring barbecue factions. Within the confines of St. Louis, they couldn't make up their minds on what style of barbecue was superior. Perhaps we had missed a similar war within the Kansas City walls. Rebecca took it upon herself to make a decision. We would dine in a section called 'the Hill'. It was a strict Italian-American district, and it was named because it had been built on higher ground. It was also the birthplace of Yogi Berra. I told the concierge that I had loved his cartoons and would keep tight hold of my picnic basket. He wasn't amused.

I informed Amy I was kidding. Yogi was a Hall of Fame catcher for the New York Yankees, not the cartoon character. She hadn't understood either reference. It was the moment I realized I was old.

Rebecca used her mobile application and we hailed an Uber driver; a happy Asian man using his family's minivan. The Hill was made up of hard-working, European, brick-and-stone buildings, built by people with thick, calloused hands. It was a Roman Catholic community.

"Now, this is a proper meal," Rebecca said. She tore apart steaming, crusty bread and dredged it through peppered, dark-green olive oil. "Food of the gods..."

"Do you think the mob owns this place?" Ruth asked. She inspected the white-table-clothed restaurant. "Seriously..."

"Forget about it," I said in a mocking Italian accent. I waved our waiter over. "But I do like an Italian restaurant operated by Italians. I think we're in a good spot."

"Dude, you're sort of chill," Amy said as she looked over at me. "You're all funny and sort of relaxed. Like, who are you?"

"'Chill'?" Ruth asked. "What does that mean?"

"It's like being relaxed while being cool," I said. I shrugged. "But I don't know how to do either." I pointed at a particular wine on the list while asking for a recommendation from the waiter. "Is that a good 'Super Tuscan', whatever that means?"

The dark-brown-skinned, dark-eyed waiter gave me an indifferent shrug. He pointed out another recommendation. I approved his choice. If a waiter had the depth to alter my recommendation, it meant he was a professional.

"Always respect a pro," I said. "They earn their money, they have regulars, they have standards, and they don't give a crap what you think."

"You don't even seem to wonder where our security detail is hiding," Rebecca said as she smelled the bread. "This is divine. I'm going to explode, but it's worth it."

"Any idea what my grandparents did here?" I asked.

Amy put on her reading glasses. She pulled out one of the diaries.

"We stayed overnight near St. Louis. Clayton. It is a big city. We will be in Kentucky soon. We are tired."

"It's not that far from here," Amy said. "They have all sorts of museums and a big park called 'Forest Park'."

"And they have?" Rebecca asked.

"Beer. Beer, my dear. Sorry, Amy. It's a thing for us *tour-ons* to get excited about," I said. I sipped the wine that the waiter had expertly poured. "We have to pay homage to beer, but this is serious vino."

"Tour-on?" Ruth asked.

"'Tourist' plus 'moron'," I said. "Think about it."

The waiter smugly walked away and back over toward another table.

"It's cool," Amy said. She nodded down at the empty wine glass as she put her hand over the opening. "Not sure what to do, but I guess I'll hang out. I'll pass tonight."

"Back in my day, expecting mothers smoked and drank," Ruth said. "Everybody turned out fine."

"Just be safe," Rebecca said. Amy smelled the bread. "No exploring for a while."

"No worries," Amy said.

"Tomorrow, we'll check out the beer," I said. "It would be rude not to go investigate. Besides, let's keep going, we'll be in *Lou-vill* soon."

"'Lou-vill'?" Rebecca asked. She sipped the wine. "When he gets around southerners, watch out."

"Totally get that," Amy said. "I didn't understand you."

"I did," Ruth said. She smelled the wine. "Is this normal?"

"Yep," I said. I shook my head over at Rebecca.

Rebecca sat back in her chair. She tapped her lips with her forefinger and took another sip of wine.

CHAPTER 34

The massive, brown-furred horses were Clydesdales. They stood passive in the midmorning sunshine. A groom walked them in a circle along a dirt path within a paddock that had a massive oak tree in the center. Their hooves, which were covered in Abominable-Snowman-like fur, had seemingly been manicured down to the last hair strand.

I had been around high-strung, muscular thoroughbreds in Central Kentucky, but they would have looked like Shetland ponies standing next to these Scottish giants. I glanced up at the aged, red-brick brewery with its iconic sign. If San Francisco and Northern California were about wine, St. Louis and the Midwest were about beer. They were known for their mass-produced and affordable brews that were found in every nook and cranny in the world.

I glanced over at my sister, who was petting a tall horse along its long nose. She looked odd to me, wearing a cowboy hat with cowboy boots, but in a sense, even with all my wealth, I paled in comparison to her. She still looked innocent and doe-eyed, and each experience was new for her. I had seen the world many times over; I knew where the ugliness lurked. I was the one who had to have a security detail follow my every movement. She was free, anonymous, and happy, because she had lived a simple life, like my grandparents. It had never occurred to me to 'keep it simple, stupid'.

"I found the only place they could have crossed on the old Route 66," Amy said. She handed me her tablet. "Chain of Rocks Bridge, but it's only for walking and biking, now."

"That's a weird-looking bridge," I said.

"I know," Amy said. "Totally, makes a sharp turn at its midpoint."

"They would have driven a bit north," I said. I traced my fingertip over the map. "And then driven south and on down toward Louisville, right?"

"Yes, let me read it," Amy said. "We made it across the Mississippi. We were scared. It was busy, like the river back in LA. We'd have drowned for sure, if the fall hadn't killed us. We didn't have a choice, but the Lord provided. We are getting closer to Kentucky. Tired."

We sat around a table after touring the brewery, drinking samples of their crisp, golden product from plastic cups. It reminded me of hanging out in high school, drinking aluminum-can tall boys until we all got 'buttered'. I was never sure what that meant, but it seemed cool at the time. I had liked that term better than 'buzzed', which seemed like we were bumblebees, or 'drunk', which seemed old and stale. I twisted the cold cup in my fingertips. It was the fuel that let us work through each 'buttered' phase as if each of us was the most handsome man in the college bar. Apparently, the modern term was 'merked', and a young, college-aged group nearby were using it to recount their own drinking memories. I had not a clue what they meant by 'yolo', and what was a 'derp'? They made me feel ancient.

"How long were they out here?" Ruth asked. She had ignored the plastic cup of beer like it was debris left on mass transit.

"I bet it took them a month," I said. "Amy?"

"Yeah," Amy said. "He rarely put a date, but I think that makes sense."

"I think we'll get on 64 and drive to Louisville," I said. "After we get some barbecue?"

Rebecca groaned at me, so we found a nearby deli with a heart-healthy chicken salad instead.

"Can we go to the Kentucky Derby?" Amy asked.

"Unfortunately, it's the wrong time of year. The race is the first Saturday in May," Ruth said.

"I thought the place was called, you know, 'Kentucky Derby'?" Amy asked. She stared past me at a group of Asian tourists who were laughing and chatting in their native language.

"That's a horse race for three-year-old thoroughbreds," I said. I glided my hands across the Formica tabletop. "The track is called 'Churchill Downs'."

"Oh," Amy said. "Can we go there?"

"Why not?" I clapped my hands and stood up. "Let's go."

As I drove along Interstate 64, we left the silvery Gateway Arch standing guard over the muddy banks of the Mississippi River. I maneuvered in gridlock, dodging big-rigs and jackhammering road construction crews, who were laying down reinforced steel, as we entered Southern Illinois. As our journey moved further from St. Louis, the traffic tempered to a slow boil and the hills seemed to cause the road to roll down and up, banked by limestone walls that the builders had blasted through to create the smooth, gray interstate. Where the land allowed, there was farmland, hidden though it was behind thick clusters of trees and bushes.

"Any place we should stop?" I asked Amy. I flipped my cowboy hat onto the passenger-side seat.

"No," Amy said. "He went dark. I do have some other stuff."

"Oh well," Rebecca said. "Dad, I need to go soon."

"Go where?" I said. "A waterfall, river..."

"You know," Rebecca said, gripping my right earlobe. "You'll have to go to sleep eventually."

As quickly as possible, I turned off the interstate and found a two-pump gas station that reeked of addiction. It wasn't acceptable to my queen or me, and we drove another five anxious miles down the interstate before I found a proper exit. We stopped at the Old Country Store that Rebecca had chosen. She ordered a coffee to go and we half-heartedly shopped for trinkets. Then, we were back on the interstate before they knew we weren't interested in Uncle Bill's 'clogged artery' special.

I steered into the left lane as I passed an old pickup truck loaded with family treasures.

"We're flying now."

"Thank you," Rebecca said. "I feel human again."

"How far to Louisville?" Amy asked. "I'm stoked to see the 'twin spires' place."

"Maybe an hour," I said. I steered back into the right lane. "Depends on traffic..."

"Where should we stay?" Rebecca asked.

"Downtown." I tapped the steering wheel. "I think there's an old hotel from the prohibition era."

"Okay," Rebecca said. She tapped on her tablet.

"'The Seal', or something," I said as I drove through a foliage tunnel. "Was there a long time ago; friend got married there. I remember it had good drinks."

We continued along the interstate to emerge at a beautiful bend in the Ohio River. As we drove toward Louisville, we crossed a double-decked steel bridge built when a Kennedy was in the White House.

"I didn't realize we were in Indiana," Amy said. "It's amazing. What's a Pentecostal?"

"Yeah, lots of people say that," I said. I waved back at Amy. "What are you reading? We're in Kentucky."

"The Seelbach Hilton," Rebecca said. "I have us set up."

Driving along the I-64 with the Ohio River to my left and, to my right, the downtown Louisville skyline, felt strangely familiar. The architecture was a blend of Southern, Midwestern, and the industrial North.

"Pentecostal?" I asked. I exited as we descended down into the city streets.

"Yeah," Amy said. "I think?"

"We're south of it," I said. "We're in a slave state."

Amy sat back and contemplated my statement. She gazed up at the tall, modern buildings towering above the flat-roofed Midwestern architecture. The long barges navigated goods along the Ohio River. It wasn't Southern enough to have stayed out of Al Capone's prohibition grip.

"I don't know what to say," Amy said. "It's a lot like St. Louis, just not as big."

"Pentecostal?" Ruth asked. She shook her head. "They weren't Pentecostals."

"No, but they did go there..." Amy said. She turned a diary page.

"I have to hear this," I said. We drove past the Louisville Slugger Museum & Factory, which had a ginormous baseball bat out front. "I've never even thought of this, but it makes sense."

"The chapel is almost done," read Amy. "I made a big mistake. We were invited to a Pentecostal service. I forgot they handle snakes. Terrified. I had Hazel on my lap. I froze. We prayed for protection. Big, big snakes – everywhere, went past us. Hazel's not happy with me. She about pulled my ears off."

"He had this almost childlike quality; trusted anybody. Grandma, not so much. He should have known better," Ruth said.

"No kidding," I said.

"Turn left," Rebecca said. She pointed for me to turn onto 4th Street. "It's at South 4th and Muhammad Ali Boulevard."

"Ah yes, the Louisville Lip," I said. I pressed down on the metal throttle.

"What?" Amy asked.

"Ali, he was known as 'the Louisville Lip'," I said. "It was an early form of trash-talking, but he could back it up. He was the boxing champion of the world and as cool as Elvis."

"Ali?" Amy asked. She stared over at Ruth.

"Muhammad Ali," Ruth said. "You know, the boxer."

"Sorry," Amy said. She gazed at the fancy hotel, which had been built the year of my grandfather's birth. "How do you all keep finding these places? This place is so swag."

"I have no idea what that means," Ruth said.

I drove along the brick street and parked under the fancy, black canopy that covered the red-carpeted steps up to the thick, imposing front doors. A team of valets opened the car doors.

"Nice ride, dude," a young valet said.

"Just keep her safe," I said, and I handed him a twenty as we walked into the grand entrance.

"Thanks, Brother," Ruth said. "I've only driven past."

"Why do I feel like I'm in Bavaria?" Rebecca asked. She walked up to the front reception area, which was made from dark marble and mahogany, as a dark-jacketed man smiled at us.

"I'll bet ya'll be from Texas," he said. He grinned at us. "Checkin' in?"

"Nope," I tipped my cowboy hat back. "California."

"Yes," Rebecca said. She placed our all-purpose AMEX on the counter. "Never mind him; he's just our driver."

Amy was reading about the hotel on her tablet. She tapped me on the arm.

"Dude, they shot the new *Great Gatsby* here," Amy said. She bounced up and down on her toes. "And some of *The Hustler*. You know, Paul Newman: very Hollywood chill."

"Way chill," I said. "Right?"

CHAPTER 35

It was a sight I had always loved, and early mornings were the best times to watch thoroughbreds being exercised. It was an art form to know how to handle and manage a temperamental racehorse that was more than five times your size. We stood near the busy, chest-high back rail at Churchill Downs as the professional riders sat light on the leather saddles and allowed the horses to gallop past us. The racehorses were under the nearby eyes of the watchful trainers, who sat atop hulking training horses like Roman generals inspecting their ranks before battle. The thoroughbreds snorted out heavy breaths and their hooves thumped into the brown dirt track. They wanted to streak down the backstretch, to race, but the riders held them just enough in check.

"What d'you think, Amy?" I asked. I had one hand in my jacket pocket for warmth and the other gripping a steaming Styrofoam cup of hot coffee. "Over there are the twin spires, above the grandstand. That's for fancy people."

"This is so rad," Amy said. She watched the horses and looked across the track at the iconic racetrack stands that had witnessed Kentucky Derbies, Breeders' Cups, and famed horses that had gone on to win Triple Crowns. "Growing up, you must've been here a lot?"

"No, this was a place for gamblers and the rich. It was also a place where people drank, so my grandparents, our family..." I said. "We would never have set foot here."

"We've been to a race," Rebecca said. She pointed to the left of the twin spires. "Sixth floor over there, behind the glass-office-building-looking place, we had fun."

"Fun?" I said. "More like fun people-watching."

"Is there anything you two haven't done?" Ruth asked. She sipped her coffee as ghosts of steam wisped past her face. "Next time, you'll invite your sister?"

"I've been everywhere, man, just ask Johnny Cash," I said.

"I don't get it," Amy said.

"The song," I said. "I've been... never mind; let's go check out the stables and enjoy that 'hay and horse poo' aroma."

"You should run for office," Ruth said. She turned and walked toward a grouping of weathered horse stables topped with green-shingled roofs. Beneath, the stables were segmented by tall stall doors, which were hung with clumps of yellow hay for the long-necked horses to snack on. The grooms were in constant motion, tending to the horses, in and out of the stretch of stalls as they were directed by trainers. "Amy, when we get to Lexington, we'll show you a *real* horse farm, with a proper barn. This place is for nags."

"She's kidding," I said.

"What's a 'nag'?" Amy asked. She looked inside a dark stall at a thoroughbred with a chestnut coat. The spongy floor was covered with fresh hay. It nudged its big head out at Amy and snorted as she backed away. "Will it bite me?"

"Go ahead," I said. I stood next to her, and we petted the warm horse behind its smooth, furry ears. The bottom half of the stall door was closed, as if we were in a black-and-white episode of

Mister Ed. "'Nag' means 'old horse'. They do bite if you make them mad, so don't do that. The real danger is standing behind them; never do that. And this isn't a nag, he's beautiful."

"Do they make glue out of them? After they..." Amy asked. She whispered, "I read *Animal Farm*, you know."

"That's harsh," Rebecca said. She stood behind us, near stacked bales of hay.

"It's frowned upon," I said. I kept scratching the horse behind its ear. "Most are cared for like kings and queens, even after they're finished racing. That's what they do here. By the way, Lexington and Louisville people don't always get along."

"We have better soil," Ruth said. I looked back at her. "It's true, look it up. The soil is the secret; a limestone layer, calcium-rich grass, rolling hills."

"You can be kinda feisty," I said. "Talk about me—"

"I'm just as competitive as you are," Ruth said as a Hispanic groom walked past us. "All they have is a race, but we're the capital. It's just that simple, you know?"

"I've heard this before. You're like a house cat," I said. "Quiet until someone starts messing with you, and then you hiss and scratch at them."

"She's not playing," Amy said. She walked toward the next stall and looked inside.

"Let's follow," I said as we dodged the groom traffic.

After we toured Churchill Downs, we drove back onto Interstate 64 and headed toward Lexington. As we made it past Peytona, I knew we were at the midpoint between Louisville and Lexington, but I felt a certain acidic sensation as we approached my hometown. I hadn't been back to stay for any length of time in decades. It was fun to act like a tourist, to roam about Los Angeles and across Route 66, but here was that same old instinctual nervous energy that had made all the difference in my life and career. My instinct was tapping behind my eyeballs, pushing me to continue the journey back to my grandfather's chapel, and I knew it wouldn't take no for an answer.

"You know there aren't any old, fancy hotels in Lexington," Ruth said. She leaned forward. "But you're welcome to stay at our house."

"Really?" Rebecca asked. She squeezed my shoulder from behind. "I thought Lexington was an old town, full of intrigue like a soap opera?"

"I know," Ruth said. "But we don't have places like Louisville; they're a big city."

"I thought there was a place downtown, from the Roaring Twenties?" I said. I was trying to figure out how to not stay at my sister's house. I loved her, but I liked to have my own space. "No worries, we'll figure something out. Got anything, Amy?"

"For sure," Amy said. She reached down into her bag. "I've got entries from into the '50s; he kind of went dark for several years, and then he picked back up."

"Feel free to read at random," I said. I drove east along I-64, and Central Kentucky emerged. It was a bucolic landscape that resembled the English countryside, with antebellum Greek Revival mansions from the time of tobacco and bourbon barons. It was littered with tobacco farms that had tall, black-tarred barns with steeply pitched tin roofs. The farmland was left quiet for the winter, as the tobacco had been hung within the rafters to air cure before being bundled and sold. I thought about the fact that the once-proud auction system – and the auctioneer cadence – had long ago gone silent in empty, downtown tobacco warehouses. As we approached Lexington, the farms transformed into the familiar rolling bluegrass pastures within curvy lines of five-rail oak fences. In some pastures, there were fenced lines *within* the lines that were built parallel to the outer line. At the crest of the hills, there were horse barns that weren't ordinary barns; they were equine palaces painted winter white, made from the finest woods, with cupolas along the slate roof lines topped with metal rooster vanes that attracted lightning from the springtime electrical storms. The open-gated entrances to the horse farms were made with thick layers of stone that descended and expanded out like eagle wings to reveal the blacktop path toward a grand main house that was hidden from view behind forests of oak, maple, and birch trees.

"Girls are growing," Amy read. "I worry. I pray for a good offertory, but I hate to ask. Hazel's busy. I worry about her. We are stretched, but our church grows. We are blessed."

"Did he write much about historic events? World War II, Vietnam, civil rights; all that stuff?" Rebecca asked.

Amy shook her head. Ruth looked at her, and she adjusted her cowboy hat.

"Really?" Ruth asked.

"Rarely. He was always focused on the church," Amy said. "Or his family, Hazel—"

"Are the fences all black tar, now?" I asked as I drove past a blue interstate sign.

"Yeah, except for Calumet," Ruth said. She tapped me on the shoulder and pointed at a road sign. "Take this exit; it's a pretty drive through Midway. We should stop and get lunch there. It's a nice area to stretch our legs."

"Oh, great idea," I said. I turned our Pierce-Arrow off the interstate system. I drove along a two-lane road, and my sister directed me to turn left down a single-lane county road. It was buttressed by stone walls and thick, fall foliage. The tree trunks were pushing the walls onto the road.

"This is amazing," Amy said. She seemed to want to reach out and touch the trees. "It's so beautiful, like a fairyland."

I stopped at a quiet intersection with a yellow caution light. In front of the car was a long rock wall that led up to the entrance of a vast horse farm.

"See those rock fences?" Ruth asked. She pointed over at them to guide Amy's eyes. "They're called 'slave walls'. You'll see them all over as we drive around Lexington."

"Whoa, they're real?" Amy asked. She got her mobile phone out and took a photo. "That's real, living history."

"Yeah," I said. "They're very real; remember, we're in a slave state."

"They learned from the Irish master stonemasons," Ruth said. She pointed down the road toward the farm entrance. "One of my boys wrote a paper for school about it. They taught the slaves how to build them to last. Dry-stone masonry. They're like perfect jigsaw puzzles; each stone was hand-selected. After a while, the slaves were the artists. They took pride in their work."

"I didn't know that," I said. I turned left, and we weaved along the double-lane road and found the village of Midway.

"This is like a village, this is history: train tracks, old brick buildings," Any said. She took photos of the quaint buildings with her smartphone. "I need pictures."

"That's why it's called 'Midway'," Ruth said. "It's halfway between Frankfort and Lexington."

"What's Frankfort?" Amy asked. She stepped past me as I held open the restaurant door. "It's cool to think the train tracks sort of connected, like the roads now."

"State capitol," I said. I sat down on a wooden chair. "I'm hungry."

"If you all will forgive me," Ruth said. She grabbed her smartphone. "Order me a tea, I'll be back. I promised Amy a proper horse farm."

"You've got her stirred up," I said to Amy. I waved at the waitress.

"Because of you," Rebecca said as she studied the menu.

"Why?" Amy asked. She put on her readers.

"I rarely visit," I said. I stared through the front window at my sister. "She's my only family. At least, the only family I trust."

CHAPTER 36

My sister waved at the security guard who had leaned out of the gatehouse, and he tipped his hat and then motioned with his forefinger for us to drive on into the horse farm. The property had rolling bluegrass pastures with a blacktop road running through it. The house was a white, neoclassical mansion built on a high spot that was large enough to provide shelter for most of New Delhi. With my sister navigating, I parked in front of a large, stone-and-mortar horse barn that looked a lot like a Greek temple with a long tunnel space carved through the center. To the left of the horse barn, within a large grass area, there were lines of granite headstones; the headstones of champion horses. From within the center of the barn's shadow, a tall man with graying hair emerged. He had a pleasant pace to his stroll, complete with his long arms dangling at his sides. His dark-brown, quilted barn jacket had the farm symbol stenciled over the left breast pocket; it was well worn, as he had used the coat to work in, and he had the sleeves rolled back. He wore comfortable, steel-toed, leather boots.

"Well, hello there," he said. He spoke with a happy Irish accent. "I'm Finn. I guess you be the missus' friends?"

"Yes, I've known her since grade school—" Ruth answered.

"Yes, yes. Now, Briar Hill?" Finn asked. He gripped my hand. "I'm the general manager; they're good people ta' work for, here in the States."

"That's it," Ruth said.

"One of the Greene girls?" I asked. I stared over at a dark-bronze statue of a horse set on a pedestal at the center of a round, reflective pond. "She had a crazy older brother?"

"Yeah, 'Billy'," Ruth said. "He's a trainer now, doin' well. She married into the family. She's a lawyer, you know how it is; everybody works on or for the farm."

"Right about that," Finn said.

"I want our friend Amy to see a real horse farm," Ruth said. She put her arm around Amy's shoulders.

"Should we start with her mucking out the stalls?" Finn asked. He chuckled with a former pack-and-a-half gasp as he pointed back at the barn with his left thumb. "I'm just joshin' wit' ya, follow me. I guess we'll start with the cemetery, it bein' right here in front of us."

"They bury the jockeys here?" Amy asked.

"No, child, there's no sign of Steve Cauthen here," Finn said. He pointed down at the first granite headstone. "These are for thoroughbreds; big-hearted champions lie here. We bury them whole, sign of respect."

"What's with all the names?" Amy asked. She kneeled down to read the rectangular headstone. "I don't understand."

"Horse buried here, name's on top," Finn said. He bent down next to her and pointed to the left. "Below, that's his dad, and that's his mom. Sire and dam. It's important genetic information, you see. We track thoroughbreds all the way back to the original three Arabian stallions and the British mares, trying to keep things pure."

"I don't understand." Amy stood up.

"Ah, long time ago, they were imported into England," Finn

said. He waved at us to follow him into the barn. "They were bred with English brood mares, which produced what were known as 'hot-blooded' horses. Come now, let me show ya."

We walked together as the sunlight reflected off the surrounding oaks and tulip poplars. Once we entered the brightly lit barn, we stood on hard, spongy rubber pavers that were held in place by smooth, gray concrete. It covered the floor like a solid, maroon blanket, all the way to the other barn door, which was open. Above us, from the tall ceiling, beneath the arched, tongue-and-groove maple, hung a row of three metal chandeliers. Finn unlatched and slid back a cherry-stained, oaken door. It had bars on the top half and it was attached to a sliding system, but it was far from a jail cell. Next to the door there was a shiny brass plate with the horse's name engraved across. The stall was wide and it was open at the top, creating good space for the horse to live in.

"Whoa," Amy said. She stared at the custom-crafted interior. "I could live in there."

"We spare no expense," Finn said. He walked into the stall, over fresh straw, holding the horse's leather halter strap. The horse bayed and nudged at him. "These beautiful beasts support the farm. They're powerful but fragile."

"Can I pet it?" Amy asked. Finn encouraged the horse forward into the center walkway.

"Pet him along his neck," Finn said. He wrestled with the strap chain as the horse kept trying to bite it. "He's in a playful mood."

"What's his value?" I asked. "Over his lifetime?"

Finn looked past me at the barn's office door, which had his name stenciled along the glass.

"This feller, north a' fifty million, US," Finn said. He walked the horse past me and outside. "They bring the girls to him. He's here to stay, season or not."

"'Girls'?" Amy asked. She appeared entranced by the muscled animal as it snorted and bayed.

"You're gettin' ahead a' me," Finn laughed. "Let's take him back inside, then we'll go take a look at the breedin' shed. That's where the money be made."

"That almost-round-shaped building," I said, pointing. It was a stone-and-steel barn with a pyramid-shaped slate roof. "It looks innocent enough..."

"Dirty mind," Ruth said.

Finn smirked at me as he walked the horse in a big circle. He checked out my vintage automobile.

"Nice ride," he said. He looked over at the curvy, shiny car. "What is it?"

"A 1929 Pierce-Arrow," I said.

"A beauty," Finn said. He nodded back at me. "I don't want our big friend here to get any ideas." He walked the horse back toward the barn. "If I take him over there, he'll get, well..."

"Ready to go," I said. I chuckled.

"That sounds Pavlovian," Rebecca said. She stepped back toward a massive oak.

"Yes indeed," Finn said. He walked the horse back inside. After, he walked us over to the breeding barn. There, he opened a square side door to reveal the barn's interior. It had a high vaulted ceiling, and the walls were padded like a psychiatric cell.

"When I hook them here..." Finn said. He blushed, hesitating. "I'm not sure I should talk about this, in mixed company and all."

"Aroused," I said. I patted him on the shoulder. "I think you mean 'aroused'."

"Behave," Rebecca said. She covered her mouth with her fingers. "Speak freely, no virgins here."

"Thank you," Finn said. He guided us to the center of the room. "We wash them before and after. Everything gets washed. We clean and clean again. Bacteria, any infection, would put us out of business. Above, in those rooms behind the windows, we watch and film the, ah, interaction."

"I'd want proof, makes sense to me," Ruth said. She stood underneath the bank of windows and pushed against the padding. "These are really thick."

"I'm confused. Film them getting it on?" Amy asked. She rubbed her belly. "You all breed horses, but you don't make money unless they win races, right?"

"That's not what makes Lexington so special; Keeneland is almost for funsies," I said. I stood at the center of the shed, where conception occurred. "Right?"

"It's complicated," Finn said. "Putting aside the regulations and prep work, we make a good amount of money. For example, that first horse I showed ya, we charge an eighty-five thousand dollar stud fee for him, per ah, interaction."

"I should have gotten paid," Amy said. She inspected the special flooring that minimized the risk of the giant horses slipping. "Sorry, I didn't mean it like that."

"You'll be fine," Ruth said. "I promise it will work out."

"Sorry?" Finn asked.

"I'm with child," Amy said. "Knocked up."

"Congratulations!" Finn said. He smiled. "Stay clear of the cemetery, and get yourself some honey. It'll make a sweet child. I promise ya'. Steer clear of anything black."

"Now you understand why I don't care about the horse races," Ruth said. She stroked Amy's forearm. "You'll be fine."

"I get it," Amy said. "This is mind blowing, but I'm not even sure I want to have this thing."

Rebecca watched Amy closely. She turned and left the breeding barn. I thought it best to change the subject.

"That's how you make money?" I asked, blurting out the obvious thought.

"But it's expensive to operate. It takes a team to breed them, and it's dangerous for them and the horses," Finn said. He waved his forefinger in a circle. "Our fee may seem high, but our fixed costs are also high. On top of that, consider the fact that we have a mare off the market for eleven months, betting she has a healthy foal. If not, as the sayin' goes, all bets are off, and, well, I get my resume together."

"How do you know who to keep or auction off?" I asked.

"I wish I had a good answer," Finn said. "It often comes down to luck, but good judgment and experience helps."

"Thus, 'the sport of kings'," I said. I stuffed my hands in my pants pockets. "Need a fortune to keep the doors open."

"Auction?" Amy asked. She stared over at Finn.

"Madam, we have annual auctions," Finn said. He nodded over at Amy. "The prized foals can fetch millions. In part, that's how we make our money."

"I see," Amy said. "You auction off the babies."

"Is this a bit more interesting than reading my grandfather's diaries?" I asked.

"I never knew any of this existed," Amy said. She crossed her arms. "I don't know what to do."

Rebecca walked back inside. She smacked her hands together.

"Should we go check out that bourbon distillery you mentioned, Ruth?" she asked. She thrust her smartphone above her head. "After, I have this to say: *Cats, Cats!*"

"What'd you do?" I asked, grinning. I looked at Ruth. "I think you did say you wanted to be invited to our next adventure?"

"They play?" Ruth asked. She shook her head. "No way..."

CHAPTER 37

After we toured the horse farm, we honed our tourism skills at a national historic landmark. The heavy, gray, stone distillery had the aged aroma I'd loved as a young man that could only be found in Kentucky. It came from the thick, oak, tongue-and-groove floorboards that held on their shoulders the stacks of bourbon barrels filled with the magic liquid. It was produced in large, copper stills made in Scotland, which would have been illegal during Prohibition when my grandparents had driven across Route 66. But in Appalachia, they would have become aware of the 'white lightning' that my grandfather described as having 'ruined many a man's spirit'.

Since I was the chauffeur, I abstained from what my grandfather would have labeled 'the evil drink', but, as Ruth and Amy observed, Rebecca was kind enough to sample my share of the auburn nectar, which had matured many years inside a fire-charred, white oak barrel. Amy was fascinated to learn about the five sources of flavor, the mash, the distillation, and the maturing processes. She had read one of my grandfather's many entries about 'the drink'. She told me he had written many times about drinking.

"The drink, it has taken another man. I did the service, but it was not God's work. The Devil had taken the man. I do not understand; he had responsibilities, a family. I prayed."

"I heard him preach about it," I said later, as I drove along the narrow, tree-lined country road that wound between and past the horse farms and the tobacco fields.

"Drink good stuff, minimize hangovers," Rebecca said. She placed her receipt into her purse. "I trust our order will find its way home."

"Hey dude," Amy said. She pointed past my face. "Hey, can I touch one of those slave walls?"

"Yes, perfect time," I said. I pulled off the road after we found a good example that Ruth could assure us was authentic, based on its historical marker. Amy kneeled down as if to pray, her hands feeling the sturdy stone walls. It was set next to the road, held in place from generation to generation, long after the master craftsman closed his eyes for the last time. She began to cry.

"Why are you crying?" I asked. I glanced over at Ruth.

"It's not just a collection of rocks," Amy said. She held her hands up like she was warming them in front of a raging fire. "I can feel their presence. I feel sad."

"You didn't have any booze, right?" I asked.

"Not even a shot," Rebecca said. She moved close to Amy. "Are you okay?"

"Yeah, I'm, like, totally here," Amy said. She sat back. "But I'm pregnant with a child from a black man. These walls are alive."

"Every child should get a fair chance," Ruth said. She nodded as a pickup drove past us. "The chance the people who made this wall didn't get..."

"I don't know," Amy said. She wiped her face. "Black, but not black enough, but not white."

"Don't be afraid," Rebecca said. She interlocked her arm with Amy's. "It's a different time."

"Easy for you to say," Amy said.

"We'll take you to Cheapside," Ruth said. She looked over at me. "Maybe tomorrow?"

"What's Cheapside?" Rebecca asked. She walked forward with Amy, back toward the car.

"Yeah, before we leave," I said. I felt the cool breeze. "It's where they used to auction off slaves, downtown."

"You warned me," Amy said. She wiped her eyes. "You warned me we were in a slave state. I was clueless. It's like ghosts are everywhere."

"Yeah, but let's do that tomorrow. Right now, let's go have some fun," I said. "Ever been to a college basketball game?"

"No, not into it," Amy said. She glided her fingertips along the car door. "Nobody goes…"

"You're serious?" Ruth asked.

"Oh, game on," Rebecca said.

"Cool," I said. "Cheer up, let's have some fun."

After we'd driven downtown, we checked into a modern hotel near Rupp Arena. Rebecca had gotten us rather expensive tickets for an annual, nationally televised college basketball game. It wasn't really a game, more like a battle, but we lived to tell the tale. Amy trudged next to me as we forged through the dense, post-game-party crowd toward the hotel's elevators. The tall, hotel atrium waterfall fountain was drowned-out by all the boisterous merriment from Wildcat fans; mixed with them were clusters of disappointed Card fans. I thought it was just another annual college basketball scrum between supposed institutions of higher learning. We were jostled along within the throng-like four fishing floats before we escaped into one of the hotel's elevators.

"Wow," Rebecca said. "That was awesome!"

"Those people were insane," Amy said. She quickly pressed the round, pale-yellow button. "I was scared. Those players are huge."

"They can be kind of Roman," Ruth said from behind us.

"Sorry," I said. "I warned you. They don't always get along, basketball being worse than the horses."

"Tell me again, how did we get so close?" Ruth asked. She had her forefinger stuck through my belt loop for leverage.

"Ask my bride," I said.

"Money and a smartphone," Rebecca said. She smirked over at Ruth. "I made it happen."

The elevator door opened, and we were separated from the masses. I laughed, leaning forward with my hands gripping my knees as the elevator tugged us away from the carnage.

"That was awesome," I said. "I'm exhausted."

"How do you all do that?" Amy asked. She looked at us as if we were three cycloptic aliens. "That was like a fight."

"She has a point," Ruth said. She hugged Amy as they stood in the corner of the elevator. "Feel okay?"

"I'm good," Amy said. "It's early..."

"I haven't felt this alive in years," I said. "Why do their games always go down to the last shot?"

"I know," Rebecca said. She clenched her fists. "I almost ran onto the court."

The elevator doors opened and we exited into the relative safety of the hotel's suite level. It was quiet. We walked into the three-bedroom suite. I waved for Amy to come over next to me in front of the windows that looked east over the corrugated, box-shaped arena.

"I know you don't understand," I said. I pointed down at the crowd that covered the city streets. "Rebecca knows me, she just knows."

"Was your grandfather this intense?" Amy asked. She stared

through the smoked-glass windows and down at the three-lane city street, which curved behind Triangle Park.

"No," I said. "He was beautifully 'chill'. Right?"

"Yeah," Amy said. "He wrote that way, really chill."

"He loved baseball; a Big Red fan. We used to talk endlessly about them," I said. "UK fan, you know, not as rabid as me."

"Yeah, I get him," Amy said. She moved away from me. "For sure, he seemed to have a California spirit. He wrote an entry. Wait here." Amy walked away, but, within a short time, she returned. "Let me read this," she said, folding over a page. "I had wondered if we should have stayed in LA, but we took a trip back. We took the grandkids. It was sad. It was all gone. God had left the city. The darkness from evil was everywhere. I am thankful we were called. Hazel agrees."

"That's him," I said. I stared forward into the night.

"He was always honest," Amy said. "Never angry; that California chill about him... didn't let in the negative stuff."

"I was there, you know," I said. I looked at Amy. She appeared mystified. "I was a kid, along for the trip. By the way, *you* don't have to have the chill."

"I know, dude," Amy said. She touched her belly. "I should have known better, I just wanted to—"

"Explore? I was chicken at your age," I said. I hugged her. "I was all icked out."

"You all never had children?" Amy asked. She searched my eyes.

"We tried," I said. I nodded back over at Rebecca, who sat with Ruth, chatting about the day. "It didn't end well. She didn't want to feel that way again. I let it go. Why do you like to explore?"

"I don't want to be tied down, but..." Amy said. She scratched at the window.

"You want control? Control of your life?" I asked. "To feel empowered?"

Amy thought for a moment.

"I don't feel anything," she said. "I just go numb, like I'm floating."

"And the father?" I asked.

"I care about him, I guess," Amy said. She turned toward me. "What would you do?"

"Not sure. Glad you turned off your phone," I said. "A human life? Feelings? I'm the last person who would understand."

"What else is there?" Amy asked. She ogled at me, whispering, "I'm an orphan. I feel safe being on my own, but a kid, that's for real, man. Yeah, I admit it, I'm scared."

"But you said you had a mother," I said.

"Yeah, I lied. It makes people not ask much," Amy said. "People can be so mean. You know, nosey."

"Like me?" I asked. I sighed. "Tell you something: I wish I had been a father. But you can't control everything, especially a child's health, right?"

"Thank you," Amy said. She touched my arm. "Evil Bob's my friend?"

"Yeah, I like you," I said. I wasn't sure what to feel, as I was old enough to be Amy's father. I thought about the distance between our ages. I had lived her lifetime twice over, but in truth, with all my money that allowed me to hide, I was just as afraid of life as her.

"Did you hate your mother?" Amy asked. "Father?"

"Tomorrow, I want to roam to some old spots," I said. I put my hands in my pants pockets.

"I'm sorry," Amy said. She backed up. "I was just, you know, curious."

"Good question," I said. "I've never had anyone ask me."

"It's cool," Amy said. "Never mind..."

"'Hate' isn't the word," I said. "It's more like I'm disappointed..."

"Why?" Amy asked. She studied my face.

"It's not about money," I said. "The reason I miss my grandparents, I guess, is because they were real."

"You're so complicated," Amy said. "What about your parents?"

"I got tired of hiding what I thought of them," I said. "As you know, I can be blunt. They didn't like what I had to say. So I closed them off."

"I can imagine," Amy said.

"I'll say this," I said. "I can accept imperfection, lack of money, that's life."

"So, what'd you say?" Amy asked.

"Good question," I said. I closed my eyes. "Years ago, I saw a photo of an old friend, a girl I liked. You know, childhood, puppy love."

"Sure," Amy said.

"I realized I had never gotten up to bat," I said. "Ever felt like you got robbed?"

"Dude, I get it," Amy said. She gripped my arm.

"Well, don't be afraid to eliminate people," I said. I clenched my jaw. "The needy, manipulative types."

"I guess I'm living that," Amy said.

"I'm not good at this, but," I said. I patted Amy's belly. "Don't be afraid to love. I was always afraid to love. I didn't even want to love a dog."

"Yeah," Amy said.

"We'll get you back to SoCal, figure it out then," I said. "The chapel isn't far from here, but thanks for playing along. I just felt I needed to do this. No idea why."

"It's a lot like this place?" Amy asked.

"No," I said. "Maybe seventy miles, but it's a world away from here."

"I don't understand," Amy said.

"Very soon," I said, "you will."

CHAPTER 38

"This place is so, so, different," Amy said. She reached up to pet the black-furred thoroughbred along its long nose. The horse was headed toward the oval-shaped dirt race track. The rider grinned down at her and loosely held the leather reins. Above us, in the trees, the red-winged blackbirds chirped a winter warning to their starling brethren.

"It's like a park," Rebecca said. "But it has horses."

"Lexington does have a horse park," I said. A gray squirrel watched us from its perch in a thorny oak tree. The long limbs were emblazoned with burnt orange leaves. "But that'll come after lunch. I have a drive-in, a parkette. I think it still exists. Get a po'boy, even though I'm not. Ha, get it?"

"Yes, funny man," Rebecca said. "You're a dork."

"This is like Disney, it's so clean. I've never seen the fall trees until this trip," Amy said. She gazed across the curved, white-painted race rails toward the nearby bluegrass countryside. "But, for horse racing, it's so, like, so zen. So chill. It even smells like flowers."

"Mixed with that horsey-poo fragrance," I said.

"Told ya," Ruth said. She pointed at the trees. "Those are white dogwoods, I have them at home."

"It's so flipping cold," Rebecca said. She had her coat zipped tight. "I'm not even awake, why can't I go to sleep before three?"

"You are who you are," I said. I waved for them to follow me along a tree-lined path and behind the tall, gray, stone grandstands. The steel roof-line beams were painted forest green, the sides covered with climbing vines that had lost their leaves for the season. We walked through the ancient-treed area and toward two circular, spongy ovals encircled in mowed bluegrass. From the end of the horse stalls, a spongy path led to the first oval. This was where the horses were to be saddled by their trainers. The other side was for the jockeys, in their silks, to walk from their clubhouse to be mounted-up on the horses that stood waiting, held in place by an experienced groom. From the oval-shaped path, they would be led into the tall tunnel beneath the stands and out onto the track. There, a regally costumed bugler with a black top hat would play a golden trumpet to announce it was race time to the crowd. It was all about understated elegance and traditions.

"They used to not have a race announcer," I said. I pointed up at the dark-green-painted press box above a line of arched windows with reflective glass. Beneath them were half-moon-shaped balconies for patrons to look down on the horse and human proceedings. "Until about twenty years ago, they used to just line them up and let 'em go after a ringing a bell. You had to pay attention, but few other things have changed."

Keeneland was a timeless race track, I thought. I'd had an old friend whose family was part of its founding. If he understood anything, he understood the thoroughbred business. Every aspect happily oozed from his DNA. I had learned a lot about the business from him. They weren't fancy people; the ladies hadn't worn weird hats. They had strong, leathery hands and reflective stares, because all they cared about were the animals. They had a clear understanding of breeding the animals; their lives and deaths. He'd told me Keeneland had been built by breeders from Central Kentucky, tired of transporting their living merchandise to New York by train. They had built Keeneland to last, and they'd built it for more than just races and gambling. After all, it was their life's blood on display around that dirt track, and, later, a grassy turf track was installed that paid homage to the British Isles. The not-for-profit track complex was intended to create a convenient sales center and to further their cause to educate the public, and I thought they'd succeeded beyond their expectations. In my eyes, it was perfect.

"Ever been to an auction?" I asked Amy. "Somebody noticed I was in town, so I got invited."

"No way!" Amy said. "Charity auction? That's—"

"No," Ruth said. She examined a row of painted concrete jockeys. "He's being funny: breeding horses, the stock, the girls, getting auctioned off for breeding."

"How kinky, bet that's a serious hookup time," Rebecca said. She dropped her empty coffee cup into a trash can, which sat next to a line of closed betting windows.

"No, no, not even close," I said. I checked my watch after looking up at the giant Rolex clock. "I think you'll find it an interesting experience."

Amy looked over at us.

"What?" I asked.

"I've read a lot of his diaries," Amy said. "But he never mentioned any of this. Why'd we come here?"

"I like your curious brain," I said. I gripped Rebecca's gloved hand. "I wanted to show you Lexington and Louisville, but then we're headed into Eastern Kentucky. It's quite different."

"You're such a schemer," Ruth said. She walked toward the Keeneland gift shop. "But I like where you're headin'."

"I don't understand," Amy said.

"Part of this is for me," I said, "and only me. I had a lot of happy memories, here. I don't have a plan, but I've always wondered... This city, this place, is so different from Eastern Kentucky. My grandparents could have easily missioned here, but they didn't."

"You're different now," Amy said. "From when we met at the library..."

"I guess. I got out of here," I said, staring up at a solitary, white-barked sycamore tree, "and I never looked back. This isn't home anymore, but, I don't know... Happy memories makes me feel connected, I guess."

Amy nodded at me. She happily stared at us.

"It's been fun," Amy said. "You all changed my life; you've changed my career as a historian."

"You're so sweet, just stay healthy," Rebecca said. "I know you'll write a good story."

"I love your joy," I said. I watched a uniformed lawn-care manager on a utility vehicle loaded with mulch followed by a team of workers. "The joy my grandparents had."

"They've been dead a long time," Amy said. "But his diaries; I kind of know them now. They lived amazing lives."

"They did," I said. "It feels good to simply be alive."

CHAPTER 39

Cheapside was a grassy, innocent-looking spot in Lexington next to the old, domed, Romanesque courthouse, which was made from native greystone topped with an aged slate roof. It was surrounded by the green, Kentucky State government historical signs that I had grown up walking and driving past as if they were as common as grains of sand on a beach. If you were an outsider to the Southern culture, or born in Southern California, and you had never been exposed to the Old South, looking up at the pale greenish-bronze of a proud Civil War general atop a horse might just be the moment you understood the Civil War had been a reality.

Amy read the historical markers aloud and she read them several times more, as if she hadn't been fully able to understand them.

"Lexington was the center of slave trading in Kentucky by the late 1840s and served as a market for selling slaves farther south. Thousands of slaves were sold at Cheapside, including children who were separated from their parents," she read. "I don't believe this!" She walked back to inspect the first historical marker. She appeared to be in total disbelief.

"No," I said. "It was quite real."

Amy inspected the bronze statue again, and, with her mobile phone, took photos and researched the confederate general's losing story.

"On the north-east corner of the Fayette County Courthouse lawn stood the whipping post established in 1847 to punish slaves for such offenses as being on the streets after 7 pm," she read. "I don't get it! Maybe I'm just hormonal. He lost, but he got a statue. They whipped people to death, right here?"

"We don't talk about it much," I said. I looked up at the weathered bronze monument. "But when I said you're in the South, this was what I was thinking about."

"Why the statue to him?" Amy asked. She looked at me. "Where's the memorial to the slaves?"

"I don't know," I said. "A lot of senseless killing…"

It wasn't a romanticized Civil War reenactment party where no one would die. Robert E. Lee wasn't a soft grandpa character from a novel and, like Ulysses S. Grant, was a hard, well-trained military man. Each had done their duty. I thought their armies had done all the talking, and the issue had been settled. It was about looking at yourself from outside to seek the truth about life. The truth about our heritage was not pleasant. What I had been numb to, though; what I had thought of as common place from growing up here, had triggered Amy's emotions. She realized it wasn't a myth.

"I have a child inside me; it would have been a slave," Amy said. She covered her face with her hands. "I don't understand."

"I was emotional, first was worst," Ruth said. She looked over at Rebecca. "The first time; my second boy was totally different."

"I'd like to see them," Rebecca said. She tried to smile. "It's been a very long time."

I acknowledged a passerby as I stood staring at the sign. It had been a nightmare for real, sentient human beings who happened to have dark skin and who had prayed to the same God as my grandparents. They must have wondered at night, sleeping on dirt floors, where their Moses was. I suspected Amy had a sick feeling, like I did. It reminded me of the first time I had toured the Anne Frank house. I was neither Dutch nor European, but if I had been standing in Amsterdam in front of that house in 1943, I would have been shot dead on sight by the Nazis. I wasn't Jewish, but I was a Jew-loving American. They had to protect the fatherland from the Jewish infestation; it was their final solution for biological purity.

If the four of us had been standing at the same street corner in Lexington, Kentucky, in 1843, before the Civil War, we would have witnessed the unthinkable. Like a large, naked man with dark skin shackled to the ground so he couldn't run away, whipped with a leather belt like a dog. I had experienced that from my own father until I was big enough to fight back, but I wasn't a captive slave who had been paraded in front of an auction crowd in all kinds of weather, full of families holding their babies, enjoying court day within the Lexington town square, beneath the oak and sycamore trees. The slave would have been paraded around like a prized bull at a stock yard, his teeth checked to prove his good health, his body examined, gawked at, to determine his worth. And then the auctioneer would have asked for bids for the future estate chattel. The same process had been repeated thousands of times, as explained by a sign at the same quiet spot where I'd stood drinking my morning coffee, an active farmer's market behind me. Those auctions had also included innocent women and their terrified children. Whole families were either purchased together or separated at the same spot, ten feet from where we stood on a sandstone sidewalk near a line of oak trees.

"Are you okay?" I asked. I put my arm around Amy's shoulders.

"I feel sick," Amy said.

"It'll pass," Ruth said. "Just part of it."

"I'm not sure," Amy said, "I want to feel it."

"You can't be serious?" Ruth asked. She touched Amy on the shoulder. "That's a life inside you."

"Let it go, her choice," I said. The downtown traffic whizzed past us as random souls walked across the street from the six-story, modern, pre-cast, concrete parking structure to investigate the market with full baskets of heirloom tomatoes, yellow corn, and jars of local-produced, golden bee honey. "My hometown is full of these historical markers. I forgot they even existed."

"It reminds me of those cobblestones in Amsterdam," Rebecca said. She walked closer. She gripped my hand. "Holocaust victims, chilling..."

"Oh yeah," I said. I nodded. "We walked over them until, finally, someone told us to look down. There they were."

"It makes me sad, this place should be sacred," Amy said. She had re-read the historical marker for Cheapside, again and again. "This was ground zero for slavery; it's like there are ghosts here, ghosts searching for their families."

"Can you feel them?" Ruth asked. She shook her head and walked closer to Rebecca. "As if they're with us?"

"Totally," Amy said. She kneeled down to touch the Kentucky bluegrass. "They're with us, all around."

Rebecca and Ruth stood together, sharing a black coffee from another shop adorned with a double-tailed mermaid.

"Lexington was a crossroads, still is," I said. I pointed into the cold breeze. "Down this street is Henry Clay's estate." I pointed in the opposite direction. "Down there is Mary Todd Lincoln's home. Behind me, Transylvania University, where Jefferson Davis went to school. Everything intersected here, it's just our history. I guess you take the good with the bad."

"No, history comes alive here, take yourself there," Amy said.

She wiped tears from her eyes. "I can feel it. I can hear the whip, I can hear the scream. Sorry."

"Don't apologize," Rebecca said. She handed the coffee cup to Ruth. "Never apologize for how you feel."

I grunted and nodded in agreement. I sipped warm coffee from a white, paper cup with a plastic lid. Amy seemed more agitated, more emotional than her normal well-below-boil temperament. Beneath her surface there boiled a passion for history. I had admired that passion when we'd first met her at the library. It was in her eyes; a passion similar to that my grandparents had held for Christian missions. I wished I had their passion.

"We forget Lincoln and Davis were born in Kentucky," Ruth said. "They likely passed each other in the streets."

"That would be weird," Rebecca said.

I stared the wrong way down one-way Main Street as I felt the whoosh of several cars passing by me. I noted a street corner from where I had taken my driver's license test. I stared up at the gray, stone-and-mortar courthouse that looked like it was straight out of something Emily Brontë would have described in her novel *Wuthering Heights*. I wondered if Heathcliff would appear behind the dark windows, which were set below a series of triangle arches.

"When I was a young man, not far from here," I said, "I used to drive down the same road, Old Frankfort Pike, that Abraham Lincoln used to take a horse and buggy on to visit his father-in-law, who owned a hemp factory that produced rope, not dope."

"You don't understand," Amy said. She pulled one of my grandfather's leather diaries out from her bag. "I didn't understand. I feel stupid." She sat down on a rolled-steel, black-painted park bench set between oak trees and surrounded by blooming chrysanthemums. She adjusted her reading glasses, pushing them back up against her eyes. "He wrote about this, again and again, I just missed it. I didn't understand what he was *really* saying." She had marked numerous sections from his diaries. She began to read as she pressed the pages down with her fingers to keep them from blowing over. "Went to Lexington, saw Negros. Sad day. Don't understand." Amy turned the page to another section within his diary that she had marked with a paper receipt for chewing gum. "They shot a black man, dead. I don't understand. Violence. They do the same thing in California. Read from the monthly news we get from LA. Why? Where is God?" Amy pushed the diary back into her bag. She pulled out another old diary. She had marked several pages with a variety of papers slips, sticky tags, and even a Kleenex tissue. "Killed ML, why? The violence, why? I don't understand. How can I protect my children? I prayed. Where is God? Are we in end times? Hazel agrees. We must trust God." She took a breath, looking up from the diary. "He wrote... He and your grandmother would talk about it," she said. "He wrote about his time; I just didn't understand what he was saying. I'm a historian, and I missed what he was saying. I am so stupid."

My sister clutched the white coffee cup. She glanced at me as she walked over and handed the warm cup back to Rebecca, who had followed her. She sat down next to Amy as a car full of children in the back seat parked behind them. The car's brakes squeaked loud enough that, were he available, I would have sent Wylie over to administer emergency repairs.

"You're not stupid," Ruth said. She hugged Amy. She shook her head. "We allow stupid. My grandfather, my grandparents, they were kind people. I miss them every day. But they made their choices; they lived the life they chose."

"It didn't occur to me," Amy said. She stared at her cowboy boots. She sniffled. "He was angry but helpless."

"No," Ruth said. She closed her eyes as she hugged Amy. "He, *they*, were not helpless. They told the truth, but nobody wanted to listen to them. Nothing has changed."

Amy stared over at people shopping for produce, strolling up and down the temporary aisles. She gripped one of the diaries. She read a section that was brief.

"Disappointed. I failed." She put the book away, glancing at Ruth and then up at me. "What was your father like?" she asked. Her face was hard, stone-like. Her blue eyes were that of the inquisitor.

"He was complicated," Ruth said. She looked up at me. "Why would you ask that?"

It was a question I had suspected would appear. After all, Amy was reading my mother's father's diaries. Nevertheless, I still wasn't prepared for it. Over the years, the decades, I had developed the non-answer skill first employed by President Eisenhower during his televised news conferences. It was a technique for answering an unwelcome question with a garbage dump of useless information.

"Let me guess," I said. I crossed my arms. "Grandpa didn't like the young man dating his daughter? That's a not-so-uncommon feeling for fathers, then and now. It would seem every father isn't supportive, for a variety of reasons. It's as common as sunrise and sunset."

"I'll vote for you in November," Ruth said. She frowned at me. "Answer her question; you can't control everything."

"You know what he did? Don't you?" Amy asked. She stuffed the diary back into her bag. "I don't understand. Why would she marry him? It makes no sense to me."

"You don't need to read that part," I said. I examined my shoes and waved at her to close the diaries. "I guess we have a conundrum, don't we?"

"Yeah, you almost didn't exist," Amy said. "She wanted, you know... but your grandparents would have none of it. Your grandmother was tough."

"What's she talking about?" Rebecca asked. She looked down at Ruth and back over at me. "What am I missing?"

"My father raped my mother, before marriage," Ruth said. She said it with the tone of a stone-cold killer. Her face was as blank as a corpse. "My dear brother exists only because of Hazel."

"Apparently, I wasn't noted in the black-and-white photos," I said. I watched a squirrel scurry up the bark of an ancient oak. "I was at the wedding that no one smiled at, but I was hidden under the bride's dress."

"That explains a lot," Rebecca said. She held her breath as she tried to master her emotions. "Now *I* feel sick."

"Amy, he turned out okay," Ruth said. She pointed at me. "Even a bastard child like my brother..."

"Let's get out of here," I said. I gripped the car key. "Well, now you know why I'm such an asshole."

CHAPTER 40

Lexington's modest skyline disappeared from my rearview mirror as I drove along the open interstate toward my grandfather's white chapel. I needed to see it. It was the one spot on earth where I had always felt safe and loved. Even though I had stopped talking to my family years before, my mother's death had left me full of empty questions. Why? Maybe it was my attempt to rediscover my childhood; maybe it was the realization that I'd left something behind that I now missed; maybe it was a feeling, a sensation, an awareness that my life mattered. Soon, the chapel would no longer be hidden from my view, no longer hidden deep within the dense Appalachian forest.

After we left Lexington, I drove through the lush, idyllic UK campus, past several groups of students walking to class that gave our curvy ride their thumbs-up approval. We stopped at an old, red-brick building. It looked like a former synagogue, with intricate stained-glass windows, that had been converted into a popular pizzeria, but after our time at the old courthouse, we lacked a big appetite. We had some breadsticks dipped in garlic butter and ordered a luscious carry-out pie. Happily, the aroma from the pie, like an aged bourbon, caused us to make it disappear and brought us all back to life. I headed down Limestone Street, past the long-gone Jefferson Davis Inn, glanced at the Southern architecture, and turned right onto East Vine and away from downtown. I decided to stop behind the Thoroughbred Park. I had always wanted to stand next to the bronze statues. The horses and riders were in a forever-frozen race toward a mythical finish pole. It was a happy, hopeful park that captured much of what Central Kentucky was about: the sense of competition, the horse farms. Amy had thought the long rock wall that shadowed the bronzes was an appropriate homage to the slave walls. I agreed.

* * *

"How about Natural Bridge?" Ruth asked later as I shifted into second gear. She leaned forward on the passenger compartment barrier, and I merged onto the Bert T. Combs Mountain Parkway. Her blonde hair was tousled by the breeze. "I think we can stay there. It would be dark, down there. It gets dark early this time of year, you know."

"Oh, yeah, I remember it," I said. I waved at a family in a modest pickup truck that had honked their horn at my shiny, chrome girl. A little, brown-headed girl who had her face pressed against the passenger window smiled over at me. Her eyes were filled with wonderment, hoping to escape beyond the truck. "Rebecca?"

"I'll find something, I hope," Rebecca said. She started to tap at her computer tablet. After a few minutes, she had found our next stop. "I found it. Give me a few, they have a resort. Well, sort of, but I think it'll work."

* * *

I hadn't prepared to hike into the dark, damp forest and up the winding dirt path, crowded-in by loose rocks and boulders, but no other route presented itself. It was whisper-quiet; the birds had flown south, and the wildlife kept out of view within what appeared to be a colorful leaf blizzard. I was claustrophobic, so the narrow Fat Man's Squeeze wasn't pleasant, but I soldiered through the tall rock formation, which was a single person wide. At the top, it was as if we had emerged from a dark hole. I sat down on a large boulder, but, as the light was fading, I didn't have long to rest, and so I lugged past a group of European tourists toward the center of the bridge. I walked under white, drifting clouds that looked like dusty chalk marks on a graying sky. The smooth, natural bridge, which had been carved by the constant weather exposure, was like straddling a huge, sandstone surfboard while surrounded in every direction by a thorny, brownish sea. Rebecca strolled near me; she glanced over at Amy and Ruth.

"If I told her this is a Kodak moment, do you think she'd know what I meant?" Rebecca asked.

"Nope," I said. I gripped Rebecca's hand. "This place is amazing in the fall, the leaves barely hanging on."

"The view is worth the climb," Rebecca said. She slipped behind me and hugged my waist. "I love you. Why didn't you tell me about your mother?"

"I try not to think about it," I said. I squeezed her hands. "I blocked it out."

"But I'm your wife," Rebecca said.

"Force of habit," I said. "Sorry."

Amy stood near the far end of the bridge. Ruth watched her take photos of its length with her mobile phone. She looked out across the rolling distances, uninhabited by any visible house, building, or road.

"Sorry, I've lost my mind," I said. I held Rebecca's arms. "Thank you for loving me."

"Stop it," Rebecca said. She hugged me tight.

"Think my sister is counseling Amy about the evil that comes with abortion?" I asked.

"Likely," Rebecca said. She sighed. "I think you'd have been a good father."

"Not sure about that," I said, "but I'm sure that you'd have been a great mother."

"I talk to my baby's ashes, do you think I'm crazy?" Rebecca asked as she pointed at Amy. "He would have been about Amy's age, now."

"No, I wonder too," I said. I stared across the forest at a sheer cliff face.

"Do you think there's really a God?" Rebecca asked. She backed away from me. "My love, you have a ripe smell from climbing, by the way."

"What? I don't know," I said. "I thought it smelled like a fine Bordeaux; a pure smell, from the earth."

"Stop," Rebecca said. "You're so weird."

It was a question I had asked myself for most of my life. Most would have thought I had lived a charmed life, but inside my mind, I lacked joy. I was consumed with winning, but even though I had won more than I lost, I had the same numb feeling from my youth. It was a curse.

"Have you ever been near a dead body?" I asked. Rebecca crossed her arms.

"What? My love..."

"They're free," I said. I walked over and kissed Rebecca on her forehead. "Before the mortuary gets ahold of them, just after they've passed on, the faces I've seen are peaceful, relaxed. They know if there's a God, don't they?"

"I've never thought about it," Rebecca said. She watched a happy couple take a group selfie. They were standing close to the bridge edge, which had no safety rail between them and its thirty-foot drop. "I really wish they wouldn't do that."

"Selfies?" I asked. I turned back around. "That sort of defines their generation."

I thought the fall leaves, which had turned red, orange, and yellow, had showed off their best as each was weaned from their mother tree. It was from a lack of moisture. It wasn't personal; the deciduous tree wanted to survive, and it could no longer feed the leaves. The leaves were no longer deep green with a perfect sheen. Their lifecycle was over, but, as they had faded, their inner beauty was left behind for all to see before they disappeared beneath a blanket of winter snow.

"I'll tell you something," I said. I looked down at the rough sandstone. "I remember the moment my grandmother died."

"You were there?" Rebecca asked. She looked at me like I had pulled the pin out of a grenade.

"Yeah," I said. I kissed her hand. "My grandfather didn't want her to die alone. Even though she was in a coma, thanks to the high dosages of drugs, you know, he thought she'd know."

"What'd you all do?" Rebecca asked. She gripped my hand. "You've never told me this, either."

"Do you like talking about our dead child?" I asked.

"Fair enough," Rebecca said.

"He took off his shoes," I said. I closed my eyes as I remembered her peaceful face. "He had us all touch her, on her leg, her arm. He got on the bed and gently hugged her, kissed her one last time."

"Why would he do that?" Rebecca asked. She pressed her forehead against my hand. "I get the kiss, but you were a kid. Didn't that mess with you?"

"No. He didn't want us to fear death," I said. I kissed Rebecca's forehead. "He even conducted her service, but the one thing I remember, it was her face."

"What was wrong with her face?" Rebecca asked.

"Nothing," I said. "She was at peace; she almost seemed to smile. It was the moment I thought God was there. I've rarely felt like that, since."

CHAPTER 41

We left Natural Bridge after breakfast. The black coffee was dense and acidic, but I liked it. A modest car crested a steep hill as we drove down the descending side of the parkway. It drew my attention enough that, above, I saw a red-tailed hawk perched atop a gray-metal light pole. It seemed to have been waiting for us. It watched us with its dark eyes as we drove past its position. It was as if it were a proud, tunic-draped Roman soldier. But then it soared into the milky haze, as if it had decided to follow us as we traveled toward Jackson. I merged onto Highway 15, which seemed to bank at a steep angle, like a racetrack. The hawk disappeared behind a grouping of naked birch trees. By instinct, I sensed it was still nearby as the vintage automobile climbed past an empty coal truck. The road snaked between the steep, brown mountains, which were covered in mature trees and jagged, dark-gray rock outcroppings. We passed the occasional family home, each with a bulbous natural gas tank behind, many of which were protected with chain link fences patrolled by good-sized dogs. I thought of my hawk friend back home, guarding our red-tiled estate, which was set on a sheer cliff edge near Carmel Bay.

"We made good time," I said. We had arrived into the outskirts of Jackson as the road turned a sharp corner at a steep mountainside. "I wonder if there's a twin-tailed mermaid nearby?"

"What?" Ruth asked. "What's wrong?"

"Nothing," I said. I drove onto what had once been a familiar route. It was now indistinguishable from every other city and town that spread across the continent, with the same fast food restaurant chains, super-saver grocery stores, and coffee shops, but for the fact it was nestled on flat ground deep within the Appalachia Mountains.

"Welcome to Jackson," Ruth said. "Everybody seems happy, today."

"What do you want to do?" Amy asked. She sat back and stopped reading the diaries. "We're close, right?"

"Keep going," I said. I stopped the car behind a dirty SUV, waiting for the traffic light to turn green. "Let's keep going? Thoughts, ideas..."

"What was it like driving here, back in 1930?" Amy asked. "These are like real roads, but just saying, this was like driving the anti-desert."

"Yeah, longest three hours of my life," Rebecca said. I looked over at Amy. "Must have been like a tree tunnel; I cannot image it during the summer. You know, with all the leaves? I'd get claustrophobic."

"It's beautiful but dangerous. Drive off the road and you're dead," Ruth said. She looked back and forth between Rebecca and Amy. "I don't know anything about the desert."

"It was amazing, but scary, and flat," Amy said. She gazed up the mountainside. "Crazy, how'd they build a road in these mountains."

We had funneled from the modern interstate system to a double-lane state road and now down to single, blacktop lanes but for the random shared center lane for passing slower traffic or for dodging hulking coal trucks. We had driven past everyday life settled near the north fork of the Kentucky River, with metal buildings for a variety of businesses and an assortment of mobile homes. But what had the roads been like in 1930? Perhaps just dirt and aggregate-surfaced connections from town to city, or city to town.

"I'm hungry, I don't think that chapel is going anywhere soon," Rebecca said. She patted me on my head from behind and indicated a chain restaurant. "But not there, no fast food. Find something fun, please."

"How can you be hungry?" I asked. I glanced up at a yellow caution sign at a turn-in for a new shopping center. We were near a new highway that was being blasted through the mountain. I pointed at the road construction. "Amy, there's your answer: dynamite and front loaders."

"Oh, cool," Amy said. She looked over at the steamrollers and trucks parked behind a long row of orange barriers, which were tied together with an orange ribbon.

"White Flash," Ruth said. "Remember? It was his favorite place in town."

"Yeah, yeah, I'm so stupid," I said. I gripped the oversized black steering wheel as I pressed down on the metal throttle. "I think I know the spot. Let me see, don't tell me."

As I drove into the tiny town, I turned the noticeable car off the local highway and toward what was once a vibrant downtown district. It was a reminder of what had been, not a picture of what now was. The big-box chains were near the main roads that we had driven past; they attracted the local penny-pinching population with bargains. The old downtown hosted an empty hardware store, an empty grocery, an empty bakery, and more empty churches. The saving grace was the elderly United States post office and the sturdy, blonde-bricked county courthouse with its greystone foundation. This was where the civil and criminal disputes were settled. It was the one blessing that had saved the shotgun-style greasy spoon with its name stenciled in black letters across the glass front door. It was set near where my grandfather had once loved to hold his own form of court. I parked within a white-striped spot, and, after we got out, I stepped up the two steps of the cracked cement sidewalk.

"It smells like grease," Rebecca said. She spied inside the burger joint. "I love it; I want to sit at the counter on one of those old stools."

"It's still here," Ruth said. She smiled up at the old, porcelain sign. "It's still here. This makes me happy."

"Yeah," I said. I gripped the metal front door handle.

They passed by me, entering the diner, with its spotless, checkerboard, vinyl-tiled floor, but I bent to the side to find the long, wooden bench along the side of the cinder-block building. It was where the old whittlers in denim overalls and railroad hats had once sat, whittling away pine, birch, and time. They had smoked Prince Albert tobacco that they had crimped within thin cigarette paper, and they had solved the local and national political issues that they read about in the *Times*, or heard from their PHILCO radios. The benches were empty.

I went inside the warm diner, which had three cherry-red booths along the interior wall. We sat together on fountain stools, resting our arms on the laminate countertop, which was held in place with a shiny, aluminum ribbon and patrolled by a pure-gray-haired African-American man with a thick mustache and a mischievous grin.

"Well, we have some Lexington folk?" he asked as he handed us menus sealed in clear plastic. "Welcome to the White Flash, even though I'm a blacky."

"You're funny," Rebecca said. She examined the laminated menu. "What's good?"

"This is not our first time," I said. I pointed my right thumb at Ruth. "We've been here before."

"Well then, I am Tyrone Chennault," Tyrone said. He reached across the counter to shake our hands like he wanted our vote for mayor. "I am the proprietor, do tell me more. I do not remember y'all, sorry."

I leaned forward with my fingers on the countertop and grinned over at Ruth. She waved back at me.

"Our grandpa," Ruth said, "loved this place. He always came here, when we came into town."

"Pardon, 'came into town'?" Tyrone asked. He pointed at us. "You ain't mountain folk, not with that car. You have to be from Lexington, and them's rich folks. I know you ain't coal people."

"Coal people?" Amy asked.

A diminutive waitress with her black hair pulled into a tight ponytail served us glasses of ice water with lemon slices. She had a dull pencil slipped behind her ear.

"Our grandparents had a church," I said, sipping the cold water. "Ahh! In Clayhole—"

"How's that?" Tyrone asked. He leaned on the counter with his elbows and interlocked his fingers. "Reverend Stephen? That your grandpa, and Hazel, right? Can't be!"

"It be," I said. I listened to the sounds from the active kitchen. "You knew them?"

"Knew them?" Tyrone asked. He backed up and stared up at the plaster ceiling. "He married us; he was the only preacher who would marry a couple of darkies. You know, back then."

"Dude," Amy said. She set the menu on the counter.

"'Dude' what?" Tyrone asked. He looked square at Amy. "That's what they called us, back then, it was better than the other. But nobody cares. Get a sense of humor."

"How long you been married?" I asked. I studied the Hispanic man working the flattop grill, which was covered with frying hamburgers with piles of red onions and steaming hash browns. "You must have been teenagers."

"We were young," Tyrone said. He stood up. "Over forty-five years, my girl has kept me. Don't be fooled, I'm older than I look. It must be from my clean livin'."

"The chapel? You all were married in his chapel?" I asked.

"Yes, sir," Tyrone said. "We was married in that little chapel. Your grandma played the piano. She was one of our witnesses. She didn't take no guff from them crazies. No, sir; she was the tough one."

"But," Amy asked Tyrone, "'darkies'?"

Tyrone glanced at me and then grinned at Amy.

"Where are you from?" Tyrone asked. He reached over to grip Amy's hand. "I like your colorful hair."

"Southern California, LA," Amy said. "It's chill, dude."

"Chill?" Tyrone said. He laughed. "Oh, child, *you* never been in the mountains."

"No, but I'm chill with this," Amy said. She nodded.

"You been watchin' too much TV," Tyrone said. "I'll tell ya. I came here after Vietnam, didn't want my kids to grow up around the foolishness going on in the cities. Back then, and even now, a good place to get shot. At first, you know people aren't sure about you, but if ya leave them be, don't be acting the fool, they'll accept you. I love it here. I love all my whitey friends, like Leo over there, all my Mexican friends, like Ricardo back there cookin', all my black friends. I'm an American, Kentucky born and bred. We are all red and pink on the inside."

"How far is it to the chapel?" I asked. I knew the answer but thought I would help distract Amy. "Thirty minutes? I was born and bred here, too, but California is home."

"I thought mountain people didn't, like..." Amy said. She looked at the other diner patrons. "You know. African-Americans, you know."

"Child, the crazies are everywhere, in all shades," Tyrone said. He pulled out his order pad from his breast pocket. "But folks here, they respected I was a veteran. Truth is, most folks just want to be left alone."

"What's your specialty?" Rebecca asked. She waved the menu like a lady's hand fan.

"Fried chicken," Tyrone said. He tapped the order pad with a blue-ink pen. "We don't use no pressure cooker. Better than any made by a fake colonel. I'm a real private first class, sweetie, it'll change your life."

"Sounds great," Ruth said. She wiggled on the old bar stool.

"Why not?" I said. I pushed the menu back across the counter. "We might need to-go boxes."

After we gorged ourselves on the flaky chicken and mashed potatoes, I wanted to take a walk down the quiet street. More than that, I wanted to take Amy for a ride deep into the hills, to discover the hollers and mountainside homes where families were awoken each morning by a loud rooster call. But, as in all things, fate intervened.

"Guess you all goin'," Tyrone said. He huffed with a throaty growl. "One last time, I know me and the misses did. I won't lie; we cried like babies."

"One last time?" I asked. I wiped my mouth.

"I don't follow," Rebecca said. "What are you two talking about?"

Tyrone looked mystified. He frowned.

"Old chapel, right?" he asked. He crossed his arms as he glanced back and forth between us. "They tearin' it down; the county took it. Seems that a bridge goin' to be built. Everybody's been over, they even had a ceremony."

"This can't be," I said. I glared at Tyrone. "Why didn't anybody call me?"

"I'm sorry," Tyrone said. "I just 'spected you knew. I didn't want to remind ya, ya know?"

"We just buried our mother," Ruth said. "Not a word?"

"The hell they're tearing it down," I said. I got up. "Pay the bill."

"I know," Tyrone said. He waved at me. "Don't give yourself a heart attack. It ain't worth it."

"You don't know me," I said.

"Evil Bob's in the house," Amy whispered.

"Evil who?" Tyrone asked.

"Me," I said. "Now, I understand why I'm here."

I pulled out my smartphone and paced back and forth in front of the diner. They sat watching me maneuver. I warned my security detail, and then I called my corporate counsel. If I had to, I'd buy out the entire town. I had the means and, at that moment, I had the conviction.

I drove out of town, past the county high school football stadium, and thrust the car into third gear.

"I knew it," I said. "This trip was not random."

CHAPTER 42

There were memories from my childhood still trapped within my adult brain that possessed the exact directions back to my grandfather's tiny, white chapel. The Pierce-Arrows' straight-eight engine thundered hotly past the small towns of Haddix and Quicksand as the road weaved its way toward Lost Creek. To our left, we swerved away from the unforgiving, dark-gray, sheer rock walls. The road slithered alongside the north fork of the Kentucky River. I glanced up as I death-gripped the vibrating steering wheel and saw the red-tailed hawk flying above the tree limbs. It shrieked at me.

    The predator bird banked left at full throttle. I smashed down on the brake and the car fishtailed right across the road, the ladies screaming from the passenger compartment at being sloshed back and forth. As I steered left, I regrouped to grab the steering wheel and continued onto County Road 476. The gas-powered automobile's welded joints moaned. As the two-lane road began to narrow, the thick tree trunks seemed to crowd closer into the blacktop surface. As I looked left, I swerved the car to the right to miss, by a thin margin, being smashed head-on by two back-to-back coal trucks. As they hammered past us, the coal dust pelted us. The car vibrated from the tires running over the roadside rumble strips. The trucks blared with their deep-throated, 125-decibel horns. I coughed to clear my throat. I wiped my face as I regained control, just before the road bent back to the right, curving parallel to the Troublesome Creek. Its cold stream was clueless, its current meandering over smoothed rocks and stones.

"Slow down," Rebecca said. She gripped the passenger barrier with both hands. "You're going to get us killed."

"You don't know that," I said. I smashed down harder on the pedal and, as I made the last turn, I saw what I had feared. Within my grandfather's cornfield sat the yellow-painted implements of road construction. I honked the bugle horn again and again and again.

"Dude," Amy said. She had her hands on her ears. "You're killing me. Dude, dude—"

As I drove past the mountainside corner, I was relieved to see my security detail's black SUV had beaten us to the chapel. I parked in front of the sanctuary's double doors, the car engine wheezing as I sprang out. They had corralled the hard-hat-wearing workers in a close circle facing the chapel, with their hands cinched behind them. Before I could speak to my security detail, a tall young man emerged from behind the church. He wore a simple, white, long-sleeved shirt, black pants, and his dress shoes were covered in brown mud. As he walked closer to me, I saw his eyes, which were a pale brown.

"Hey there," he waved at me. "I don't think these men mean any harm. Do they?"

The security detail stared over at me, asking for instructions.

"They are here to do harm," I pointed at the chapel. "No one touches this chapel, no one."

He nodded with his hands folded behind.

"It is a house of God," he said. He reached forward.

"And who are you?" I said.

"I'm Reverend Landrum; I'm the new preacher here. But call me 'Clyde'. And who might you be?" he asked. He nodded over at my car. "Hey, that's quite a car, and you brought friends. I'm glad to meet you all."

"My grandfather was Stephen," I said. I released his hand.

"That's awesome," Clyde said. He hugged me. "I'm stoked. I'm thankful you are here. What a blessing, your timing is perfect."

"Exactly," I said. I nodded back over at Rebecca. "See? I'll save the church. They won't mess with me, or you, I promise. I have this under control."

"Maybe unhook these men, first," Clyde said. He held his hand out toward the construction prisoners. "Please?"

I looked over at the security detail and nodded. They cut off the cords. The men stood up and rubbed their wrists.

"Who's in charge?" I asked. I walked over toward them. They all pointed back over at Clyde. He waved for me to follow him. He looked over at the workers.

"Go home," Clyde said. "Live to work another day."

He grinned at me as he encouraged the ladies to follow him into the sanctuary. He closed the chapel doors behind us. To his left was a small shrine to my grandparents. We walked past another set of six-panel double doors and inside the sanctuary.

"What am I missing?" I asked. I coughed from stirred up dust. The oak floorboards creaked. He leaned against the last wooden pew.

"It's true," Clyde said. He patted an ancient back-bench pew. "This is where all Baptists sit for worship service. I kid you not."

"I get it! You're funny," Ruth said. "Backseat Baptists."

"Can I get an 'amen'?" Clyde asked.

"I don't get it," Rebecca said.

"This is, like, for real," Amy said. She glossed her fingers across the pew's back support. "You weren't kidding; it even smells, you know, musty. This is real history."

"Why?" I asked. I stood up tall with my arms crossed. "Answer me, before I crush you, and them."

Clyde bowed his head, he whispered a prayer and put his arms up in surrender.

"No one comes anymore," Clyde said. He pointed up at the modest pulpit my grandfather had preached from. "I preach to an empty room, but I'm ok with it, for now."

The door behind the pulpit opened and a black-haired woman walked toward us with purpose. Clyde held his hand out.

"We're physicians, we minister. We're here to follow in your grandparents' footsteps," Clyde said. He hugged the petite woman. "May I introduce my wife, Acacia?"

Acacia appeared as young as Clyde, but she was brown skinned with dark eyes. She had a bright, wide-toothed smile that seemed to draw us closer.

"Hello, sorry, but as you can see, we are in the middle of a process here," Acacia said. She shook our hands.

"Answer," I said. I stared down at Acacia, and back over at Clyde. "Now."

"You're rather intense," Acacia said.

"Calm down, Brother," Ruth said. "Hear them out."

"Okay, okay, tell me what you see," Clyde said. He stepped back to reveal the modest chapel with its high, pointed ceiling and a row of oak pews banked by tall windows on either side. I stepped forward into the right aisle.

"My grandmother used to play that piano," I said as I walked. "He carved a heart inside it. In short, nothing that some updates and a fresh coat of white paint won't fix."

"Where did you come from?" Ruth asked. She inspected Clyde and Acacia. "I'm with my brother, whatever he says."

"Oh, we're missionaries," Acacia said. She smiled. "Like your grandparents, we're from California. We went to Biola, you know."

"Biola? We were just there, on campus," Rebecca said. "We talked to a man."

"Deano," I said.

Clyde and Acacia looked at each other and nodded.

"Yes, we know of him, in administration," Clyde said. "We met there, before we went to medical school."

"But how did you get here?" I asked. "And why are you messing with my grandfather's church?"

"Ah, we were called," Clyde said. "From prayer, we guess, but an earthly call also came."

"I know what that means, it's code," Ruth said. "Same with our grandparents. They were 'called' to minister, too. Answer him. Why?"

"No, you don't see," Clyde said. "The school was called by someone. They told them about your grandparents. They needed help, just thought Biola might remember them."

"We happened to read the opening," Acacia said. She shrugged. "It was on a bulletin board, just random, we decided to investigate. And, well, we love it here, we love the people. We feel so chill."

"That is so chill," Amy said. She bobbed up and down, but then she grimaced.

"Yeah, chill," Clyde said. He smiled and pointed at Amy. "SoCal? You don't look well."

"I don't feel chill," Amy said.

"You understand each other?" Rebecca asked. "This is all so 'chill'? I feel so old."

"Then you can understand," I said, "why I'm angry."

"Absolutely," Clyde said. "We mean no disrespect."

"Can I help you?" Acacia asked Amy.

"I'm listening," I said. "But you're not tearing this place down."

"I'm good," Amy said.

"Actually, we got here just in time," Clyde said. "They were going to demolish this chapel. The city council, some legalese, I don't know."

"Eminent domain?" I asked. I stepped back.

"That's it," Clyde said. "They want to build a bridge, out there." He shuffled his feet as he pointed toward the front window and at an old bridge that appeared to be more rust than steel.

"I see," I said. I looked out of the window that was held in place by rotting muntins. I pointed up at the cemetery on the side of the hill. "They're buried up there, in that cemetery."

"We know," Acacia said. She touched my shoulder. "We walked up there, we prayed at their graves."

"The government had bought the land," Clyde said. He put his hands together. "The church board agreed it's the seed money to build a clinic. The city promised we can use the land if we build a clinic."

"We believe we can heal the body," Acacia said. "And heal the spirit, we don't have all the money, yet, but with God's grace..."

"Cool, awesome," Amy said. She felt her belly. "A free clinic, I'm stoked. Sort of."

"Amy?" Rebecca asked.

"I'm okay," Amy said.

"I think your grandparents would approve, right?" Clyde asked. He nodded at me and then at Ruth. "Sorry, though, this won't be a free clinic. We're not a charity, but we will be charitable. And we want to keep the church foundation; the engineers say it's solid greystone, perfect to rebuild from."

"I'm not sure what they'd say," I said.

"I should read from his diary," Amy said. She pulled out a

dusty volume. "He was upset, she needed care, but even she couldn't get it in time."

"What are you talking about?" Clyde asked.

"We, well, *Amy* has been reading my grandfather's diaries," I said. I encouraged Amy to read one last time, but her hands shook.

"Amy?" I said. "You're not okay."

Amy waved me away, her readers cockeyed across her nose.

"She has the cancer," she read. "She kept it hidden from me, feared we lacked the money. I failed her. I should have been a doctor, or stayed in LA. Maybe we'd be rich. I pray, pray, pray. All I know to do is pray. I am a fool."

"Stop. I'll make you a deal," I said, but I was concerned about Amy. Rebecca stood next to her, holding her arm. "I can help."

"Thank you, Brother," Ruth said. "I guess your prayers are answered."

Clyde held his hand up. He looked down at Acacia.

"No," Clyde said. "We're not a charity. We were called to build something that will last. Easy money is no foundation."

"We are physicians," Acacia said. "God trained us to take care of his children and ourselves. We will build our family and our clinic here through God's grace, not charity. What we create will outlive us."

"No argument here," I said. I looked back over at Amy and Rebecca. "But instead of taking the city's word, I'll buy the chapel. And the land. I'll deed it back, for free."

"No," Clyde said. "We plan to rebuild it. We need the wood. I appreciate your offer, but no. We must follow God's plan; a plan that we believe in with all our hearts."

"We will waste nothing," Acacia said. She looked curiously at Amy. "I must examine her, now."

"While you all talk, if you don't mind," Amy said. "I feel dizzy, I need to lay..."

"Of course," Acacia said. She held her hand out to Amy, but

she was too late. Amy fell back into Rebecca, and Rebecca fell back against a pew.

"She's with child!" Ruth said.

"Clyde," Acacia said. "Hurry."

Amy's eyes wobbled. Clyde quickly grabbed her and carried her into the chapel's back room. We followed a trail of red blood drops.

"Acacia, get the door," Clyde said. "Hurry…"

"Please, God," Rebecca said. She began to cry. "No, please."

CHAPTER 43

All I could do was watch Acacia and Clyde attempt to save Amy's life, to try and save her unborn child's life. It was as if my feet were frozen to the floor. They had her resting on their bed, in their small living space. She appeared peaceful, not unlike how my grandmother had looked on her deathbed, just before she passed. I thought it might be Amy's deathbed, and the look that Clyde gave Acacia told me the same story. He encouraged us to walk back inside the sanctuary. Acacia stayed behind.

"How long has she been pregnant?" Clyde asked. He wrapped his stethoscope around his neck. "A few months?"

"We don't know," I said. I searched for answers from Ruth and Rebecca.

"Yeah," Ruth said. "She didn't say."

"We gave her some aspirin," Clyde said. "We think she hemorrhaged. Does she have family? I may need to get consent to treat her."

I nodded as I stepped forward.

"What can we do?" I said. "She has no one, she's an orphan. Tell me what you need."

"I thought she had a mother?" Rebecca said. She wiped away tears sourced from an unlimited stream.

"No," I said. "She told me she made it up, to stop the questions. It helped her hide."

Clyde stared past me. He whispered a few words, a prayer.

"Pray it's not what I think it is," he said.

"Tell us," Ruth said. "I hate not understanding."

"If her fallopian tube ruptured, she'll need surgery, but the coma's another issue," Clyde said. "My instinct is it could be diabetic ketoacidosis."

"She could die?" Rebecca asked. "And the baby?"

"This is extremely dangerous," Clyde said.

"Tell me what you need," I said. "Tell me. I can have a helicopter here in minutes."

"What we need? Luck, pray for luck," Clyde said. "We have only the basics here, we didn't anticipate this. I might have to terminate."

"Abortion?" Ruth asked.

"Yes," Clyde said. He stared at Ruth. "I'll do what I have to do to save her life."

"But, an abortion," Ruth said. "That's a human life."

"And that young woman is bleeding to death," Clyde said.

"I'll get a helicopter," I said. I pulled out my mobile phone, but I didn't have any cell service.

"Put your phone away; a helicopter does us no good, we need to stabilize her first. She needs blood," Clyde said. "Otherwise, she'll die on the way. Go through her stuff, maybe she has an emergency number, it might tell us who to call, maybe her blood type?"

We converged at the car. Ruth pulled open Amy's suitcase. Nothing. She'd packed clothes, books, and personal grooming products, but nothing with any indication she had any condition like heart disease, diabetes, or even what her blood type might be. Nothing.

"Driver's license," I said. I smacked the side of the car. "Yes, of course, the back of her California driver's license. Find it."

"Where's her purse?" Rebecca asked. She scratched around the back seat. Nothing. We searched the car and tore through her suitcase again. We searched all through the car, again and again. Nothing.

"Inside, retrace her steps," I said. I pointed at the front doors. "It's inside the chapel, that's it."

We ran back inside. After a brief search, we found her bag under the back pew. Ruth crawled underneath and dragged it out, seizing the license and flipping it over. She took it to Acacia, who looked down at the license.

"That's unlucky," Acacia said. "We have nothing, nothing here. It should be here, everyone should know this."

"Please, God," Rebecca said. She kneeled down on the hard floor. "Please, what more do you want from me?"

Acacia thought for a few vital moments. She looked up at the exposed, wooden ceiling.

"Are any of you O negative?" Acacia asked. "Do you know? Look at your licenses."

I pulled out my license and flipped it over.

"I'm O negative," I said. I stood still, my face was flushed. "I'm O negative."

"Come," Acacia said. She grabbed me tightly. "Now!"

Acacia took me by the hand and dragged me through the sanctuary, into the back room. She sat me next to Amy. Clyde moved over next to me.

"He's O negative," Acacia said. She swabbed Amy's arm at the elbow.

"Do I have your consent?" Clyde asked. He held the large

needle in his gloved hand. It was connected to an intravenous line that was, in turn, connected to Amy. "Do I?"

"Do I have a choice?" I asked. "Yes."

"No, just sit quiet," Clyde said. "We got lucky; I had an IV kit, costs five bucks, five bucks for a life."

"Yes, yes," I said. I felt the needle sting. I watched my dark-red blood cycle from my arm, through the translucent tube, and into Amy's arm. Her face was still peaceful. I started to cry. I didn't know why. "What do I need to do? I'll do anything for her."

"Nothing, just sit still," Clyde said as he closely examined the line. "I prayed for luck, and I got you. O negative: perfect blood type for emergencies."

"God gave you what we need," Acacia said.

"Oh, yeah, sure," I said. I tried to breathe slower, as if it made any difference. But then I felt a presence in the room. It was the presence that I had felt the moment my grandmother had died. It felt like someone had put a warm blanket over me. I felt peaceful. I sat quiet and still, my shoes flat on the wooden floor. I assumed the worst. I thought of my dead baby.

In time, Amy began to stir, her eyes moved under her eyelids. She began to breathe rhythmically. Acacia checked her heart rate, she felt her forehead. She nodded over at Clyde. After the longest hour of my life, I heard a Life Flight helicopter's blades thump as it descended from the sky. Clyde unhooked me from Amy. The medics rushed inside and wrapped Amy in a blanket, then carefully placed her on a metal gurney. I followed the gurney outside. Rebecca and Ruth stood near me as we followed the crew. Amy opened her eyes. She stared up at us as they moved her closer and closer to the loud helicopter.

"Your grandparents would be proud," Clyde said. He patted me on the shoulder. "I guess you drove all the way out here to save Amy."

"Whatever you need," I said. I shook my head. "Whatever you would have me do."

I ran over and looked down at Amy just before they slid her onto the helicopter.

"Thanks, Evil Bob," Amy said. She winked at me.

"Anything for a friend," I said. I gripped her hand as the medics moved her away.

"Stay," Rebecca said. "Come back to me."

She gripped my shoulders as they loaded Amy into the helicopter. We watched them close the door. It powered up, ascended, and disappeared behind the brown hillside. It was quiet.

CHAPTER 44

The sounds from the helicopter had faded. I closed my eyes and sucked in a deep breath. My shoulders ached. I prayed for Amy. I prayed for her unborn child. I gazed up at the clouds. I hadn't noticed the clouds were gray. They seemed like bruised cotton candy after the fair had left town. It was quiet.

"Happy?" I asked. I shook my head. I thrust my fist into the sky. "That what I'm supposed to do?"

"Who are you talking to?" Ruth asked. She stood next to Clyde and Acacia.

"Them," I said. I looked up at the hillside cemetery where my grandparents' bodies were buried. Where my mother's body was buried. I pumped the car's gas pressure, checked the dials, and tried to start the engine, but it just gasped back at me. Maybe it was out of gas, maybe it was out of patience, or maybe it just wanted to be left alone. I pulled out the key and threw it down.

"Fine," I said. I slammed the car door shut and started to walk toward the rusting bridge.

"Where are you going?" Rebecca said. She grabbed at me, but I pulled away and moved down the two-lane road.

"Let him go," Clyde said. He stepped behind Rebecca. "Come, we should pray."

"I need to talk to them," I said. I started to jog. "Call Wylie, get the car fixed."

I jogged across the bridge. The Troublesome Creek flowed beneath it. No cars or trucks passed me, though I would have welcomed the gruesome death. It was cold. It was quiet, but for a constant breeze that whistled a warning through the tree limbs. I walked past a ranch-style house as I tried to breathe; it was at the base of the hill, where the cemetery sat. I stared up the steep hillside, which was covered with thick bluegrass and ancient trees, and noticed the wide, gravel road that wound left-to-right up to the plateau. The gravel rocks were bigger than I had expected. I had to kneel down and climb with my hands and knees. My hands were covered in white chalk, brown dirt, and sweat. About halfway up, I had to stop. I sat on the grass, gasping for air. The earth was damp. My hands were scuffed-up; they throbbed and shook like I had an essential tremor. After a few minutes, I gulped, nodded, and sucked in a deep breath. Then, I restarted my journey up to the cemetery. After a few more minutes, I crossed over where the road ended, near a locked metal gate. Before me were the marble tombstones, with dates chiseled under the names. I walked up to the wire fence. To my left, my mother's freshly covered grave. To my right, my grandparents' shared eternal spot to watch the daily human and animal goings-on within the pie-shaped clearing where their chapel sat. As I trudged around to their tombstones, I gripped the fence. A red-tailed hawk shrieked at me; it was perched atop a barnacled oak branch that spanned the cemetery. It stared down at me with its black eyes.

"What do you want?" I asked the animal. The predator bird appeared curious. It didn't move as I climbed over the wobbly fence. I stood above my grandparents. The bird just watched me. It seemed unruffled. I remembered the moment I had watched their coffins deposited into Mother Earth. I sat down and leaned back on the metal fence post. I covered my face with my dirty, moist hands.

"Why am I here?" I asked.

In the distance, from the forest, within the darkness between the trees, I thought I heard music being played on an out-of-tune piano. An out-of-pitch voice followed. It was high and male, his words familiar.

"We're marching to Zion, beautiful, beautiful Zion." And then, "Rock of ages, cleft for thee."

"Why am I here?" I asked. I kneeled forward. I glossed my hand across the polished surface, tracing my forefinger through their carved-out names and dates. "I'm sorry. I'm sorry I failed you."

I began to cry. I hated to cry. I screamed: I screamed to be left alone, I screamed for my childhood, I screamed back at the bird. It just stared. I had emptied my lungs, and I collapsed. My head hurt. I hugged the ground. From behind me, I heard truck wheels roll over the gravel. The brakes squeaked, the doors swung open, and then they were closed, followed by the sounds of hesitant footsteps. I didn't look up at them.

"Why am I here?" I asked. I got back up onto my knees. "I could've killed her."

"That's quite a bird," Clyde said. He reached down and grabbed my shoulder with his long fingers. "Without you, Amy might have done something different, but we'll never know, will we?"

"It reminds me of home," I said. I stared up at the predator bird. Its eyes were dark at the center, but they were auburn around. I had always just thought it had black eyes, but I'd been wrong.

"You know, some consider it a divine messenger," Clyde said.

He released his grip. "I don't know about that, but it's interesting to wonder, right?"

"Amy reminds me of our child. He died as a baby," I said. I put my hands on my knees. "He would have been about the same age now. A boy; an innocent baby. God took him. I never forgave God."

"You've never said anything," Rebecca said. She reached through the fence to touch me. I felt her fingers caress my neck. "Why?"

"What kind of father would I have been?" I asked. I stared down at the thick grass. "Why does everyone I love have to die? I don't understand. I hate this feeling."

"Brother, you'd have been the best," Ruth said.

She and Acacia moved in behind Rebecca. Clyde kneeled down. I glanced up at him.

"Breathe easy, Brother," Clyde said. "Life's about living; let God control things."

"I wonder what he would have looked like, now?" I said. The tears streamed down my face. "I wonder what he would have been like."

"I know a verse," Clyde said. He looked up into the heavens. He had a wonderment about him that reminded me of my grandfather. "'Do not be afraid, for I am with you.' Some dude named 'Isaiah' wrote that. I don't know, it seems to work, but only God knows the answer."

"My mother's dead," I said. "She never understood me. Don't think she wanted me around, but the one person *I* wanted around died?"

Clyde nodded.

"Life's not about answers, it's about living with our choices," he said. "The 'why this', the 'why that'... I'll not insult you with platitudes. I guess that I wish I understood the 'why', but I don't."

"Would you have aborted that child?" Ruth asked.

"Yes," Clyde said. He looked back over at her and nodded. "Yes."

"I don't understand," Ruth said. She crossed her arms.

"I'm not Solomon," Clyde said. He looked over at Acacia. "We had the mother in front of us. She was unable to answer. Do we let them both die? We are physicians; we deal with reality. We are not philosophers. All I can do is pray for the wisdom to make the right choice, to make the right decision, and then learn to live with it."

"Yes," Acacia said. She hugged Ruth. "We pray for God's grace and wisdom. We get answers we don't understand."

"What's it like to feel love?" I asked.

"Just look into Rebecca's eyes," Acacia said, "and be quiet."

"I love you, Bobby," Rebecca said. "We'll be all right."

I pulled up a handful of bluegrass and threw it out in front of me. It blew back into my face.

"Love you," I said.

"Let it go, Brother," Ruth said. "Let it go."

"I guess it's time to go home," I said. I tapped on the tombstone and stood up. I looked down the hillside at my grandfather's white chapel. "Let's go..."

Clyde stood next to me and put his arm across my shoulders. He pointed down at the chapel.

"It must have been an amazing place, back in their day," he said. "Tell me about it."

"Yeah, it was a happy place," I said. "It was, but they're all gone now. I guess that's life."

Clyde nodded as he stared down at the chapel.

"What if I were to say," Clyde said, a hard look in his eyes, "you take the wood, leave the foundation with us?"

"Why?" I asked.

"I don't know," Clyde said. "You tell me."

And I saw in my mind the answer I had searched for as I had

driven across the deserts, the prairie land, the mountains, and away from the ocean.

"I'd like that," I said, slowly shaking his hand. I smiled. "I know what to do."

"I thought so," Clyde said. "By the way, an investment *would* be welcome, just so long as you believe in our endeavor. We're sure, not proud."

"I can do that, I would be..." I said. I smiled at Rebecca and Ruth, "...Excuse me, make that *we* would be, happy to help you build your clinic." I pointed down at the chapel. "Let's take it home."

"What?" Rebecca asked. I looked back at her.

"Not *our* home," I said. "It's home already, in my mind. You'll see."

"God does work in mysterious ways," Clyde said. "Amen, Brother."

THE END

Two years had passed since our journey from Los Angeles, across Route 66, and to my grandparents' chapel. It was now but a fond memory. We had invited my sister's family to stay with us for Thanksgiving, but on Black Friday, we flew down south to LA.

As we stood together under the all-too-typical Southern California sun, the simple, white chapel seemed to welcome the warmth; it seemed to welcome no humidity. I hoped it had been reborn – reborn to reflect my grandparents' hearts. It gave me a peaceful sensation that there was something out there, beyond me; a powerful, silent presence. I wasn't scared anymore as I stood within the noisy sounds of daily downtown Los Angeles' life; as we stood on the street corner for what had once been the intersection of 5th Street and Hope Street. I looked back and stared up at the pyramid above the LA Public Library, built during my grandparents' time.

"Thank you, Brother. I think they would have liked to know that was across from their chapel," Ruth said as she hugged me. "This has been my best Thanksgiving ever."

"Mine, too," I said as I hugged her back.

"Mine, three," Rebecca said as she held Amy's boy. "He's perfect."

"I'm a mother," Amy said. She bounced up and down. "It's so mind blowing. Me?"

"He is perfect," I said. I looked over at Wylie. "We did good?"

"I love babies," Wylie said. He grinned as he played with the child's soft fingers. "You did good, Boss."

"Totally," Amy said. She hugged Wylie. "I wish our new friends were here."

"Yeah, me too," I said. "Hey, they gave in and let me name it. I chose 'Hazel's Clinic'. It just opened, so they couldn't get away. Some excuse about how their ministry was too important to take time away."

"Where have I heard that before?" Ruth asked.

"I know," I said. "Like they've been reincarnated."

"That's wonderful, Boss," Wylie said. He brushed his thick mustache with his hand. "And you did it in a 1929 Pierce-Arrow. What a machine, what a machine."

"Yeah, and thanks for retrieving her. Sorry, I was mess," I said. "I think she'll just stay in, in Carmel, going forward, right?"

"Yeah," Wylie said. He nodded. "Good idea."

"I guess I was meant to be there," I said. I reached over for Amy's hand. "Luck counts…"

"Totally, totally," Amy said. "Thanks for saving my life, Evil Bob."

"Thank divine intervention," I said. I stepped toward the chapel. "It was something else, Amy. I was just the vessel with the right blood type."

"I think Clyde felt sorry for you," Rebecca said. She winked at me. "You were kind of pathetic."

"I guess money does have a purpose," I said. "But you're right. I was just sad. Sorry, I just didn't want their memory to die. This was the only thing I could think to do, at the time. I have no idea why."

"I think they're here," Ruth said. She smiled. "I can feel them. They're here. They're happy."

I had paid for everything, though I was surprised the local real estate investment trust's board of directors had accepted my recommendation. Actually, at the time, I was stunned, but it's now just a hazy memory. Perhaps they thought I'd lost my mind and it was an easy method to keep me quiet. I don't know. I'd have thought it was just a weird set of coincidences, but there was that presence I couldn't describe, as if it whispered to me. It seemed to always be nearby, now. I had learned there aren't words to describe what cannot be described; even trying to think of a few words was a disservice to its presence. I couldn't explain it, so I just kept the sensation to myself. I thought the chapel silently spoke for it, and it spoke for my grandparents. It had guided the instincts my grandfather had told me to listen to. After the board had agreed, I had only one stipulation: that they would display my grandfather's chapel as a nondenominational historical representation of unity, kindness, and understanding. I wrote the words for the plaque.

'This is a no-name chapel. All are welcome.'

I stood at the same front door that I had walked past many times as a child. It now rested beneath the tall skyscrapers. I reached forward to touch the one happy constant from my childhood. Next, I looked across the sanctuary and studied the simple, eternal flame that I'd had built into the exact spot from which my grandfather had preached his good news for forty-two years. The simple flame was fed by two nearby fires. It was my way of remembering my grandparents as individual people and then as one. But, most of all, it allowed the chapel to share its glow late into the night; a reflective glow that might attract someone in need. Perhaps someone who felt lost, just like I had.

"Dude," Amy said. "See? I told you; history's alive."

"You don't think I've snapped?" I asked Amy.

"No way," she said. "You preserved an important part of history. And part of your family history. It's chill."

"You sure you don't want our names on the memorial plaque?" Rebecca asked. "You did this. No one will know, otherwise."

"No, let people focus on the chapel," I said. I turned and looked over at her. "That would be our vanity talking. They didn't believe in vanity."

"Very well, my love. I'm just happy to have my Bobby back," Rebecca said. She kissed Amy's boy on the cheek. "Life is so precious, so magical, so misunderstood."

"It was just what I thought I was supposed to do. I don't have an answer, it's just a feeling," I said. I pressed the warm, white-painted wood.

We held hands and gazed at the modest chapel as people of all races and faiths walked inside to investigate the newest piece of historic art on the downtown LA scene. It had once stood sentinel to great wars, societal upheaval, weddings, funerals, and crowded potluck dinners. It had once stood as a testament to grace on a pie-shaped piece of land near a bend in the Troublesome Creek.

The chapel was born because a Kansas girl had faith in her Kentucky boy, a boy that she just happened to have met in 1926, on the street corner of 5th Street and Hope Street.

A few days later, after my sister had returned home, under an auburn-colored sunset, we dressed in white. Rebecca and I waded waist-high into the cold Pacific Ocean. Frothing waves surged along our private beach beneath the rocky cliffs. But, as we moved further out, it was as if the ocean had expected us, and it became calm and resplendent. The birds were quiet, the wind was soft; it was almost silent. I had invited everyone I knew who had the one quality I lacked: faith. We stood with our Hindu, Jewish, Buddhist, and Christian friends. Our Muslim friends forgave us for the cremation, but prayed for us as they watched from the cliff edge. I wanted to give our child every advantage in death that I hadn't given him in his brief life, so I had even invited a Native American, as my grandfather had been part Cherokee. He'd told me that was the reason why he'd rarely had to shave.

The waters were full of life, and it smelled strongly of salt. We each held a bag with some of our child's ashes inside – a child we had never gotten to know, a child long-since gone, but a child who had caused us to simply wonder. And, if we stripped our feelings bare, a child who we had loved unconditionally.

As each friend said a prayer or practiced a ritual, we each lit a candle, which floated within cypress baskets. Then, we emptied the ashes into the water. The baskets were taken by the gentle ocean currents, and we watched the innocent candlelight fade into the darkness.

Rebecca and I held hands as we cried. We gave our boy back to God, and I sensed that familiar presence hug me. That night, we celebrated a life.

* * *

The next morning, I sat in my backyard drinking black coffee from a tall mug and watching the tides ebb and flow. The red-tailed hawk was perched high above me on a thick live oak branch. It watched me with its black-and-auburn eyes, and it surveyed Carmel as the bay transformed from darkness to light. The gray fog blanket seemed to have been swept off the land and rolled back into the ocean as the sun warmed my face. The humpback whales emerged from the dark, blue depths, and a happy, blond-haired boy played with his golden retriever along the frothing beach. I stood up and turned to walk back toward Rebecca, who stood near the thick, wooden door to our kitchen. As I approached her, two white doves encircled me. Then, they flew past me and disappeared into the bright sunlight. I smiled at Rebecca. I was finally home.

Made in the USA
Columbia, SC
23 December 2017